MARKED

BOOK 1
IN THE
SOUL GUARDIANS SERIES

KIM RICHARDSON

AWARD-WINNING AUTHOR OF *MARKED*

www.kimrichardsonbooks.com

ISBN-13: 978-1461017097

ISBN-10: 1461017092

Fourth Edition

More books by Kim Richardson

SOUL GUARDIANS SERIES
Marked Book # 1

Elemental Book # 2

Horizon Book # 3

Netherworld Book # 4

Seirs Book # 5

Mortal Book # 6

Reapers # 7

Seals Book # 8

MYSTICS SERIES
The Seventh Sense Book # 1

The Alpha Nation Book # 2

The Nexus Book # 3

DIVIDED REALMS
Steel Maiden Book # 1

For my mother Danielle,

In Horizon

MARKED

SOUL GUARDIANS BOOK 1

KIM RICHARDSON

CHAPTER 1

REBORN

"WAIT FOR ME!" Kara jogged along Saint Paul Street. She
pressed her cell phone against her ear with a sweaty hand. "I'll be
there in two minutes!"

With her heart thumping against her chest, her black ballet flats
tapped the cobblestones as she avoided oncoming traffic. Her
portfolio swung at her side. She jumped onto the sidewalk and ran
through the crowd.

"I can't believe you're not here yet," said the voice on the line.
"You had to pick today of all days to be late."

"Okay, okay. I'm already freaking out about the presentation.
You're not exactly helping, Mat."

A laugh came through the speaker. "I'm just saying ...this is
supposed to be the most important day of your life. And you,
Mademoiselle Nightingale, are late."

"Yeah, I heard you the first time...*Mother*. It's not my fault. My
stupid alarm didn't go off!" Kara dashed along the busy street, her
long brown hair bouncing against her back. The smell of grease and

7

beer from the pubs reached her nose and her heart hammered in her chest like a jackhammer. She knew if she missed the presentation, her hopes of landing a scholarship were over. She didn't have any money for college, so this was her only shot.

Over the heads of the crowd, Kara could just make out the sign, Une Galerie. Stenciled elegantly in bold black letters, the name hovered above the art gallery's majestic glass doors. She could see shadows of people gathered inside. Her chest tightened. She was only a block away now.

"You know, the presentation won't wait for you—"

"Yes, yes, I know, it's not like I *planned* this. Now I'm going to do my presentation out of breath and disgustingly sweaty. Not exactly the kind of first impression I wanted to make," Kara growled into the phone, trying to catch her breath.

For a horrible moment she thought she wasn't going to make it on time and considered getting off the sidewalk to run along the edge of the street instead. She looked back to see how bad the traffic was.

Then her heart skipped a beat.

Less than half a block behind, a man stood motionless and indifferent to the wave of humanity that flowed around him. He was staring at her. His white hair stood out against his dark gray tailored suit. Kara frowned.

His eyes are black, she realized.

A chill rolled up her spine. The man melted into the crowd and vanished, as though he were a mere trick of the light. The hair on the back of Kara's neck prickled as a sense of foreboding and the urge to scream filled her. Who was this man? And why was he looking at her?

"I think I'm being followed," Kara spoke into her cell phone after a few seconds. Her mouth was dry as a feeling of dread welled up inside her.

"You always think you're being followed."

"No. I'm serious. I swear…this guy is following me—some psycho with white hair. I…I think I've seen him before. Or at least my mother has…"

"We all know your mother is a little *nutty* sometimes. No offense, I love your mom, but she's been seeing and talking to invisible people since we were five. I think it's rubbing off on you."

"Listen. I was with my mom yesterday on Saint Catherine Street, and she said we were being followed by someone. What if this is the same guy? Maybe she's not as crazy as everyone thinks." Kara wondered if there was a little truth in her mother's visions. She loved her mother very much, and she hated herself at times for thinking her mom belonged in a loony bin.

Mat laughed. "Are you serious? It's bad enough that your mom sees spirits and demons. If you start believing in all that, they'll lock you up."

"Thanks for the vote of confidence. Remind me why you're my best friend again?" Kara decided to drop the subject. After all, the strange man was gone and her fear of him was melting away with every step, replaced by nerves and restlessness for her presentation. She focused on the gallery sign as she ran. "Okay…I can see you now."

Mat was leaning against the gallery's brick exterior. His head was turned toward the glass doors. He pulled his cigarette from his lips and blew smoke into his phone's receiver. "I think it's starting. Hurry up!"

Kara felt her cheeks burn. Her heart pounded in her ears and muffled the sounds around her. She took a deep breath, hoping it would calm the fluttering in her stomach, and she sprinted onto Saint Laurence Boulevard. Her cell phone slipped out of her hand and hit the pavement.

"Crap!" Kara crouched down to grab her phone. "Stupid phone—"

A flicker of movement appeared in the corner of her eye.

"WATCH OUT!" Someone shouted. She stood up and turned around.

A city bus hurtled towards her. She stared, transfixed. The bus kept coming.

An arm reached out to her. She saw a split second image of two monstrous headlights.

And then it hit.

Thirteen tons of cold metal crushed her body. She didn't feel any pain. She didn't feel anything at all.

Everything around her went black.

A moment later, Kara was standing in an elevator.

At first, streaks of white light obscured her vision. She blinked and rubbed her eyes. The elevator was elegant...three sides appeared to be made of handcrafted cherry panels decorated with golden-wing crests. The smell of mothballs lingered in the air, like her grandma's dusty old closet. When her eyesight improved, she realized that she wasn't alone.

On a wooden chair facing the elevator's control panel, covered in black fur, and wearing a pair of green Bermuda shorts from which protruded two hand-like callused feet, sat a *monkey*.

It spun on its seat, wrapped its feet around the backrest of the chair, opened its coconut-shaped mouth and said in a very business-like manner, "Hello, Miss."

Kara's jaw dropped, and she swallowed the urge to cry out. She stared at the beast, terror rising up inside her. The creature's words rang against her ears, foreign and impossible. The elevator seemed to spin about her. There was nowhere to run; she was trapped in a wooden box.

His hairless face crinkled into a grin so that he looked like an oversized walnut. His square head sat directly on powerful shoulders. He raised his chin and looked down upon Kara. His yellow eyes mesmerized her; and although she tried, she couldn't look away.

A cascade of emotions ran through her: fear, revulsion, and anger. Confused, she couldn't make sense of it all. The monkey had in fact spoken to her like it was the most natural thing in the world, and now it was watching her as though *she* was the one that was unnatural.

Kara's nails dug into the soft flesh of her palms, and after a minute she was able to force some words out of her mouth.

"I'm dreaming. Yes, that's it. I'm having a strange, mind-blowing dream of a talking monkey." She shook her head and rubbed her temples. "And it's definitely the wildest dream I've ever had." Her throat was dry like she hadn't had a sip of water in weeks. She tried to swallow, but all she could do was contract her throat muscles.

The monkey frowned, a low growl rolled from his throat. "I'm not a *monkey*, Miss. I'm a chimpanzee. You mortals are all the same. Monkey-this, monkey-that. No respect, always getting above yourselves. You forget what you are now. You are not as important as you think."

Just then Kara realized her hands were shaking and didn't know whether it was from fear or from anger at the way the chimpanzee was addressing her. She clamped her fingers into fists and kept a straight face. "I meant no offense, Mr. Chimpanzee. I'm just having a very strange dream that I probably *won't* remember at all when I wake up." She shrugged. "This is probably some past experience I had as a child at the zoo that's resurfacing somehow. I wonder what it means…"

The chimp glared at Kara with a mixture of disdain and indignation. "You're most definitely *not* at the zoo or any such wildlife park. And you may address me as *Chimp* Number 5M51, if you please." He raised his chin importantly. "You'll be arriving at your destination momentarily." And with that, he turned his attention back to the control panel.

Gradually, Kara began to feel more awake, as though she had woken from a long, deep sleep. Reality slowly crawled back in along with the fear that perhaps this *wasn't* a dream. She bit her lower lip as she told herself to *think*.

"Um, what destination? What are you talking about? Where are we going?" she asked, her eyes focused on the talking chimpanzee. Panic soared as she tried desperately to squelch the screaming in her head, but it wouldn't go away. This *was* a dream...wasn't it?

Chimp 5M51 turned his head and smiled, exposing rows of crooked yellow teeth. His eyes locked onto hers. "To Orientation, of course. Level One."

"Orientation?"

"Yes. All mortals who have passed must go through Orientation. That's where you're going." Chimp 5M51 clamped his feet around the edges of the chair and extended an abnormally long arm in the direction of the elevator's control pane. He pointed to the brass buttons.

Kara leaned over for a better view. The panel read:

1. Orientation

2. Operations

3. Miracles Divisions

4. Hall of Souls

5. Department of Defense

6. Council of Ministers

7. The Chief

A feeling of dread slowly rose up inside her. She stared at the panel, dizzy, her knees weak like she was about to collapse. "This...this doesn't make sense. I...I'm dreaming. This is a dream!"

Kara shut her eyes and pressed her back against the elevator wall, trembling. "It *can't* be happening. It just *can't*. I need to wake up now. Kara, you need to *wake* up!"

"You're dead, Miss."

Kara opened her eyes. The word *dead* echoed in her ears like some sick joke. The weight of his words started to pull her under. She was drowning. She fought against the overwhelming feeling of panic, like a need for air.

"I'm not dead!" she hissed, and gave a shudder of dismay. "I'm right here, you stupid baboon!"

The chimp was unconcerned. "Think what you must," he said, as he lifted his chin. "But think about this. Can you remember the events before this elevator?"

Kara floundered, trying desperately to remember. Bits and pieces flashed inside her brain: a white light ...metal ... darkness ...

The bus.

Kara dropped to her knees. The city bus had hit her...pulverized her core and crushed her like a tomato. But then she remembered something else, something that didn't make any sense. It was coming back to her now, like a faded memory sharpening into a clear picture. It flashed before her eyes...she saw an arm reach out and touch her during the bus crash. Someone had tried to save her...

"See? You're dead," said the chimp matter-of-factly, and Kara detected a hint of amusement in his voice, as though he enjoyed watching her struggle in misery and confusion.

As she pulled herself together, she pressed her hand against the left side of her chest, she couldn't feel a heartbeat. She pressed down on her rib cage. Nothing. She clasped her wrist. No pulse. No beating. No movement at all.

"See. No beating. No heart...like I said, you're dead," declared the chimp again. Kara felt herself wanting to punch him.

But before she could make sense of what was happening, she was thrown off balance as the elevator stopped abruptly.

"Level One. Orientation!" the chimp announced.

"Wait!" Kara pushed herself away from the elevator wall and wobbled up to the chimp. "I don't understand. What's Orientation?"

With his finger still on the button, he turned his head. "Orientation is where all the new GAs are categorized."

Kara stared stupidly into chimp 5M51's yellow eyes. "What are GAs?"

"Guardian Angels."

"Huh?"

Kara heard the swish of doors opening. A hint of a smile reached the chimp's lips. He raised his arm and pressed his hand on her back. Then she flew out the elevator.

CHAPTER 2

ORIENTATION

KARA BELLY-FLOPPED ONTO a cold stony surface. Face glued to the floor, she raised an eyebrow. The floor vibrated against her cheek. She winced as chaotic noises hit her ears, as though thousands of voices were speaking at the same time.

Carefully, she lifted her head off the ground and looked around. Her jaw dropped.

She was surrounded by people. As she jumped to her feet, she saw they were gathered inside an assembly hall the size of ten football fields. Lines of people of every shape, size, and ethnicity twisted through a maze of offices and corridors. The air was humid, and it smelled remarkably like the ocean.

Kara turned just in time to see the elevator with chimp 5M51 disappear back into the ground. "Well, there goes one monkey I'm not going to miss," she muttered to herself.

The commotion was louder than a rock concert. Kara pressed her hands to her ears. There were thousands of them, and they were all dead...just like her. They pushed and shoved one another, itching to get to the front of the line. This wasn't exactly how she had pictured the afterlife, especially not with self-satisfied apes. But then again, she had never really given much thought to the spirit world, or death for that matter. She was only sixteen and she had felt invincible.

Kara was alone, lost, and *dead*. She knew she should be feeling something like happiness. After all, she'd just discovered that life after death existed. But she couldn't. Beside her, an oversized middle-aged man chatted happily with an old bald man. *They* looked pretty excited. Most of the walking dead around her seemed overjoyed, except for a few people who looked like she felt—nauseated and horrified.

Not knowing what else to do, Kara joined the line nearest her. She stared at her feet. She wasn't up for a chat, especially with some stout dead old guy who was prancing around as though he'd just won the lottery.

But she wasn't *ready* to die just yet …she wasn't *finished*. All her hopes and dreams—vanished into thin air. The soundless empty hole where her heart once lived was cold. She knew her life was over.

"Ahem." Someone cleared his throat.

Kara kept staring at her feet.

"Excuse me, Miss. Are you feeling okay?" the man persisted.

Was there any hope that she could avoid *sharing*? Couldn't she just disappear?

Unfortunately for Kara, it appeared that he wanted to share. "You know, it's really not *that* bad," continued the voice.

Kara stole a look and saw that the voice belonged to the fat old man. His face was plastered with a lopsided grin. He licked his pink lips in anticipation. "We're in Horizon! Alive! Can you believe it! Well, sort of alive. We're dead, but alive. Isn't this great?"

Kara lifted her head. She tried to fake a smile, but the corners of her mouth were sewed in place. "Yeah. It's really great."

The man beat the air with his arms. "This is *so* exciting!" And, with great effort, he leaped into the air and twirled. His tiny legs kicked underneath his gigantic undulating belly. He hovered for half a second and then landed with an echoing *boom*. "Who would have thought that Horizon actually existed? Life after death…it's *real!*" If he wasn't already dead, Kara was sure his heart would burst out of his chest like red, chunky sauce and hit his neighbor smack in the face.

She studied the man for a moment. "What's Horizon?"

He stopped twirling to give her an answer. "Utopia. Shangri-la. Zion. Elysium. Horizon is the afterlife. It's real, and we're here. Isn't this wonderful?"

Kara scowled as the man spread his enthusiasm to his next victim in another row of the dearly departed. She felt a presence behind her and turned to see that at least a hundred newly expired folk were bringing up the rear. The noise level increased, if that was actually possible. Kara hung her head and tried to cry, but no tears would come. She crossed her arms over her chest and stared into space.

Time seemed to have no effect at Orientation. Before she knew it, she was next in line to enter one of the score of office buildings that surrounded the acres of happy dead. She wrinkled her face and stared at the building. From the outside it looked like a regular office—beige painted walls draped with beige colored paintings, beige industrial carpeting and glass windows with beige horizontal blinds.

Creative.

The door was the only thing that looked out of place. It was ancient, with a mammoth sized wooden frame, and it was decorated with a brightly lit neon sign which read: *Oracle Division # 998-4321, Orientation.*

Kara frowned. She wasn't sure whether or not she should knock. Sooner or later she knew she would have to make up her mind, for thousands of impatient dead people were anxiously pushing her against the door.

She sighed. "Okay, here goes nothing."

Making a fist with her right hand, Kara raised it to the door. As her hand lingered in the air, the door swung open with a screech. The office was jam-packed. She sneaked in and stopped. A salty gust of ocean fragrance embraced her. Hundreds of scattered papers covered the ground and littered the desks. Filing cabinets filled the office, stacked on top of each other, twisting all the way to the ceiling—and then there were the giant crystals balls.

It was like a crazy bowling alley. Huge glass balls rolled across the office flattening everything in their path. Tiny old men ran balanced on top of the spheres like circus acrobats, their silver gowns flowing behind them. Using their bare feet, they maneuvered the balls effortlessly in all directions. Like single entities, man and ball moved as one.

The crystal balls bumped into cabinets, and the men rummaged through the contents. They tossed their long white beards over their shoulders, flipped through papers, and caused an avalanche of white parchment. Kara's eyes darted to a drifting sheet of paper that was making its way down towards her. She jumped up, caught it, and read:

Guardian Angel: Peter Jones
Class order # 4321
Rank: Rookie 2nd year, W-1 Guard squad, (lowest rank)
Assignment: Elizabeth Grand. 5585 Sherbrooke Street, front entrance.
11:42 am. Crushed skull by slipping down 2 flights of stairs.
Status: Pass. Saved charge. Soul untouched.

Kara shook her head. She bent down, picked up another paper from the floor and read it. It was similar, except this time it was Tina Henderson who had saved Affonso Spinelli from choking to death on a meatball at Luciano's Porte Vino Restaurant.

Were all these papers about guardian angel assignments? She let the paper slip from her hand. She snooped around the filing cabinets. Papers rustled under her feet as she moved around the office. Along the way, she discovered several smaller rooms from which more men emerged treading above their glass spheres like oversized unicycles. They all appeared very much engaged at the moment...

"KARA NIGHTINGALE!"

Kara nearly jumped out of her own skin. Her legs wobbled as she made her way through the towers of filing cabinets and followed the voice. Around the corner to her left, she spotted another office. The door stood ajar. There, above a large crystal ball, sat another one of those men, surrounded by piles of paper. He jumped down to a great semi-circular wooden desk. He wore a frown on his brow and gestured impatiently.

"Come in. Come in. No time to waste. Lives to save!" he said in a strange, high-pitched voice.

Kara dragged herself inside the cramped office. More cabinets were stacked on top of each other and spread across the walls. A five-foot round pool was mounted in the back corner. The aroma of salt water was strong in the little office. A low *tick tock* distracted her. Following the sound, Kara spotted a huge grandfather clock leaning against the wall to her left, its long pendulum swinging from left to right.

She walked over to the desk and stood with her hands at her sides, biting her lips. She opened her mouth to speak...but shut it again. Alive, when she'd get nervous, her heart would pound so hard against her chest that it would sometimes hurt. But not this time. No hammering or pounding, only nervousness with a silent core. It didn't feel normal.

She forced the words out of her mouth. "How...how did you know my name?"

The old man finally stopped ransacking his desk and grabbed a file. His eyebrows shot up on his forehead. "Ah, yes, yes. Here it is. Kara Nightingale ...age sixteen ...hit by a bus ...pretty nasty way of dying ...so sorry about that ...soul was already chosen to be a guardian ..." He stroked his beard and was silent for a moment.

Kara cleared her throat. "Um...excuse me, sir? Um...what am I doing here?"

The man's head snapped up. "Doing here? Why...you've been chosen, that's what! And now we need to get you started on your new job. Okay. Let's see here...what's the assignment again...? Oh dear. I think I've forgotten." His face cracked into a grin. "It's not as easy as it seems...to see into the future. You tend to get the present and the future mixed up. Now, where is that piece of paper?"

Kara frowned deeply. "I don't understand...what new job? I have a job?"

The file slipped from the man's hands. He fell forward to collect the papers. "Oh! Right!" His face lit up. "Well, you're *dead*, obviously. And you've been preselected to become a guardian angel. To work at saving lives. Isn't that wonderful?" He crumpled the papers in his excitement. "And today is your first day on the job." He scratched his bald head. "Or is this your second day? Oh dear."

Kara stared at him in frank disbelief. "Me, a guardian angel?" She remembered movies she'd seen with guardian angels protecting men and women from evil. She wondered if she would get a pair of wings.

"Well, let's see here…right. As a rookie you'll be stationed in the W-1 Guard Squad of the Guardian Angel Legion, lowest rank. Your duties today will be to *observe*. Your combat training will commence *after* the orientation period is over…after your first trip." His kind eyes glistened as he looked upon Kara.

She watched him warily, his words ringing in her ears. The realization chilled her. She tried to speak, but her lips were glued together. A shiver rolled through her and she wasn't sure if it was because of the excitement of the situation or pure fear.

"Your Petty Officer will enlighten you with the details." He closed the file, slammed it down against the desk with a *bang*, clapped his hands, and bellowed, "David!"

Kara glanced sideways and turned her head. A handsome teenager, a year or two older than her, popped into the doorway. His broad shoulders were covered by a brown leather jacket which hung closely around his muscular build. He strutted his way towards them. Two golden stars marked his forehead, just above his brow.

"Yes, oracle? You called, Your *Holiness*?" Smiling widely, he combed the top of his blond hair with his fingers. He stopped beside Kara and gave her a wink. His laughing eyes were the color of the sky. Normally Kara would have blushed, but seeing as she was without blood flow, she felt a strange tingling instead from the tip of her head all the way down to her toes, as if her body were under attack by hundreds of prickling needles.

The oracle jumped up and extended his arms. "Clara, meet David McDonald. David, meet Clara Nightingale." His eyes darted from Kara to David. "*She* is to be your new rookie."

"Uh…it's *Kara*, not Clara."

The oracle stared at her as if she had said the strangest thing. "Oh, right! Forgive me, Kara."

David laughed. "They usually get it right after about a hundred times."

Kara studied David's face. His lips parted and twisted into a sly smile. He clasped her hand in his and shook it. She felt an electric current flow from her fingers to her toes. His hand wasn't the blood-warm touch she remembered feeling when shaking a mortal hand, but it wasn't cold either. It was perfectly cool.

"Hi. It's nice to meet you, Kara," he said, as he flashed a row of dazzlingly white teeth. "And it's *McGowan*. Not McDonald." He let go of her hand and lifted the collar of his leather jacket, but his eyes stayed on her.

"Um, hi …it's just …let me get this straight," stammered Kara. "I'm getting a new job as a guardian angel, and you're going to be like my boss? Is that what's happening here?"

David's eyes sparkled warmly as he watched her face. "More or less. Yeah." He marched up and grabbed her dossier from the oracle.

"I think I'm losing my mind."

"No…you're just dead."

Dead, Kara thought. She wanted to dissolve on the spot. She might be dead, but her core could still feel pain. She didn't want to be dead. She wanted to be alive…

"Come closer, Clara," said the oracle. He steered his crystal ball away from the desk with his feet and came towards her. "It is time for you to take the oath! Or did you take it already? Oh dear. Here I go again, mixing everything up! Have we been here before?"

Kara shook her head. "Uh…no. What oath? I never took an oath."

"Oh good," sighed the Oracle. "It is the oath all guardian angels must swear to. A sealed oath, which can only be broken if the soul dies." A sudden glow emanated from the crystal ball, bathing the oracle's feet in a soft white light. The brightness subsided. A cloud-like mist formed from inside the globe. It swirled around, changing its form with every twist. The oracle pressed his wrinkled hands together in front of his chest, his eyes still fixed on Kara's. To her great surprise, they started to change color, morphing from blue to brilliant golden.

Kara's eyes widened as she backed away. "Wait. What if I don't *want* to become a guardian angel? Can't I just go back home?" This was all happening so fast that she wasn't sure she wanted to be part of it.

The oracle shook his head. "I'm afraid not. This is how it has to be…there is no other way. Your life as you knew it is over. Today you're starting your new life and your new job."

Kara blinked, her mind working overtime. It had to be better than doing nothing, being *really* dead. And then there were the broad shoulders of Petty Officer David…

"Come closer," said the oracle sternly.

Fighting the urge to run away from David and the oracle, Kara stepped forward. "Wait a minute…I think you're making a mistake. I don't think I'm the right person for this job…"

The oracle put a finger to his lips and nodded imperiously. "The Chief has chosen *you*, Clara, to join his army, to become one of his guardian angels—a true and sacred honor." His golden stare hypnotized Kara. "Now, you must repeat after me."

Kara nodded.

The oracle continued. "I, Clara Nightingale…"

"It's Kara."

"Oh no! Did I get it wrong again? My memory is not what it used to be." The oracle smiled and wiped his brow.

"Let's start this again." He cleared his throat. "I, *Kara* Nightingale, declare myself servant of the Legion of Angels. I will perform my duties as a guardian angel wholeheartedly. May the witnesses of my oath hold me to it."

Kara felt foolish but repeated everything word for word anyway.

"We will hold you to it," declared the oracle and David together.

And then something strange happened. First, the oracle's skin started to blaze a soft golden color, and then he leaned forward and pressed his thumb on Kara's forehead. His touch burned a spot between her eyebrows and sent a sizzle of electricity from her head to her fingertips. She felt heavier somehow, as though the simple touch had weighed her down. After a moment, the oracle leaned back and Kara watched his eyes slowly return to their natural blue color. The crystal ball shimmered and then lost all of its brilliance.

She reached up and touched her forehead, running her fingers along the spot where she had felt it burn. Her brows drew together.

She could feel the outlines of a star...just like David's. The oracle had branded one on her as well.

"I have a *star* on my forehead?" said Kara, which was more of a statement than a question, as she rubbed her brow. A tiny smile reached her lips and she felt herself relax.

"It is the symbol of the Legion of Angels. You are a guardian angel now...you swore the oath." The oracle steered his crystal ball back to the other side of his desk and sat back down. He glanced at the clock. "And now *you* have a job to do. Time is of the essence! Daniel!"

David flipped a black duffel bag over his shoulder and strutted over to the pool. "That's me. Come on. The faster we get this over with the better. We only have a half hour to get to Mrs. Wilkins before she dies." He climbed up the little ladder hanging over the edge of the pool and stepped onto the ledge.

Kara frowned. "Hold on. You mean to tell me that to reach Mrs. what's-her-name, we have to jump into the pool?"

"That's exactly right," answered David as he lowered his bag and jammed the file into it.

It was too weird. But then again, she *was* dead—walking, talking, with a golden star burned into her forehead.

Kara took a few tentative steps towards the pool. "Wait a minute...how come *I* wasn't saved? Where's *my* guardian angel?" Images of her life flickered inside her head...her family, her friends, her paintings. "Why wasn't there anyone to save me?"

David zipped up the bag and threw it over his shoulder. He flicked his eyes down at Kara and grinned widely. "You *were* saved. Well, your *soul* was, that is."

Kara rubbed her temples in a desperate attempt to calm herself. "This is not making any sense. I can barely grasp the notion that I'm dead and standing here having this conversation with you. And now you're telling me that my soul was saved, just not my body?"

His eyes were thoughtful as they rested on her. "That's right. Your soul was chosen. You were destined to become a GA. It was just a matter of time before you died and were shipped up to Horizon like the rest of us. We're running low on guardian angels, you see, and you were next on the list." He winked.

"I was *chosen?*"

"Yup. By The Chief himself. Thinks you've got what it takes to do the job. And, speaking of the job, we have to go…" David threw out his hand and beckoned her to join him.

Kara clamped her hands around the metal pool's cool railing. "You said you knew that woman was going to die. How is that possible?"

"You forget where you are. Oracles can see into the future. It is their gift. They know days before that someone is about to die. So they assign a guardian angel to save that person's soul. It's your job to save them, no matter what, before the demons devour it."

"Demons?" Kara's eyes widened as she felt her body tense up. It took a few seconds to gather herself. "Are you kidding me?" An image of her mother flashed in her mind's eye. She turned her attention to the oracle, who was ignoring their conversation completely. His eyes were gold again. He stared into space, still as a statue. Kara wondered if the little man was scrying into the future at this very moment.

"The oracle's busy now. He's doing his job; now it's *our* turn." David grabbed hold of Kara's arm and pulled her up the little staircase, settling her next to him. His gaze narrowed. "Now listen carefully. Are you listening?"

"I'm all ears." But Kara couldn't shake off the feeling of dread. Demons were her mother's favorite subjects—a crazed woman's imaginary foes...right? "No...no one said anything about demons." She tried to put on a brave face for David, but she knew it wasn't working.

"Don't worry," his expression softened. "Nothing's gonna happen. It's a real easy assignment, trust me. The legion wouldn't assign something that was too risky to a rookie on their first day. We'll be back before you know it."

He smiled and studied her face, and for a moment Kara was lost in his handsome features. His blue eyes glistened. "Up here, water is important. Remember that. It's the gateway between Horizon and Earth...it's how we travel." He flashed another smile, his teeth exposing their radiance. "So we have to jump in. You ready?" He grabbed Kara by the elbow, edging her forward.

Kara stared at the pool's reflections, imagining demons in the deep water, waiting for her, waiting to devour her soul.

"All right then," said David, "on the count of three..."

"What? Wait! I'm not sure I want to do this..."

"One ..."

Kara jerked her arm around, desperately trying to rid it of David's iron grip.

"Two ..."

"No wait!" squealed Kara. "I can't swim!"

"Three!" David pushed himself off the ledge and jumped, dragging Kara down with him.

She splashed into the water and sank to the bottom. The water didn't *feel* like water at all, more like fog, or a heavy mist, like when you've stayed too long in the shower. Kara could breathe easily, somehow, probably because she had no lungs. She turned her head and tried to look for David, but she began to spin fast—horizontally—with ear-piercing shrieks as whitish bubbles seemed to consume her. White light exploded all around her. Shielding her eyes, Kara managed to look down. The light was coming from her. Her entire body was illuminated by fluorescent white light. She felt a sudden pull and watched her body disintegrate into millions of brilliant particles. Then she started to float away.

With a last flash of light, everything around her disappeared.

CHAPTER 3

THE M SUIT

KARA FORCED HER LIDS open and looked around. She frowned.

The shadows of the world around her were a hazy blur, as though she had opened her eyes under water. She felt dizzy, almost like the time she stole a bottle of wine from her parents' wine cellar and drank half the bottle. But this was different. She was trapped in a strange body. She searched inside this body and found herself. She willed the body to move...she moved her fingers, then her arms. This new body felt like she was wearing it on top of her other self—a skin-tight suit.

As the dizziness lessened, her nerves calmed. She concentrated on her hearing. She could hear the distant sounds of traffic and the soft murmurs of people talking. She blinked. Shapes became focused. It was as though she were watching the world through someone else's eyes. She looked down at her new body and pressed her hands against her chest. Nothing. No beating of the heart, no lungs compressing. Empty.

Her eyes slowly adjusted to the shadows around her. She was in a humid alleyway that stank of last week's garbage. She followed the smell and spotted cats eating from the metal dumpsters. Tall brick buildings masked the light. Shapes moved within the shadows. Kara recoiled as two grubby looking men eyed her from a dark doorway, whispering at each other.

Then something touched her shoulder.

Kara jumped backwards and nearly fell.

"Relax, Kara, it's me." David reappeared. He wore the black duffel bag on his back. His cheeky Colgate smile made his face a little too handsome. And when she realized she was staring at his lips, she turned away so he wouldn't see the flush she felt staining her cheeks. Then she remembered. She couldn't blush. She had no blood.

"How are you feeling?" he asked, as he clasped her shoulder. "Dizzy?"

Kara grimaced. "Like my sixteenth birthday hangover."

David stared into space, a silly grin on his face. "Yeah …those were fun times."

Kara lifted her head. The world around her was in focus now, but the ground still wavered slightly. She felt excited to be back, even if it was only for a short while. At that moment she realized how she'd taken life in general for granted when she was alive. How easily life could be taken away, how fragile life truly was. Had she known she'd be dead that morning of her presentation, she would have done things differently. She would have been kinder to her mother…

David sighed and turned back to Kara. "But that's normal. It'll go away in a few minutes."

He let go of her shoulder and dropped the duffel bag on the pavement. He bent down, rummaged through the bag, and pulled out a map. After studying it for a moment, he stuffed it back and pulled out a brown leather wristwatch. "Good, we're only a few blocks away." He leaped to his feet and strapped the watch around his wrist.

A breeze masked the dumpster smell for a moment as it brought in exhaust fumes and the scent of hot pavement from the busy street. Kara brushed a strand of hair behind her ear. She brought her hand up to her face and studied it, wiggling her fingers, focusing on the fact that she was in a body that didn't belong to her.

Back in Horizon, before taking the big plunge, she remembered feeling like her old self, just without the internal organs...but like herself. But now back on Earth, after her death, this body felt alien. She wasn't sure she'd ever get used to this.

"The M suits take some time to get used to the first time. Believe me, I know." David clapped his hands together. "Man, I remember my first time...I went totally mad for a while. I even lost my Petty Officer. No, wait, he lost me." He laughed, his eyes sparkling.

Kara smiled. His laugh, the sound of his voice was intoxicating. He reminded her of the college boys she'd seen around the city: young, beautiful, and full of themselves. They oozed an *eau d'arrogance*. Most of the high school girls drooled over these boys.

She had labeled them "The Untouchables." David was one of them. He was *very* handsome, with a strong athletic build. She felt uncomfortable being so close to him, but at the same time, she felt a thrill at their closeness. Their eyes met for only a second, and Kara was sure he had just read her mind. He smiled.

"But you know, after a few suits, you'll hardly feel them anymore…they kinda become part of you, like skin." David straightened out his jacket and flipped the collar up. "Yeah…that's more like it."

Kara frowned. "What do you mean by *M* suits?"

"Mortals. Humans. Earth dwellers. If you're not part of the Legion, you're a mortal."

"So you're saying I'm wearing a *human* suit?"

"Yup."

Kara made a face. "That's totally disgusting." She shook her head. "I still can't figure it out. How did we get here?" Her brown eyes searched his face.

"You see," explained David as he studied her, "when we jumped into the pool back in Horizon—remember? Right, well, we were *transported* to Earth." He lifted his arms and pointed to his chest. "In these babies."

"Right…in these body bags," said Kara, and she looked down at herself. She studied her arm. She pulled back her sleeve and passed her hand over her skin. "Feels…different?" she said and looked up into his eyes. "Like I'm not totally connected to it yet."

David nodded as he smiled at her. "I know. It's the same for everyone. You'll get used to it."

"So these bodies just *magically* appeared?"

He laughed. "You're funny. But...ah...*no*. See, when we travel between Horizon and Earth, we need to submerge ourselves in water...the pools, remember? Water serves as a gateway between the two worlds. It also allows us to create our M suits and then shed them later. Don't ask me how, it just does. And we call the process 'Vega.'"

Kara blinked. "I'm a puppet without the strings." Her mind wavered inside her mortal body, anticipating movement. She shifted her weight from one leg to the other...a thought was all it took now. The body responded. Like water sucked into a sponge, her spirit was absorbed entirely; body and soul moved as one. She didn't need to will her body to move anymore. It was quickly becoming second nature to her. She rested her hands on her hips. Perhaps it wouldn't be as difficult as she first thought. "I think I'm getting the hang of this."

David watched her and grinned. "In Horizon we don't need flesh and blood bodies, our bodies are immortal. You're still the same person you were, just not in the same mortal body. You think and feel exactly the same. It's like you never left your old body. But our mortal bodies are gone...and as a GA, you have to submerge yourself in M suits to walk on Earth...your soul would die without them. Think of them as another version of your old body. But I have to admit, I love wearing suits...they make me feel invincible."

Kara felt her mind ease with every passing moment. It wasn't so bad after all, this new life that was starting to emerge.

"Okay, wow …so where do we go from here?" asked Kara, as she practiced moving her limbs. She took a few steps, staring at her feet, grinning. She had to admit, it did feel pretty awesome once you got used to it.

"We have less than *fifteen* minutes to get to Mrs. Wilkins before she slips and takes a nasty fall over her dishwasher's open door. That's how she's supposed to die and it's our job to stop that from happening. You ready?" David cocked an eyebrow.

She looked up into his grinning face and shrugged. "Not really, but what choice do I have?"

David laughed. "None. But don't worry, I'm here with you." And then he added smugly. "I happen to be one of the best guardians, so you could say that you're in luck."

Kara shook her head, a smile played on her lips. "Really? So why would the Legion stick one of their best with a rookie like me?"

"Because it's all part of the job," said David, his eyes flashed mischievously. "I'm the hottest thing in Horizon, baby." He threw the black bag over his shoulder, straightened out his jacket, and strode off. "Let's go," he yelled back.

"Sure thing, hot stuff," laughed Kara.

She ran to keep up, trying not to trip on her new legs. Soon the alleyway disappeared, and they found themselves in sunlight, facing a busy street. Tall palm trees decorated the length of the street on either side, like enormous lampposts. Their leaves ruffled in a light breeze, bringing forth the smell of the ocean. Instantly, Kara knew she wasn't in her hometown anymore. She spotted a metal street sign at the corner. "Northeast 5th Street" was stenciled in white at the top on a green platform. She had never been here before.

"Where are we?" asked Kara after a moment. She stared at a giant aloe plant.

"Fort Lauderdale, Florida," answered David. He strutted up the street with ease, and Kara assumed this wasn't David's first trip to Fort Lauderdale.

They walked along 5th Street, zigzagging through crowds of shoppers. The smells of onion, garlic, fish, and spices surrounded them. She imagined a juicy cheeseburger.

"Can we eat? I mean do we *need* to eat? Like...can we taste food?"

"No. These are mortal suits, not real mortal bodies. We don't eat. We don't need to."

"That sucks...I was hoping to try a slice of pizza or something."

"You could try...but it'll be like eating paper."

"I think I'll pass. Thanks."

Kara followed David closely. She still felt uneasy about wandering the streets in a new body. She looked passersby in the face and wondered if these people noticed something different about her. "Do you have a mirror on you?"

"Why do you want a mirror?" David stopped walking and met Kara's eyes.

"To see myself. I'd like to see what I look like." Kara wondered if there'd be traces of her accident still visible on her.

"Oh…of course. You want to make sure *you* are still *you*. Come over here." David walked up to a parked car. He made sure no one was looking. "You can check yourself out with this." He pointed to the side mirror.

With her nerves prickling at the idea of being disfigured, or looking like someone else, Kara leaned in and took a peek, immediately feeling a sense of relief. "I look exactly the same? Same eyes, nose, hair? I can't see any traces of my—" She decided not to bring up how she died, at least not yet. She wasn't entirely sure how she felt about revealing something so intimate to a stranger. She met David's eyes. "I look the same. How's that possible?"

"Because you're you."

"But what happens if someone I know sees me?" Kara pictured her mother's frightened face. She figured she'd probably die of a heart attack, seeing her dead daughter wandering the streets like a zombie.

David grabbed Kara by the elbow and steered her away from the car. "They won't because you don't look *exactly* the same to them. You'll appear a little different. You'll have the same brown eyes and brown hair, but you'll look like a cousin or something."

"I don't have any cousins."

They walked along another block until they reached North Andrews Avenue and turned south. Couples with children passed them by, and Kara thought of her own family. At that moment she felt miserable. She missed her mother. Even though she was a little mad, she was the only mother Kara ever knew. She imagined her mother's grief-stricken face and wished she could tell her somehow that she was okay.

"Do you miss your family?"

David was silent for a second. "Sure I do. I miss them all the time, but I wouldn't trade my life in Horizon for anything. I love my job. We're part of an elite group...chosen to keep the mortals safe. The rush I feel on a mission...you can't get that same feeling doing anything else. It's dangerous, and I love pushing the limits. I'm good at it. It's like ...this is what I'm supposed to be doing." His face lit up, and she felt herself drawn to those piercing blue eyes.

Kara wondered if David had had many girlfriends back when he was alive. She knew the answer to her own question and realized she was being silly. But another question burned in the back of her mind. "Can...can I ask you something?"

"Sure. What do you want to know?"

Kara avoided his eyes, and before she could stop herself she asked, "How...how did you die?"

"Oh, that," laughed David. "Well, it wasn't anything spectacular. I drowned."

"You drowned! Oh my God. That's a horrible way to die."

"Well, actually, I drove my parents' car off a bridge. So it was a little more bad-ass but stupid in the end."

Kara imagined the scenario in her head. "What was it like? I mean...to drown? Did you suffer? It must have been terrible."

"The last thing I remember was a feeling of flying—which was really cool, by the way," said David. "Then the car hit the water, and I hit my head on the steering wheel. I blacked out. And then I woke up with a monkey breathing down my neck."

"Right, the chimp in the elevator." Kara shuddered. "Not sure I'll ever get used to that."

David adjusted the bag on his shoulder. He paused for a second before continuing, his expression thoughtful. "What about you? What do you remember about your death?"

The concern in his voice made her nervous, and she scratched the back of her neck. "I didn't feel anything when I died—I mean, I didn't feel any pain. I remember the bus coming at me. I remember thinking it was too late to run out of the way…then it hit. The next thing I remember, I was in an elevator." She shook her head. "I thought I was dreaming."

"I think we all go through that." David pointed. "There it is, 187 North Andrews Avenue, apartment number three." He glanced at his watch. "We don't have much time. Quickly." He jogged to the front of the gray stone building and ran up the metal staircase, three floors to apartment number three.

Kara stared up at him from the bottom of the stairs, feeling both excited and terrified. But she ran up the stairs, her body completely in tune with her. This was her new life now, she better start getting used to it.

"The key to a successful assignment is to do the job *quickly* and discreetly. Save the mortal…and get out. No need for any demons if you save the mortal."

"Um, these demons," said Kara, "what do they look like?" She couldn't help but cringe while she waited for the answer. If demons existed, there was a slight chance her mother saw them too.

"Depends. There're lots of different kinds of demons. Some can look like monsters from your worst nightmares, and others can look just like you and me—mortal."

"With black eyes?"

David narrowed his eyes. "Yeah...how did you know?"

Kara's head spun. She tried to gather her thoughts. "My mother saw them I think. She called them demons. She said they were after us. I mean, we all thought she was nuts. I never saw anyone or any demons. I wanted to believe her. I tried so hard. She made it sound so *real*...but I couldn't. I spent most of my life hiding her away from everyone so they wouldn't put me in foster care. See, my father died when I was five so it's just...it was just the two of us."

"Well, she wasn't crazy." David cocked his head to the side. "Some mortals can see spirits and demons. They're called Sensitives. They formed a secret mortal society and have been dealing with the Legion for hundreds of years. Your mom is probably one of them."

"Sensitives," repeated Kara. "I guess you're right." Her guilt weighed her down. Her mother wasn't crazy. She remembered her mother screaming and pointing to invisible foes, and now Kara was filled with regret. Her mother had been telling the truth all these years. It only made Kara feel worse.

David watched her, concern in his eyes. "Kara? I need you to focus."

She looked up at him. "I am."

"Good. Now, watch and learn." David rang the doorbell.

After a moment there was a screeching noise as the intercom went on.

"Yes...?" answered a woman's coarse voice.

David cleared his throat and gave Kara a wink. "Hi, Mrs. Wilkins? My name is John Mathews. I'm here with my friend Karen. We're from Saint Thomas' high school, and we're collecting donations for the swimming team. We're sure to win this year..."

There was a loud *scrch* from the intercom. "Oh! Yes, yes. Of course. Come on up!"

The door buzzed and vibrated as David pushed it open. "Her son used to be on the same swimming team. Let me do all the talking," he whispered, "your job for now is to observe. Just follow my lead and everything will be fine."

"Right." Kara followed him into the building. The air was thick and had a faint stench of lingering mold. She wrinkled her nose. Dirty brown stains painted the light gray walls, and leftover gum was smeared into the cruddy, carpeted stairs. Dead cockroaches the size of mice lay on the floor next to the walls, and live ones disappeared into tight crevices. Voices from the neighboring apartment's television seeped through the walls.

When David reached the top of the stairs, he turned around. "And another thing," he said. "Mortal suits are temporary. They only last a few hours. Staying on Earth too long will give the demons our location. The longer we stay here, the easier it is for them to find us. They can sense us. That's why we have to hurry. But don't worry, demons don't just show up. We still have lots of time to do our job. But if ever you do see one, *don't* panic." He studied Kara's face. "The worst thing you can do is go ballistic and scare the mortal. She's not supposed to know anything about demons—or about us. We have strict rules about these things. Besides, I'm here to protect you. Do you understand?"

Kara nodded, biting her lip, although she wasn't entirely sure she *wouldn't* flip out if she saw a demon coming her way. "Okay. Um, the demons, can they hurt us? I know we're dead but…" Her mind travelled back to when she was a child. "When I was little I used to have horrible nightmares about monsters. I used to see dark shapes following me all the time. My mom would say that they were demons, and that they wanted to eat my soul. Is that true? Jeez, listen to me…I'm such a spaz."

"You're not a spaz," said David, his eyes suddenly kind. "You're a guardian angel…and not a bad looking one either."

Kara rolled her eyes, pretending that she didn't enjoy that comment. "But seriously, can they hurt me now…or are we, like, *invincible*? Do we have *special* angel abilities?"

David faced a door covered in peeling white paint. "Demons are the only ones who can take a guardian angel's soul. If a demon takes your soul then you stop existing, and there's no coming back. But with training, you'll develop your abilities. Look, for now, just leave the demon to *me*…if there *is* one. Today it's watch and learn."

Kara struggled to stay calm. She didn't want David to think she was a wimp, especially not on her very first day on the job. "But what do I do if I see one?"

David knocked on the door. "You won't. At least not today."

Kara sighed as she concentrated on David's relaxed demeanor to ease her mind. She realized she had no idea what she would do if she saw one and hoped David was right.

The door creaked open to reveal a plump lady in her sixties. "Hello, dears…come in, come in," she said, as she waved them in. "So, you're both on the swimming team?"

"Yes," said David and Kara in unison, as they entered a small entranceway. Kara could see parts of a kitchen from where she stood, partially hidden behind walls that opened up to the left to reveal a dining and living area. The small apartment reeked of dingy carpets, potpourri, and a smidgen of cat pee. How she missed her grandma.

Mrs. Wilkins surveyed the young couple. "Hmm. Well, you're a nice looking pair, aren't you?" Smiling, she wiggled her oversized body excitedly, sending waves rippling all the way down to her feet. "My Stanley always came home from practice dying for some juice. I'll fix you some." She turned slowly and teetered towards the kitchen.

David glared at Kara. Shaking his head, he showed her his watch and mouthed, *No!*

Kara peeked into the tiny kitchen and spotted the dishwasher's open door, and on display, a row of sharp knives flickering in the kitchen light, sticking out from the plastic cutlery basket in the dishwasher—the murderer.

"Um, that won't be necessary, ma'am," said Kara. "We ...we just had some coffee not too long ago," she lied, putting on her best fake smile. "We're not thirsty, really."

Mrs. Wilkins halted and turned around, looking mildly disappointed. "Oh. I *see*. You young people are always in a hurry."

Kara scratched the back of her neck. "Um, yes...but thank you very much." Grinning, she stretched the corners of her lips as far as they would go, hoping it was enough to convince the woman.

Mrs. Wilkins frowned and studied Kara once more. She pinched her lips together. "Well, then. I'll go get my wallet." She wobbled down the wallpapered hallway and disappeared behind a door.

"That was close," breathed David. He glanced at his watch and grinned. "Well, Kara, today is your lucky day. One minute left, the charge is safe, and there are no signs of demons." He stood close to her, his arm brushed up against hers. "This was an *excellent* first assignment. Man, I'd kill for a beer right now."

Something moved in Kara's peripheral vision. She turned her head. In a dark corner of the hallway, down past the door where Mrs. Wilkins had disappeared, Kara saw a shadowy shimmer. At first she wasn't sure she saw anything at all...maybe her eyes were playing tricks on her. But as her sight adjusted to the darkness, the shadow appeared again. It was little more than a shifting fog that flashed and disappeared. As it glistened in the dim light and flickered in and out of sight, it took solid form long enough to expose fragments of a corrupted and twisted body. The shifting shadow glided towards them.

Exactly like her nightmares.

CHAPTER 4

DOWN THE TOILET

DAVID DROPPED HIS BAG. He shoved both hands into it, pulled out a long silver dagger with his right hand and grasped a brilliant white orb in the other. "Kara, move!"

But she couldn't. Glued to the spot, Kara's body suddenly turned ice cold, as though the temperature in the room had dropped by twenty degrees. Weakened by the evil the creature oozed, Kara felt icy hands tighten around her neck, suffocating the life out of her. "What's happening?" She brought her hands to her throat and felt the weight of the demon pull her down. Darkness lurked inside her, threatening to consume her mind.

But Kara wasn't about to let this ugly demon kill her. She was stronger than that. With her inner strength, she strained and fought against its evil. After a moment, the cold released itself and dissipated.

"Quick…behind me!" David pushed Kara hard to the ground. He ran past her and planted himself in the middle of the hall, swinging his weapons before him.

And at that moment, Mrs. Wilkins decided to join the fun.

"What's all this *racket*?" She bellowed as she bounced into the hallway between David and Kara. First she saw David, who was holding a very large dagger, and then she turned her attention to Kara on the floor a few feet behind him looking very pale.

"Good Lord!" Shrieked Mrs. Wilkins, cowering against the wall. "What are you trying to do with that knife?" she cried. "Are you going to murder us…cut out our innards and sell them on the black market?" she squealed as she clutched her chest.

"Lady, we're here to *protect* you!" cried David, his eyes locked on to the shadow.

Mrs. Wilkins followed the direction of David's eyes and saw the demon at the end of the hallway. She gave out a yelp. Taking on a solid form for a moment, the demon showed its true self, a putrid core of intertwined monsters. Wormy tendrils formed legs that it used to propel itself towards them. It shimmered before changing back into black mist.

"Go back to the Netherworld, shadow demon!" David thrust the white orb before him. Brilliant rays of white light shot out of the globe. They flew straight at the shadow demon. They hit. The demon let out an ear-piercing cry as its solid form reappeared, covered in light. Convulsing, it flickered and changed back into a black cloud, then vanished.

"Kara!" shouted David as he turned around and faced her. "Take Mrs. Wilkins outside…quickly…before more demons come!"

Kara blinked. She stared into David's face, her feet glued to the ground. Images of demons flashed inside her head...her childhood nightmares were real. Her mother had been telling the truth all along. The demon that tormented Kara in her dreams, time and time again, had just appeared a few feet away from her. She shook herself out of her trance and forced herself to concentrate on David's words. She had to do something. Mrs. Wilkins' body was trembling, her face screwed up in complete terror and bewilderment. She needed Kara's help. Kara was the *guardian,* after all. Compelled to do the right thing, she pushed herself up and jumped towards Mrs. Wilkins, tripped, and fell flat on her face.

Mrs. Wilkins, on the other hand, decided to move. Trampling over Kara she stumbled into the kitchen, screaming like a banshee.

"Kara!" yelled David, as he saw Mrs. Wilkins wobbling into dangerous territory. "Mrs. Wilkins is in the kitchen. The *dishwasher.* Keep her from it!"

A chill prickled on Kara's M suit as she felt the temperature in the hallway drop again. She lifted her head off the ground and flinched as another shadow demon appeared behind David. "David! Behind you!" She pointed towards the corrupted creature.

The shadow demon glistened back to a mist and grabbed David from behind, enveloping him in a black cloud. For a moment, Kara thought the demon had devoured him—there was nothing but a black fog where David had stood. Suddenly, the creature materialized back into its true self and David emerged. He leaped into the air as he fought the shadow demon off with his

49

dagger, stabbing and slicing off parts of the creature. Black liquid sprayed the walls.

"Get—to—Mrs.—Wilkins…" he panted as he fought the demon.

"Right," said Kara. She had to try to keep the lady away from the dishwasher. She struggled to her feet and staggered to the kitchen. She spotted Mrs. Wilkins hiding under the kitchen table, praying.

Kara fell to her knees, inches from the table. "Mrs. Wilkins, come, come with me…we have to get out of here." She grabbed hold of the old woman's droopy arm and pulled. "Please, we have to go!" she urged.

But Mrs. Wilkins wasn't moving. With her eyes wide, she just rocked back and forth, praying silently. Kara could hear David still fighting the shadow demon. She knew she had to move fast. She yanked Mrs. Wilkins with both hands, pulling as hard as she could. But nothing happened. Kara couldn't pull her out from under the table.

And when Kara thought things couldn't get any worse, she felt a chill as another shadow demon materialized in the kitchen, two feet away from Mrs. Wilkins's crying face. Nasty black cloud-like tentacles rippled along the kitchen floor, slipping their way towards them. Mrs. Wilkins screamed and rushed out from underneath the kitchen table, sending chairs and Kara flying back and crashing into the wall.

Kara watched the events as they happened as if she were watching a movie clip in slow motion. Mrs. Wilkins clambered out from under the kitchen table, slipped, and flew two feet in the air. Her body hovered for a moment—and crashed face first onto the open dishwasher door. With a loud *crunch*, the dishwasher's door fell off its hinges and flattened under Mrs. Wilkins' weight.

Kara stared open-mouthed as Mrs. Wilkins lay spread-eagle on the kitchen floor, knives protruding from her bloody scalp. Her unspoiled left eye fixed on Kara, accusingly, as though this was her fault. After a moment the woman's body sparkled, as though her skin was painted with millions of tiny diamonds. The diamonds then detached themselves and hovered above the body, slowly coming together in a ball of light, like a tiny sun.

Something moved in Kara's peripheral vision. As she turned, she watched in horror as the shadow demon crawled towards the dead woman. Without thinking, she pushed herself up and ran towards the ball of light. Something inside her told her to protect it. But after three strides, she felt something grab a hold of her left foot. She fell flat on her face. Then her body was lifted in the air by her feet and thrown across the room. She hit the wall with a crash and fell hard on the floor. Kara struggled to her feet and whipped her head around. A pulpy mass of flesh with exposed veins slithered on the kitchen floor. Blood red tentacles lashed out, like an overgrown octopus. Multiple heads and mouths *with razor-sharp teeth covered its body.* The demon ignored Kara and crawled towards Mrs. Wilkins.

Stiff as a statue, Kara watched in horror as the creature's tentacles wrapped themselves around the woman's feet and pulled itself up, inches from the ball of light. Its misshapen form rolled onto the dead woman's corpse. Its touch corrupted her body, and her skin turned immediately black and rotted away, peeling. The shadow demon pulled itself up towards the light.

"No!" howled David, appearing suddenly in the doorframe. He ran towards Mrs. Wilkins.

But it was too late.

The shadow demon shimmered and grew. It then threw itself forward, swallowing the ball of light completely, and vanished.

David ran towards Mrs. Wilkins and looked down at her blackened body.

"Oh…this is *not* good." He dropped to his knees. "We've lost the *soul*. I'm going to get sacked," he said, as he narrowed his eyes. "I shouldn't have let this happen. I should have seen it, been more prepared. This is my fault."

He jumped up and started to kick the dishwasher. Mrs. Wilkins's shriveled body rebounded as it jiggled and bounced up against the door. Black ooze dripped out from the corners of her mouth.

David shook his head. "Wait a minute…I don't understand? How did they get here so quickly? It doesn't make any sense."

A chill rolled up inside Kara at the panic in his voice. "What…what do you mean? David, what are you talking about?"

"The demons. They never show up that fast. It usually takes an hour or so for them to sense us. But this was like…they *knew* we'd be here."

After a moment, he looked up at Kara, his eyes wild. "We have to get out of here." He stood still for a moment, then sprinted out of the kitchen and vanished into the bathroom, leaving Kara staring open-mouthed.

"Quickly, this way," yelled David from the bathroom doorway. "It's clear." He disappeared inside the bathroom.

"I don't have a good feeling about this." Kara struggled to her feet. "Ow!" She felt a sharp pain on her right ankle. She lifted up her pant leg. A tiny black mark in the shape of a spider web traced her ankle. "What the...?" She rubbed her finger across it and felt no discomfort. The pain was gone. She rolled the bottom of her pant leg back down and took off after David.

When she reached the bathroom doorway, David was kneeling beside the toilet convulsing, but he wasn't puking his nonexistent guts. Instead, raging mad, he rummaged through the contents of his bag and pulled out a file. He shoved it in Kara's face. "Here, take this...you'll need it. We're going to Level Four. We have to tell them we've *lost* a soul and it's not going to be pretty. Get ready."

Kara stared down at her shoes, feeling miserable. She wasn't entirely sure what this meant, or what she had done, but from the crazy expression on David's face, she figured losing a soul was *very* bad.

"I'm sorry," she managed to croak. "I...I—tripped and then I couldn't pull her out. I kept pulling and pulling, and then I tripped again and the demon..."

"Don't worry about that." David straightened up and he threw the duffel bag back over his shoulder. "Right now, the best thing for you and me is to get out of here." He lifted up the toilet seat with his foot. He glanced up at Kara and cocked his head towards the toilet. "You go first, I'll cover you." He jumped over and stood in the doorway protectively, watching.

"What? What are you doing?" cried Kara, flabbergasted, her eyes bugging out of her head. "You don't want me to—you can't be *serious*. That's disgusting."

David turned to face her and said sharply. "We really don't have time for this. Haven't you noticed the demons here—*hello?*"

Kara blinked. "You're crazy. No, you're insane. There's no way I'm touching that. It's nasty."

"That's what they tell me." David turned his head and watched the hallway, then turned back to Kara and met her eyes. "I need you submerge your head in *water*, and I'm not going to wait to draw you a bath. Do you *really* want to wait around and see if the shadow demons decide to come back? Because they will, you can count on that."

Although she didn't want to admit it, Kara knew David was probably right. Reluctantly she leaned towards the toilet and clasped her hand on her mouth "It stinks. Are toilets normally that small? I'm not sure my head is going to fit in that." She grimaced as she gawked at the yellow water and the slimy brown ring around the inside.

"It'll fit." David sighed loudly as he dropped his shoulders and looked up at the ceiling. "You're not going to catch a disease or anything, you're dead remember? You're going to have to get used to it. It's your new career. Quickly...I'll be right behind you." He came forward and edged her towards the toilet.

"Wait," said Kara desperately. "What happens after I put my head in it?" She pointed to the toilet.

"You'll be back in Horizon, on your way to Level Four," said David after a long pause. "You'll be safe. I promise. Now, let's go. Come on." He pushed her forward.

There was a sudden loud *crunch* from the kitchen.

Kara winced. She turned and looked at David with her eyes wide. He jumped into the hallway, his dagger clasped in his hand. Kara strained her legs to move and stepped into the doorframe. Sticking out her shaking head from the bathroom doorway, she realized the noise was only Mrs. Wilkins's shriveled up body slipping a few inches off the dishwasher's door.

David jumped back into the room and pushed Kara forward towards the toilet. "Okay, that's it. Don't make me throw you in there." He cocked an eyebrow. "I will if I have to...trust me."

Kara wobbled over and stared down at the empty toilet. "I can't believe I'm about to do... what I'm about to do. We need water—right."

She clasped the file against her chest. "I can't catch anything. I'm already dead." She shut her eyes. "It smells like roses...big, beautiful roses like at Nanny's house." Kara pinched her nose, plunged her head in the toilet, felt her millions of molecules separating, and vanished.

CHAPTER 5

THE HALL OF SOULS

KARA FORCED HER EYES OPEN. She stared at a gray marble floor. Half of her face was squished against the cool ground. She felt her knees folded under her and her butt in the air. Walls with wood panels surrounded her. She pushed herself up and sat on her heels.

An enormous primate sat in the operator's chair. Although he was sitting, his frame reached the top of the elevator's ceiling, his bald head grazing the top. His long hairy arms brushed the floor and his fat behind drooped on both sides of a wooden chair. Bright orange fur toppled over his red slacks and covered every inch of him...a jumbo-sized orangutan.

Kara scrambled to her feet and checked herself out. She studied the orangutan for moment and cleared her throat. "Hey there," she said and gave a little wave. "You're not chimp 5M51."

The orangutan rotated its head in Kara's direction. It blinked, and then whirled around in the chair to face her. A small pair of round spectacles rested crookedly on the bridge of his flattened nose.

"What floor, Miss?" It lowered its head to be at eye level with Kara and pushed the spectacles up with an exceptionally long finger. "Hmm?"

Kara raised her eyebrows. "Right ...um ..." She glanced down at the crumpled file still clutched against her chest. "Uh...I think I'm supposed to go to Level *Four*?" She looked behind her half expecting David to suddenly appear. She wished he was here with her.

The primate watched her. His watery eyes darted to the file she held near her middle. In one slow movement, it lifted its arm and pressed the number four brass button on the control panel. Long strands of orange hair swayed below his arm. "Level Four!" He said loudly, his peach colored eyes bewitching her.

"Thank you," she managed to say staring at the floor. "So ...you work with chimp 5M51?"

"Chimp!" interrupted the primate furiously. "*I* am no *chimp*. Do not mistake me for one of that *dreadful* lot. My species is superior. *I* am an orangutan. Orangutan 7PT9, if you please," he said as he puffed out his chest. He straightened his spectacles and wrinkled his face in contempt.

"Okay then, orangutan 7T-something-something...?"

Kara sighed as she waited in a long and uncomfortable silence. The elevator ascended to a higher level. She noticed the orangutan staring at her. "Why do you keep staring at my head?" she said after she couldn't bear it anymore. "Is my head on the menu or something? What is it?"

The orangutan dropped his eyes and stared at the floor. "Hmm...no reason. I wasn't staring at your head."

"Yes, you were."

"No, I wasn't."

"You just did it again. I saw you."

"I don't know what you're talking about." 7PT9 lifted his chin and faced the control panel. His left eye stared at Kara.

Kara bit her lip. "Whatever." She hid her head behind the file. Her hands shook. "Stay calm. Level Four can't be as bad as Level Three," she said to herself.

Her mind flashed back to what had happened to Mrs. Wilkins moments ago. Images of shadow demons flashed before her eyes. A tiny ball of light hovered above Mrs. Wilkins's dead body. Kara frowned and lowered the file. She wasn't sure she was guardian angel material. She wrapped her arms around her chest. What happens to guardian angels who've lost a soul? Kara leaned against the panel. Her body trembled. She waited.

Suddenly the back of Kara's head bounced and hit the panel as the elevator jolted to a stop.

"Level Four: Hall of Souls," yelled the orangutan.

"Okay, here goes nothing. Wish me luck!" Kara clasped the file against her chest and stepped up to the elevator doors, only to feel a sudden tug on her head.

"Ouch!" Kara rubbed her injured scalp. "Are you crazy! What? Is my head a dandruff buffet to you? What is *wrong* with you *monkeys!*" she yelled.

The orangutan lifted his chin in the air. "Ah, correction…not *monkey*, Miss, but *orangutan.*" He turned and faced the control panel. "Level Four," he called again as he sucked his fingers.

Kara glared at the orangutan. "Cannibal," she hissed under her breath.

"Tasty," replied the primate.

The doors swished open. Kara stepped forward. "Wow…"

She stumbled out of the elevator with legs made of jelly. She stood in a never-ending ebony sky. The Hall of Souls sparkled like a great field of fireflies. It reminded her of the sky above the farmer's fields behind her grandma's house at night, of watching the lightening bugs as they lit up the black skies like twinkling stars. The corners of her mouth curled up.

Kara trod forward on black marble floors. As she ventured deeper into Level Four she came to realize that her fireflies were, in fact, millions of dazzling spheres hovering in the air. Soon she found herself surrounded by light. Brilliant globes floated all around her, as though Christmas lights draped down from the sky. She peeked through the glowing spheres and caught a glimpse of something huge and white. It flickered in the midst of the great hall. The white shape glistened and grew brighter, like an enormous flame. A humid breeze caressed her cheeks. Soft humming filled her ears. She closed her eyes and sighed.

"Whoa!" cried Kara as someone crashed into her. She tripped and fell to the ground, then rolled over onto her elbows. Her aggressor walked away in the opposite direction and disappeared behind a wall of light. "Excuse *me*," growled Kara. She struggled to her feet. "What am I...*invisible?*" She marched on, then stopped dead in her tracks.

Hundreds of golden-haired children scurried around the majestic space. They made their way through thousands of floating globes and carried what looked like large glass jars. Their Forget-me-not-blue robes swished behind them. Kara stared at their identical faces.

Three-wheeled vehicles sped erratically across the floors, driven by the same golden-haired kids. The back seats of the little cars were overloaded with more glass jars. They clinked together as the vehicles dashed through the walls of light and out of sight.

Kara was surrounded by a Cirque du Soleil extravaganza. She peered over the kids' heads. A sparkle caught her eye. She walked towards it. After a moment, she stepped into a clearing. A desk chiseled from a large block of glass stood on a raised platform. Catching the light from the globes, it sparkled like a giant diamond. A great man sat behind it.

Kara's feet vibrated below her and the mass of glowing globes hummed in unison, as though millions of fireflies took flight at the same moment.

But where was David? Had something happened to him? He was supposed to be right behind her. She shook her head, trying to purge the images of David being ripped apart by demons.

"Uh …excuse me?" said Kara to a flock of kids. She forced a smile reminiscent of David's. "Hi …can you help me? I'm not sure what to do with this?" She held up the file.

They ignored her and walked away, as though she was invisible.

"Thanks for nothing," yelled Kara. Tapping sounds caught her attention. She turned around. "David? Ah…not David."

A pair of guardian angels with golden stars on their foreheads emerged from a wall of shining spheres. They marched past her, looking somber, and headed towards the glass desk. Kara decided to follow them.

They walked in single file towards the desk. It glimmered like a crystal in the sunlight. A rainbow of colors spilled onto the black floor. The desk was covered with books, with a large flat-screen computer monitor sandwiched between them. A massive man with a furrowed brow sat amongst the clutter of books and papers. He was dressed in a white robe, open in the front with a high gold-trimmed collar, his long sleeves folded on the desk. Gold cloth trimmed the wide cuffs. His face was handsome and serious. A golden glow emanated from his pale skin. And as Kara tiptoed closer, she noticed his forehead was marked with a golden shield, crisscrossed with two silver swords. He terrified her.

The two guardian angels dragged themselves up to the desk and spoke with their heads bowed. Kara stayed a few feet behind them. She fumbled with her file. The thought of addressing this man made the hairs on the back of her neck stand up. Perhaps no one would notice if she ran away. After a moment, the man looked up and gave them a malicious and calculating look. One of the angels held out a file. The man grabbed it and flipped it open. In a quick movement, he beckoned to the driver of one of the three-wheeled contraptions. The vehicle swerved around, sprinted towards the dais, and jolted to a halt. The guardian angels climbed into the back seat. With their heads bent awkwardly, they squeezed themselves into the tiny space. They raced out into the fields of glowing spheres. Kara stared after them.

"Where's David?" whispered Kara. Her body tickled unpleasantly. Her mind was working hard. She bit her lower lip. Her hands shook and she teetered back and forth on her heels like a seesaw. After a moment, she edged forward. Her eyes were glued to the large man's hands. She halted with the file clasped tightly to her middle. She waited. He didn't seem to notice her at first. He studied the pages of a thick, leather-bound book. Kara recalled images of her once-upon-a-time-happy life back on Earth—alive—where angels and demons existed only in her paintings, and where she was enjoying a juicy piece of pepperoni pizza, with grease dripping down the corners of her mouth...

The giant man lifted his perfect head and examined her. "Name, class order, and rank," demanded a booming voice.

Kara forced the words out of her mouth. "Uh ...I-I'm, Ka-Kara ..." she stammered, crumpling her file with trembling fingers. "Um, I don't know my class order, but I know I'm a *rookie?*" She pushed herself up.

His flaring blue eyes searched her for a moment. He held out his hand in front of her. "Give me the file," he commanded.

Kara obeyed and handed him the file. Her hands shook, and she clenched them into fists.

The man sat back and flipped through the file. His head snapped up. "You are the rookie, Kara Nightingale. Your class order is # 4321. You're back from your first assignment...where is your Petty Officer?" He lifted his brows and looked behind her.

"Um ...I'm not sure. He was supposed to be right behind me..." Kara said nervously. She turned her head around, searching behind her. "He...he told me to come here to Level Four. That's all I know." She clasped her hands behind her back and fumbled with her fingers.

The man eyed her in silence for a moment. He looked back down at the file. "Tell me, what is the name of your Petty Officer?"

Kara blinked. "David McGowan."

With eyebrows raised, the man pursed his lips and looked up at her. "I see," he said flatly. "You're with *David*."

"Ah...do you know him? Are we in trouble or something?" She let her arms fall at her sides. "Do you know where he is?"

"I will have to report this." At that moment his hands moved over a keyboard. His brows dropped slowly and shot up every few seconds as he typed. After what seemed to Kara to be a very long five minutes of staring at someone's fingers there was a loud *tap*, *tap*, and Kara turned to see David jogging up to her.

"Ah...there you are, Kara," said David, smiling widely. His hair was a bit messy, Kara noticed. But other than that he appeared fine. He turned to the giant man, "Hello, Ramiel. You miss me? Oh, Mighty One?"

Kara glared at him. "What took you so long?" she whispered. "I'm dying here."

David dropped his duffel bag on the ground. "I was delayed. You know...demons."

Ramiel glared at David. His blue eyes blazed. "Well, David McGowan, I see you haven't lost your sense of *humor*," he said coldly. His face twisted in discontent. Kara stole a quick look at David, just long enough to catch him winking at her. She turned around.

"I see you have *abandoned* your rookie on her very first assignment? I'm sure Lieutenant Archangel Gabriel would be interested in this information," said Ramiel. "Never playing by the rules...are we, David? Believe you are *above* the rules? You're not setting a very good example for your rookie. Putting her life in danger isn't good for your record." He waved a large finger annoyingly at Kara, and then his eyes moved to David. He gave him a reproachful stare.

David smiled, studying Ramiel's face. "You're always so kind to me, Your Lordship. But don't worry, she was never in any danger. I took care of it."

Ramiel cocked an eyebrow. "We hope you will guide Kara and help her embrace her duties as a guardian angel...without the loss of her soul or *rule* breaking."

David flashed his perfect teeth and put on an innocent look. "Me? *Rule* breaking? Never, Your Blessedness! I am a true believer in playing by the rules...you just remember that," he beamed.

Ramiel's expression darkened. His beautiful face creased in contempt. With a loud *screech* he pushed back his chair and stood up. He towered over Kara and David easily. "As I understand it, you're on very *thin* ice already as it is, David. Unfortunately for you, the Legion is tired of your mess. You lack discipline. I better not hear of any foolish business like jumping out of airplanes or going after seven higher demons by yourself! What kind of example are you setting for the rookies?!" he roared.

Kara wondered how many other rookies David had trained before her. He couldn't be that bad, could he?

David lifted his right hand, palm facing Ramiel. "Cross my heart and hope to do die—oh, wait a minute. I'm already dead," he laughed.

Ramiel's scowl was frightening. Kara had a feeling that, if he wanted, he could probably squish her and David into jelly. Instead he threw the file at David, who caught it easily. "There is a *soul* to be burned." He sat back down and immediately returned his attention to his keyboard.

David opened the file and scanned through it. He closed it and turned to face Kara. His beaming face transformed quickly to a gloomy one. "Um...this burning soul business isn't the most pleasant, you know. But, hey...better get it out of the way. Let's go." David turned around and grabbed Kara by the arm. He pulled her along with him.

"What?" Kara blurted out, as she wiggled out of his grip. "Wait, uh...David, can you tell me what's going on? What am I supposed to do here? What did Ramiel mean by, *'there's a soul to be burned?*'" Kara had a terrible feeling *her* soul was the one to be barbecued.

"Huh? Oh, right. Don't worry about Ramiel. *Archangels* think they own the place, just because they report to The Chief in person. Think that makes them *special*. Just a bunch of swollen-headed morons, if you ask me," he sneered and turned on his heel. He set off towards the fields of brilliant globes.

Kara chased after him. "So...soul burning...what's that? The thought of burning anything makes me nervous."

"You've lost Mrs. Wilkins' soul...so we have to go burn it. We have to throw the dead souls into the white fires of Atma. They can never be reborn."

"Souls can be *reborn*?" said Kara in awe. She couldn't picture it.

"Of course... when a mortal body dies, the soul is reborn into another mortal body when a new child is born. And the process just keeps going, over and over again, unless the soul gets killed...like Mrs. Wilkins'. Then it's finished—finito—they're goners."

Kara felt as though she had just been punched in the gut. Her legs stiffened. "I...I killed her. I killed her soul—this is all my fault." She imagined Mrs. Wilkins reborn as a cute little baby. Her throat tightened. "She'll never be reborn because of *me*. I...I killed her."

"It's not your fault. Don't torture yourself. Listen...these things happen, it's part of the job."

Kara dropped her shoulders. "Well...this part *really* sucks."

David shoved his fingers into his mouth and whistled loudly. A three-wheeled car jerked to a stop. Kara followed David to the waiting car and squeezed herself into the back seat after him. He opened the file and showed it to the driver, who nodded and then stepped on the accelerator. The engine roared loudly. Kara and David flew against the back seats, their cramped bodies squished together in an extremely uncomfortable body tangle. As the driver zigzagged his way around the great hall, Kara suddenly wished she had a stomach full of partially digested food, so that she could throw it up all over the driver.

Tall white flames wavered and danced up ahead, like a giant candle. The flames grew in size as they drove past them. The car raced on. It flew down invisible roads and paths in an endless blackness. Finally, it stopped. Thousands of globes sparkled all around them.

Kara looked around. A tall white fire burned in a majestic stone fireplace behind them. To Kara, it looked like a fire that belonged in a fairy tale. She wondered if she could touch the flame.

David yanked himself out of the vehicle and walked towards a wall of glowing spheres. He paid particular attention to a blackened globe which hung inches from the ground. Unlike the other sparkling spheres, no illumination came from it.

Kara pulled herself out of the car. The driver remained seated and stared in the opposite direction. A salty smell filled her nose, and her mind flashed with images of the ocean. She walked over and stood next to David. "What's the matter with you? You look like someone just died."

David leaned over the dark sphere. He sighed and was silent.

"What's going on? Why is everyone so frantic out about this black ball?" She looked at it suspiciously. "What's so special about it?"

Kara moved closer towards the dark globe. Immediately, she felt a wave of desolation pass through her, as though someone close to her had just died. She was overcome with sadness, which frightened her. She took a step back. "What…what *is* that?" She shook her head and tried to shake the feelings away. "David…what's happening? Why do I feel like this?"

He knelt down and carefully grasped the sphere in his hands. "You're feeling the loss of a life. This soul belonged to Mrs. Wilkins. When the soul is killed on Earth, it also dies in Horizon. The life lights have gone out. All that's left is this blackened shell. Here…take it," said David as he pushed himself up and stretched out his hands.

Astounded, Kara took another step back. "You want me to hold it? I don't want to."

"You have to. You were the guardian angel of that soul. You're responsible for it." David grabbed Kara's right hand and pressed the globe into it.

As the cold sphere touched her skin, Kara was hit with an alarming number of different emotions, as though a collection of feelings from thousands of years had exploded into her all at once. She staggered and nearly dropped it.

"Careful now, don't *drop* it," said David, as he grabbed Kara by the arm and steadied her.

"This feels so weird. What am I supposed to do with it?" Kara trembled as the emotions ran through her body.

"Throw it in the fire. Dead souls need to be burned in the white fires of Atma," answered David, and gestured behind them towards the huge stone fireplace. It towered fifteen feet above them. Tall white flames flickered hundreds of feet in the air.

"It's better if you make it quick, *trust* me." David walked towards the impressive fireplace. He dragged Kara by the elbow with him. "This part of the job really sucks. What you do is…you need to throw it in the fire."

They reached the fire and stopped. Kara blinked several times. The brightness of the flames hurt her eyes, like when she used to stare at the sun without blinking.

David studied Kara's face. "And better do it fast."

Kara raised her eyebrows. "Wait. Why do you look so tense? What's going to happen once I throw it in?" She had the horrible feeling that things were about to get a lot worse.

"Um, I can't really describe it…just do it," said David as he sensed her reluctance and pushed her forward with his hands against her back.

Wide-eyed, Kara took a step forward. She grasped the dead soul in her shaking palms. Kara approached the white fire. She was surprised to feel no heat. It was white hot, but she felt nothing…no burning sensation against her skin. She lifted her hands before her and threw the dead soul into the white fires.

The ground shook.

Millions of screaming voices exploded inside her head, as though all the existing souls cried out in excruciating pain the moment she dropped the globe into the white flames. Kara's body burned from the inside. The screams tormented her. They pulled at her soul. Images flashed before her eyes: a dark woman working in a field, a young blond girl riding her bike in a manicured suburb, an old woman bargaining for fish in a loud market. A sudden passion rose inside her as she saw images of a beautiful red headed woman kissing her lover. More images of different women flashed inside her brain. They screamed as their souls slowly pulled away from her, dying. She swayed on the spot, as the thunderous emotions ransacked her being. And then the feelings and images disappeared. She fell onto the hard floor.

Kara opened her eyes a moment later, only to see David's concerned face inches from her own. "It gets easier, I promise. I passed out, too, the first time. You don't look as bad though. Okay, let's get you up." He yanked her back on her own two feet.

"That was..." she said in a harsh voice as she tried to regain control, "...very interesting. When do I stop shaking?"

"It'll pass in a few minutes. I know how painful it feels..." David reached out and pressed his hand against her back, rubbing gently in a circular motion. "It's really the worst part of the job."

Kara lifted up her head. Their eyes met and locked. Her skin prickled as she felt warmth spilling throughout her being. Tiny electric shocks zapped all the way from her head to the tip of her toes. She pulled her eyes away. There was a long and uncomfortable silence. She didn't dare look into his eyes again. So instead, she spoke to his boots. "When do we leave? I don't think I can stand another minute here."

David removed his hand from her back and stepped away. He stretched. "Right now."

"Good." Kara felt sick, if that was even possible in her guardian angel body. "Where are we going now?"

David clasped his hands together and rubbed them. He beamed. "Now comes the fun part." He danced on the spot. "You and I are going to Operations."

CHAPTER 6

OPERATIONS

ON THE ELEVATOR RIDE to Operations, Kara watched silently as two identical monkeys operated the control panel. The size of common house cats, they were completely covered in black fur except for two white streaks along the sides of their backs. More white covered the bottom half of their faces, like an old man's beard. Long bushy tails wrapped around the chair's back rest. In a flash, one of the monkeys leaped off the chair and dashed across and around the elevator walls. It brushed the top of David's and Kara's heads before settling back beside its brother. It put something in its mouth and started chewing.

Kara rubbed the top of her scalp. She wanted to choke them. "You little *creeps!*"

"*Don't worry about it, I got this,*" whispered David from the corner of his mouth.

Kara glared at the monkeys and put her hands on her head, protecting it from the furry cannibals. She blinked. A black shape rocketed across the walls—and then stopped. Its tiny feet dangled in the air as David grabbed a monkey by the throat.

He brought the monkey to his face. "I will pull off your tail and then your brother's tail if you try that again...rat. *Believe* me."

And when he let go of the monkey, it scurried away and climbed back onto the chair, facing the panel. It stood still for a moment, then turned its head and stuck out its brown tongue. Its twin gave them the finger with its four hands.

"You're making this too easy for me, you little rats." David took a step forward.

"Okay, we'll stop," said the monkeys in unison. "We promise we'll be good." Both monkeys flashed a set of yellow teeth and wrapped their arms around each other. Somehow, Kara wasn't convinced. She covered her head with her hands, just in case.

After a very long three minutes of obscene theatrics from Tweedle Dee and Tweedle Dum, the elevator jerked to a stop. The doors swished open, and Kara stepped off the elevator. Her feet pressed into soft ground.

Kara lifted her head and looked around. Operations was like the Sahara Desert. Rolling hills of ruby red sand stretched out for miles, rippling like giant Ruffles potato chips. A soft breeze tickled her forehead, and she wiped her bangs away from her eyes. A strong salty fragrance filled the air around them. It reminded her of the times when she was about ten years old, running across the beach at her grandparents' cottage, chasing the waves. Kara smiled. It was her happy place. Fluffy white clouds raced each other across a baby blue sky and out of sight.

Kara turned at the sound of the elevator disappearing into the ground, as though a patch of quicksand had swallowed it up. She followed David down a slope leading into a populated area in the middle of the red desert. Her feet pressed deep into the sand with every step as they got closer. Soon she was walking through a maze of tall white pyramids. She squinted. "What are those?" Kara side-stepped closer to one of them and stretched out her hand. Her fingers pressed right through it. She frowned. "Is this some kind of white sand?"

"No. It's salt," answered David.

Kara took a handful. She opened her fingers and watched the tiny white crystals escape through the gaps. She wiped her hand on her jeans and ran to catch up with David.

"Why is all this salt here?"

"It's for the pools."

"Right. And ...why is that again?" asked Kara.

David smiled. "It's for protection." He stared into Kara's eyes. "Salt is a weapon against demons. It acts as a repellent, sort of. It hurts them, and we can use it to kill them, too."

Kara nodded her head. "Good to know."

Loud thumping and squeaking noises surrounded them. Kara peeked around one of the pyramids. Hundreds of large construction-like trucks dumped huge quantities of salt onto the ground. The vehicles wheeled themselves right into the salt pyramids and sucked out the salt with long metal hoses, like giant vacuum cleaners. Massive round glass containers rested on their backs. They filled up with salt. Her eyes darted to the drivers. They were the same yellow-haired kids from the Hall of Souls.

David noticed Kara staring at the drivers. "The little guys are cherubs."

"Cherubs?" repeated Kara. "Aren't they supposed to have wings and fly around like cupid?"

"Don't believe everything you read."

Before she could open her mouth again and ask more questions, David grabbed Kara by the elbow and urged her forward. She followed him through the jungle of the salt pyramids. After a few minutes, they came to a clearing with thousands of open blue tents arranged in rows across a flatter part of the red desert. Long white drapes of cloth on poles rippled in the breeze atop each of the tents, like enormous flags. The tents were alive and loud with the clatter of steel on steel and the clamor of fighting. Hundreds of guardian angels fought each other in combat practice. They stabbed and sliced with shiny silver swords. The clanking of wood hitting wood grew louder as she spotted other angels hitting and blocking each other with wooden staffs. Puffs of red sand shot up in the air. The combatants kicked up their feet and plowed them into their opponent's chest.

Kara studied David's face. "Am I going to learn all that?" She pointed to the fighting.

David turned his head and looked at her. He smiled. "All GAs are required to learn basic combat training. Today's your first day. "

Kara's face twisted in a grin. She felt tiny sparks of excitement. "I always wanted to learn how to defend myself...like learning some martial arts or something. I think it's cool." She skipped alongside David and increased her speed.

Some tents sheltered desks, spread out in rows as in a classroom. Guardian angels sat behind them with open books. Oracles stood on their crystal balls at the front of each of these classrooms and addressed the angels.

The salty ocean fragrance lingered in the air. Kara pressed her shoes into the red sand and followed David. She stretched her neck in every direction, not wanting to miss anything. Groups of oracles rolled past them. They conversed amongst themselves, carrying large books that left long paper trails behind.

After a few minutes of walking, they reached a gully where hundreds of round pools spread out in rows and disappeared beyond the red dunes. Shining metal staircases leaned against them. Loads of guardian angels jumped into the pools at the same time, like an international diving competition. Flashes of white light hovered above the pools, and then disappeared.

Kara and David walked through the crowds of angels and oracles to a tent filled with every kind of weapon imaginable: swords, bows, daggers, maces, axes, and glowing white nets. They all dangled from hooks screwed into standing wooden panels, like large tool walls. Tables were covered with shiny blue arrows and white crystal orbs of every size. David unhooked two long daggers and hid them inside his jacket.

"What am I supposed to use?" Kara glanced at the hundreds of weapons hanging from the panels. "Hey…what do I use? Yes, very good, David."

With a stupid smile plastered across his face and making sure he had Kara as an audience, David was juggling three orbs. He threw them higher and higher into the air. "Pick a sword or a dagger…" He caught the orbs one after another and bowed. "Whichever you want."

Kara shook her head. He was beginning to grow on her. She saw a small golden scabbard amongst the rows of larger swords. She walked over to the panel and lifted it from its hook. It had a gold handle with wing cross guards. She clasped her left hand around the scabbard, and pulled the blade out with her right hand. A flicker of light shone on the golden blade. She turned it in her hand. Stars appeared to be etched into it. The sword felt strangely familiar in her hand, and very light.

"So, you've picked this one, eh?" said David, as he moved beside her.

Kara looked down at the shiny sword and grinned. "Yup. I like it. It *sparkles.*" She twirled it in her hand, as she would one of her paintbrushes. She sliced the air as she brought it down. "I'm ready to cut me up some demons."

David pressed his right hand against his chest and screwed up his face. "I'm so proud of you, I could *cry.*"

"Please don't. So…where to now?"

He jumped up in the air. "Now you're talkin' like a true GA. This way."

David grabbed Kara by the arm and pulled her out of the tent. He dragged her with him until he found an empty tent. Then he balanced himself and pulled off his boots with his feet. "It's better if you take your shoes off."

Kara looked down at her black ballerina flats. "Right...these aren't exactly combat material." She pulled off her shoes and wiggled her toes in the red sand. The soft sand felt wonderful against her toes.

"The Legion has a few basic maneuvers that all GAs have to learn...real easy stuff." David pulled off his jacket and threw it on the wooden table near the end of the tent. "I'll teach you how to attack, to parry, and how to riposte." He walked to the middle of the area beneath the tent, where the form of a circle was drawn with a white powder. He stood with legs apart. "Above all, you need to learn how to protect yourself. Once you've mastered this, then I'll teach you the fun stuff...how to *hit* and *vanquish* demons." He stretched out his right arm and gestured with his hand for her to come where he stood. "You have to know where to *cut* them...where it hurts."

"I can't believe I'm actually going to do this." Kara stepped forward and stood in the circle facing David. "Um...this should be interesting." She studied David's grinning face. "I must warn you...I sucked in gym class." She twisted her sword in her hand. "Never had good eye-hand coordination."

"You'll do fine."

"You might lose an eye."

"The ladies love an eye patch."

"Okay then, I'm ready, Captain Hook."

David flashed a smile. "First, always make sure to have sufficient distance between your feet…"

Kara mimicked David's feet position and stood with her legs apart.

"Good. And keep track of all the moves your opponent makes. Now, I'm going to show you how to parry. When you parry, the blade should be closer to the body like this…"

David clasped the sword with both hands and pointed the blade down with his wrists pronated, "…for self defense. You should always be looking for an opening to counter the attack. You ready?"

"I think so."

"Okay, I'm going to raise my sword and come in for an attack. Let the swords hit."

David moved forward and with a *clang* he hit Kara's sword with his own.

He stood facing her. "Now you want to sidestep and wrap your sword around so that you're holding it over your head…and ready to strike back. Like this…"

David rolled around, forcing Kara to follow his momentum. She came up around him and held her sword over her head, deflecting David's strike.

"I can do this." said Kara. "I can really do this."

David studied her face. "You see …you want to try it again?"

"Yeah. This is amazing. I can't believe it …"

"If you don't stop smiling soon, your face is gonna stay like that," laughed David.

Kara flashed a frown at David. "What's *wrong* with my smile?"

He raised his eyebrows, a huge smile of his own plastered across his face. "Nothing. Smiling is the second best thing you can do with your lips."

"Hey!" Kara shoved David forward, grateful for the non-existent flush on her cheeks. "Let's go." She tightened her grip on her sword and tried hard not to look at his lips.

David showed Kara how to disarm her opponent by twisting his blade and leaving him no choice but to drop it. She tripped on her own feet a couple of times and fell flat on her face, which was totally normal. But what felt abnormal to Kara was the fact that she didn't even break into a sweat and never got tired. She had no need for water, for food, or even for sleep. Like the energizer bunny, she kept on going and going and going. And for the following days— what Kara believed to be days—they spent every hour going over the hitting and blocking techniques.

"Keep your guard up," yelled David. He slashed Kara across the arm with his blade. A deep wound.

Immediately, Kara dropped to her knees and covered the cut with her hand. She stared open-mouthed at her arm. "You-you *cut* me? You cut my arm?" She glared at David, who only stared back.

His face crinkled into a smile. "Relax, it's nothing..."

"Nothing? You practically sliced my arm off!" Kara narrowed her eyes and looked back at her wound. She bit her lip, closed her right eye, and peeked with her left eye through her bangs. She prepared herself for the worst. But as Kara lifted her hand from her injury, she fell over backwards. A flash of brilliant light obscured her vision. She blinked. Rays of white light poured out from the gaping wound, as if a flashlight shone through the cut.

"What the...?" The wound started to heal itself. It pulled the edges of the cut together slowly, until not even a scar remained, as though her skin had stitched itself together. "I'm going mad." She stared at her arm. "Holy shi..."

"Ah! None of *that* here," laughed David, "you don't want Gabriel to hear you, *trust* me."

"But, my . . . my arm? My skin? It just...fixed itself." Kara couldn't believe her eyes; she felt as if she had just witnessed a really good visual effects stunt.

David pulled her up on her feet. "You're an *angel*, what did you expect, blood? You have no blood. You're not *human* anymore."

"Right...I...I forgot. I'm not human anymore." Kara stared at her arm where the cut had disappeared. She passed her hand along her skin. She smirked. "It's amazing. I can heal myself."

Kara was surprised to find that she enjoyed the training sessions with David. Her many injuries healed themselves, and remarkably, she developed a knack for it. The moves suddenly made sense. Her reflexes were good, and she could keep up with David.

A crowd of GAs grew slowly and formed a circle around Kara and David. Her neurons acted up. She felt prickling all over her body. She hated having any kind of attention on her. A tall and powerful-looking older teen guardian angel stepped out from the crowd. He walked up to David and Kara with a grin on his face. His brown hair shimmered in the sun. Two golden stars flashed on his forehead.

"Wow, pretty good for a rookie. But then again, your teacher lacks discipline...any rookie could beat him," he laughed as he turned and encouraged the crowd to laugh as well. He turned his handsome face and eyeballed Kara.

"Care to test your skills on me? Unless of course, *your* Petty Officer is afraid I'll make him look bad in front of his peers?"

He flashed his gleaming white teeth at David. A few GAs snickered.

David pursed his lips. Kara saw hatred in his eyes as he stepped up to the angel. "Don't you have a hair appointment or something, Benson? Stop wasting our time, douche bag," he said, as he shifted his sword between his hands menacingly. He looked at Kara momentarily and gave her a wink.

A second later, Benson pulled out a gleaming silver sword. "Always a wise-ass."

The crowd around him dispersed. His face twisted up in concentration. He bared his teeth in a snarl with his eyes glued on David.

"What is this, a testosterone fight in Horizon?" Kara took a step towards them, lifting her hands in the air with her palms facing outwards. "Okay, boys, let's not do anything stupid. We're in a *happy* place, right? There's no need for this."

Benson turned his attention to Kara. His tawny eyes glittered as he stared her down. He studied her with a strange look in his eyes.

"I see why you've picked this one…she's *pretty*. We all know what you do to the pretty ones."

Kara frowned and watched David's reaction. She couldn't read his face under all the angry wrinkles.

"I'd mind my own business if I were you," David growled.

"It is my business. She was my *friend*. I knew what you were doing to her!"

"What?" said Kara. "David…what is he talking about?" A sudden feeling of jealously welled inside her. She tried to shake it off, but somehow it was getting worse.

And without warning, Benson charged forward and kicked David hard in the stomach. Kara watched in horror as David stumbled backwards. He regained his balance quickly and stepped back into the fighting circle, his blade grasped tightly in his hand.

Benson's face cracked into a sly smile. "I'm surprised the Legion even gave you a rookie, after what happened to Sarah. I always said you were going to get one of us killed! What you did to her was unforgivable. You broke our most *sacred* law."

He turned his head and read the puzzlement on Kara's face.

"Oh? So she doesn't know? You're better off looking for another Petty Officer, Rookie. *Love* affairs are forbidden in Horizon."

Kara looked at David and saw a flash of fury in his eyes as he threw himself at Benson.

"Angels!" an oracle bellowed, "What is going on here?" Kara watched the oracle roll over towards them. She had never seen an oracle look so outraged.

"Nothing, oracle," answered Benson, with the face of an angel. "We're practicing combat maneuvers…that's all."

The oracle's blue eyes went from Benson to Kara to David, before going back to Benson. The oracle pursed his lips and cocked an eyebrow. "It didn't look like practice from where I was…and I've *seen* it many times before! A bit *harsh*, don't you think? You are not savages…you are angels. It's time you behave like them."

"We need to be able to defend ourselves…in extreme conditions…" said Benson. "Nothing we can't handle."

"You *can't* handle anything." David met Benson's glare.

"*Your* methods are not safe. They're insane. Your rookie will *die* because of you," spat Benson as he clasped his sword. His knuckles turned white.

"That's enough," yelled the oracle.

The ground shook. The light from inside his crystal ball seemed to darken.

The oracle twirled his beard around his fingers. "Everyone out. You have jobs to do and souls to save. Let's go!" Immediately, the crowd dispersed.

Benson threw a finger in David's direction. "You'll *pay* for her death! Filth like you doesn't belong in the Legion." Kara watched in silence as Benson marched out of the tent and out of sight. A few of his minion GAs tagged along behind him like sad little puppies.

"It really upsets me to see you angels not getting along," said the oracle. "And as for the two of you," he said as he pointed a skinny finger, "you have a bus to catch." Then he steered his glass sphere around and rolled away.

David stared at his feet. His expression changed like clouds before a storm. Kara wanted to ask David who had died, but something told her now was not the time. Instead, she settled for the obvious. She bent her body sideways and searched David's face. "Why does Benson hate you so much?"

"Because I'm better looking," he answered, as he met her eyes and winked.

"You're so full of crap. You know that?"

David's face cracked into a smile. "And that's why you *love* me."

"Oh, *please*. Did he hit you on the head or something? I think you're suffering from a bit of brain fart."

"Maybe," laughed David. "Okay, I think that's enough training for a while. You're more than ready for your next assignment."

They walked in silence through the red desert. Kara's mind filled with unanswered questions. But some in particular kept coming back. Who the heck is this Sarah? And what happened to her?

CHAPTER 7

FISH NETS AND SALT SHAKERS

DAVID LED KARA DOWN a little slope into the heart of the desert. They made their way towards a large white tent resting in the midst of a sandy red ocean. A large powerful man with short black hair sat in a chair.

"Is that another Archangel?" asked Kara.

"Yup."

"Thought so. They're all, like, really... *big*."

"Big men with bigger egos."

The Archangel's dark brown skin contrasted against his white linen top and trousers. Her eyes moved to his face. It was beautiful, as if some higher power had sculpted it to perfection. She forced herself to look away.

In the light wind, sheets of paper fluttered across the top of a great wooden table that ran the length of the tent. Kara counted ten oracles rolling on their glass globes, rummaging through files along the table. A line of about fifty guardian angels waited patiently on the other side. Some angels stood at the front of the table. They each conversed with an oracle. After a moment one of the oracles gave an angel a file, then the angel nodded and marched out of the tent. He walked down a gully and headed towards the pool area. A few minutes later, the guardian angel climbed up a metal staircase and jumped in without hesitating.

A loud *tick tock* sound found its way to Kara's ears. A large brass grandfather clock stood in the background...it read two o'clock.

She followed David to the end of the line and looked up at him. His face cracked into a grin. She rolled her eyes and turned her head towards the pools. Silhouettes of GAs jumped into the waters of their next assignments. Kara and David stood in silence for a while. The waiting was driving her mad.

"So...what's the next assignment?" Kara asked.

"Don't know yet. We'll know what it is once the oracle gives us the job file."

Kara sighed. "Right ...do you think it'll be easier or harder this time?"

David shook his head slowly. "I'm not sure."

"Hmm."

Kara's mind flashed to the mysterious Sarah. She couldn't get her out of her head. Who was she? Did David break the sacred Horizon laws and had an affair with her? Could angels fall in love? She fought the strange jealous feelings creeping inside her. When Kara looked towards the grand table, they were finally at the head of the line and David addressed the Archangel.

"Hey...what's up, Gabe?" David bared his teeth.

There was a long pause before the Archangel lifted his eyes from his paper and gazed upon David. Kara saw him fully. Tall and powerful, with fierce black eyes that seemed to pierce through you. His face was dark and commanding; a magnificent beast of a man and as dangerous as a grizzly bear. His face was twisted in a scowl. "It's *Gabriel*," growled the Archangel as his mood darkened. "Ah, and here is our *famous* delinquent." The Archangel Gabriel towered over them, narrowing his eyes.

Kara bit the inside of her cheek. Does anybody like David in Horizon?

"Ha, ha, ha...very funny, Gabe," David said and turned to give Kara his trademark wink. He rolled his head back to Gabriel. "So ...got anything good for us?"

Gabriel's dark brown eyes flashed with resentment. "That depends on what you mean by *good*. But something has come up which might suit you, and your *particular* way of doing your job."

Kara felt a poke at her side. David raised his eyebrows. With a goofy smile painted across his face, he gave her two thumbs up. She smiled back and nodded. While David shifted with excitement, Kara studied Gabriel. He got up from his chair and walked over to an oracle to his right. They exchanged words, and after a moment Gabriel came back with a file clutched in his hand. He glanced at Kara for the first time, for about two seconds, and then he glared back at David.

"This assignment should agree with your rookie," boomed the Archangel, "as it is simple and should not have any *complications*."

Kara noticed the emphasis on the word *complication*. Gabriel stepped forward and thrust the file at David.

"Seems simple enough," said David after a moment, a slight lifting at the corners of his mouth. "And right up our alley." He closed the file.

Gabriel's hands turned into fists. "Remember our last conversation, David."

Kara realized that wasn't a question.

"No fooling around, you understand? I'm tired of covering up your messes. If you don't smarten up and take your job seriously, you'll be stricken from your GA post." He pointed a large finger at David. "This is your *last* warning!"

David kept smiling. "It's all good, Gabe."

"I'm *dead* serious, David!"

David rolled his eyes. "Ha, you're already *dead!*" He placed his right hand on his chest. "Don't worry, Gabe. I'll be a good little soldier—I promise."

"David, stop it! You're going to get us in trouble," whispered Kara.

"Don't worry...Gabe loves me," whispered David through his teeth.

"You're so full of crap! Oh no..."

The Archangel turned his attention to Kara. His dark eyes focused on her unnaturally, as though trying to break into her mind. He blinked and looked back to David. "After this *simple* assignment, I want you and your rookie to report back to me. Understand? She still needs more combat training."

Kara followed Gabriel's gaze over to the closest blue tent, where two guardian angels fought one another with swords. Their feet moved quickly in the sand, kicking up little clouds of red dust. Their weapons collided with loud clatters.

The oracle's voice woke her from her trance. "What are you waiting for? Get to it!" he yelled and clapped his grubby little hands together. "No time to waste! There are *lives* to be saved!" He turned around and looked at the clock. "Quickly now, you have less than an hour!" He waved his short arms in the air as he urged them on.

David turned and faced Kara. "Let's go." He walked out of the tent with Kara at his heels.

"DAVID!" bellowed Gabriel. "Remember what we discussed!"

"Sure thing, Gabe," answered David as he turned back around. He grabbed Kara by the elbow and steered her out from the tent.

Kara glanced back and met Gabriel's eyes, and saw a flash of suspicion in them. She quickly looked away.

After they replenished themselves with weapons in the weapons tent, Kara followed David down a slight slope to one of the many pools. Loud *plops* could be heard in every direction as hundreds of guardian angels plunged into them. Kara grimaced. A splash of salt water hit her face. She heard a motor running and turned to see a contraption that looked like giant vacuum cleaner. It rolled up to a neighboring pool and spit out the salt from its belly into the water.

"This place just gets on weirder by the minute," Kara said.

David placed himself behind a short line of guardian angels and waited to climb up to the pool's deck. "You ready?"

An old man five pools down pressed his hands together in front of himself, squatted, and with great effort he leaped into the air and belly-flopped into the water with a huge smile on his face.

"I'm not sure," said Kara. Water spilled out and around the edges of the pool. "What happens if I fail again?" Now Kara watched an Asian couple holding hands as they jumped into the pool together yelling, "Woo hee!"

"You won't. Trust me." David nudged Kara on the arm with his fist.

But somehow she wasn't convinced. She had a premonition that this new job wasn't as easy as she first imagined it to be, and a lot more dangerous.

David searched Kara's face for a moment, and then pulled himself up the metal staircase attached to the pool. "You'll see, it's going to get better, I promise. Stick with me and I'll show you a great time." He knelt down and passed his hand in the water. "Come on in, the water's great!" He beamed.

Kara sighed and climbed the staircase. She stepped onto the ledge and settled herself beside David. She opened her mouth to speak, but closed it as soon as her lips parted.

Benson stood on the edge of the neighboring pool. He stared at David with an expression of disgust, as though he had just bitten into a sour fruit. He stood there, his body hard and motionless, like a statue. Only his eyes moved as they looked David up and down. And then David noticed Benson. To Kara's surprise, he regarded him with disgust as well. Both men stared at each other down from a distance, as in a western pistol duel. But Kara saw pure hatred in

David's eyes as he glared at Benson. He turned his head away and looked at Kara. "Okay, you ready?"

"Uh—what was *that* about?" Kara said, still staring at Benson. "You guys look as if you want to rip out each other's throats." She turned and looked at David.

He met her eyes. "Nothing worth mentioning. Benson's a douche bag."

Within seconds, Benson pinched his nose, bent his knees, and jumped into the water. His body lingered for a moment through the moving waters, and then he started to spin horizontally. Seconds later, his entire body sparkled in brilliant white light. And then Benson vanished. No sooner had he performed his disappearing act than another guardian angel stepped up to the ledge and took the plunge. It was like watching a line of falling dominoes—angels kept jumping into the pools one after the other.

"We really should go," said David. He edged forward, ready to dive in. "We have to jump in at the same time. We can hold hands if you want…?"

"No thanks. I'm good. Can you stop smiling please?" Kara stuck her hands at her sides and bit her bottom lip. "We'll jump in at the same time."

"Okay then. On the count of three."

Kara nodded. She stared at the reflections on the water's surface. The water was a sheet of diamonds, sparkling in the sun light.

"One …" said David.

One, echoed Kara in her head as she tried to suppress her nerves.

"Two …"

Kara felt tiny electric shocks move around in her body—her nonexistent nervous system acting up.

"Three!"

David and Kara leaped into the air and plunged into the pool at the same time. Water splashed all around as they sank to the bottom. Kara opened her eyes and turned her head to the right. David was covered in light. A muffled sound escaped his mouth as his lips flapped together. He lifted his left hand and flipped his thumb up. Then Kara's vision blurred as she felt her body starting to spin. She kept her eyes open. Whitish bubbles floated in front of her and white light illuminated her body. Brilliant particles detached themselves one by one from her body—and then everything around her vanished.

Kara opened her eyes moments later. She sat in the back seat of a parked car. Cracked brown leather covered the seats. The only light came from the windows, which were nearly completely covered with gray grime. She crinkled her nose. It smelled like dirty old shoes and cigarettes. She blinked. Her vision adjusted itself to her new surroundings. David sat comfortably in the front seat. The leather seat screeched as he turned around to face her.

"How you feeling?" he asked, his face worried. "You okay?" He was almost angelic in that soft light, not at all the cocky soldier she was getting to know, but a beautiful creature from the heavens. She wished he'd stop being so concerned.

Kara pursed her lips and nodded. "I will be after the spinning stops."

She took a moment to get used to the dizziness. "That's weird." She said after a moment. "The dizziness is gone...I'm not spinning anymore. What the...?" She moved her hands. "I feel in more control of this body than I did the first time. It's still weird—super weird—but much better this time. A lot better." Her lips curled into a smile.

"That's great. The dizziness goes away after you've done about five Vega—after that, piece of cake. You won't feel a thing." David smiled at her, teeth bared.

Kara rubbed her forearm and pressed her hand against her mortal flesh. "Wow, this is still so weird!" She passed her hand gently on her skin. "It feels synthetic. Like there's a layer of saran wrap on top. Creepy," she laughed. She let go of her arm and looked around the car. "So ... where are we?" She strained her eyes to see outside the car windows.

"Let's find out." David grabbed the file from inside his leather jacket. He flipped it open on his knees. "Okay," he said after a moment, and looked outside his passenger window. "I think we're on Saint Hubert Street...yeah, I see it! We need to be on the corner of Notre Dame and Gosford Street in..." David glanced at his watch, "...in about forty minutes."

Kara looked out the window. "I know where we are. We're in Old Montreal! Most of my art classes were in this area. All the best art galleries in the city are here." She pressed her nose against the dirty glass.

"You were an artist? Before the…"

"Yup. Well … more like a wannabe artist." Kara turned and met David's eyes. "I was on my way to a really important competition…when I got squished by the bus."

"Ouch…that's pretty nasty." David looked away. "Was your boyfriend waiting for you…at that competition?"

Kara's mouth opened but nothing came out. She composed herself. "Uh…no, I didn't have a boyfriend. My best friend Mat was waiting for me, actually." She noticed David had a strange expression on his face.

"Were you guys close?"

"Close? Well, yeah. He was practically the only real friend I had. Whenever I brought new friends to my house they usually ran away screaming."

"Because of your mom and her demons?"

"Yeah, but that wasn't the only reason. I don't know how to explain it—and you'll probably think I'm crazy—but sometimes my mother would *disappear* before my eyes and reappear seconds later…somewhere else. Like one minute she's in the kitchen, and then the next, she's in the bathroom. And I can see by the look in your eye that you think I'm nuts."

David shook his head. "No. I'm trying to understand what you're saying. Your mother would just … disappear?"

"Yup. The only explanation that makes sense was that I probably suffered from recurring blackouts. You know, like loss of time? I'm pretty sure my brain was protecting itself from my mother's insane behavior. At the time I didn't know anything about

Sensitives. This whole demon thing was probably too much for me."

David flicked the file with his thumb. "I don't think they were blackouts."

"What?" Kara leaned forward. "What do you mean?"

"In fact, I don't think *you* had anything to do with your mother's disappearances." David rubbed his chin. "I'll have to check with Gabe...but if what you're telling me is true...your mother is a guardian angel."

Kara's head spun. David's words hit her hard. She struggled with her thoughts. "W...what? But...no...that's impossible. My mother never *died*. She can't be an angel."

"Yes she can." David gave her a warm smile. "You just didn't know."

It took a moment for Kara to speak again. "I...I don't under...what are you saying?"

"I think your mom's a guardian angel. Like you and me. You wouldn't have noticed when she died. Her soul went straight to Horizon. And they probably sent her right back at that same point in time...before she died, and made it look like she didn't die."

"Okay, I'm confused."

"Try not to think about this now; we'll figure it out later. Let's concentrate on our mission." He glanced at his watch again. "We have less than thirty-five minutes."

"How am I supposed to concentrate when you tell me my mom might be a guardian angel?!" Kara held her face in her hands. "All those years I thought she was nuts. I even wished I could run away…away from the madness. And . . . all along . . . all this time . . . she was helping people and fighting demons. I feel like such a jerk."

"Don't. You didn't know. And I might be wrong. Kara, listen to me. We'll look into it when we get back to Horizon…I promise. But now we really have to go."

"Okay." said Kara. She'd have lots of time to feel sorry for herself later. She brushed her bangs out of her eyes. "Um, what's the mission—the job thing?"

David passed her the file. She read:

Petty Officer: David McGowan

Guardian Angel: Kara Nightingale

Class order # 4321

Rank: Rookie 1st year, W-1 Guard squad, (lowest rank)

Assignment: Mr. Jean Tremblay, on the corner of Notre Dame and Gosford Street, sidewalk. 15:07 pm.

Crushed by a two ton concrete block when a cable from a giant crane snaps.

David pushed open the passenger door with a pop. "Let's go." He whirled his legs out of the car and pulled himself up and out.

Kara struggled out of the car and gave David back the file. "Uh, you know… if we can't stop the crane from collapsing it's going to get a little messy."

"The messier the better!" David beamed. He pushed Kara's door closed. "We're only a few minutes away by foot. Follow me."

And with that, he turned on his heels and walked southwards on Saint Hubert Street. Kara followed closely behind, her mind filled with thoughts of her mother.

They arrived on the corner of Notre Dame and turned right, heading west. The street was packed with the usual business types: women and men in expensive suits, carrying café lattes in one hand while chatting on their cell phones with the other. Taxis honked loudly as Kara and David zigzagged through moving cars in the crowded street. The taxi drivers were making obscene gestures through their windows at the jay-walking pedestrians.

Kara smelled the exhausts fumes. "Mmm…it's good to be back."

David laughed. "Nothing like a good whiff of city streets to make ya home sick."

They arrived at Gosford Street about ten minutes later. A giant crane towered over the city's buildings. Its long metal neck reached for the sky. It rotated slowly, carrying a large load hooked on its metal cable. Men in dark blue uniforms and bright orange construction hard hats shouted over the loud thumping noises and roaring engines. The construction site spilled over an entire block.

Kara watched as a single man with an orange hat waved the pedestrians along with a striped white and black flag. His face was sunburned, and it cracked into a million wrinkles when he took a drag from his cigarette. A huge round belly sprouted out of him, hanging low above crooked legs. To Kara, he looked like a very ugly pregnant woman.

"Well, we have about twenty minutes to kill," said David, as he glanced at his watch. "Enough time to get ready." He looked up and down the giant crane, studying it for a moment. "The crane will probably rotate this way ... and then the cable will snap at around there." He pointed north. "That concrete block is big enough to splatter someone all right. Wow, that's gotta hurt."

Kara stood and watched the passersby, waiting for the event *du jour*. She tapped her foot on the ground. "David—you really think, with my new training, I'll be able to handle the demons? I mean—I feel stronger, and I have these new skills ... but will it be enough? David...?"

David waved at two voluptuous mortal women, who happened to be waving and smiling back.

"You've got to be kidding me! David!" Kara punched him.

"OUCH!" cried David, as he rubbed his arm.

"That didn't hurt, you *liar*." She couldn't help smiling.

David continued to rub his arm as he grinned widely. "Yeah, well, you have *man* hands!"

The two women watched David with suspicion in their eyes. Then they stared at Kara and whispered to each other, wide-eyed. After a moment they walked away, but not before giving David the evil eye.

Secretly, Kara hated those women—the voluptuous kind, sculpted by the hands of a higher power, perfect in every aspect, impossibly beautiful: long silky hair and healthy-looking curves in the right spots, the exact opposite of the straight lines from her tomboyish body. The boob-fairy had never visited Kara, even with all the money she had collected and hidden under her pillow. Nope. The boob-fairy skipped her house and magicked all the other girls from her high school with great-looking chests. No wonder David had eyes for the other girls…there was nothing to look at over here.

What happened next was purely incidental. She didn't know what possessed her; the words just busted out of her mouth, and before she realized what was happening it was already too late. "Who's Sarah?" *Oops.*

David winced, clearly not expecting it. "Huh?" He turned around to face her, his face twisted in distress.

Kara wished she hadn't asked, and stared at a spot on his shoulder. "Me and my big mouth. I'm sorry, I shouldn't have asked."

"No, it's all right." David sighed and was silent for a moment. "Sarah was a rookie, like you…and my friend. We worked on missions together. And we were really close."

"I see."

"No, not like *that*. We were just *friends*. But then rumors started spreading about our alleged affair—which wasn't true. Romance is forbidden in Horizon. We're told to be soldiers, not lovers. If you're caught, you're banned from the Legion forever—I've heard stories that they even take your soul away. So, anyway…the Legion got involved. They tried to separate us, but we always managed to hang out anyway and go on jobs together."

"So, what happened to her?" Kara asked softly. "Did she…die?"

David stared at the ground. "After we'd completed one of our missions, we decided to hang out longer on Earth. It was Friday night, so we went to a few clubs. You have to understand something...we were all mortals once, and sometimes we still long some of those mortal feelings: the naivety and carefree attitudes. We wanted a break from our responsibilities. Anyway, we had far too many drinks, we both made some new mortal friends of the opposite sex, and we forgot who we were and how long we'd been out." He was silent for a long moment before speaking again. "And then when they came, we were weak and unprepared."

"Who came, David?"

"Demons. I fought them off me, but when I reached Sarah...it was too late."

The images of shadow demons devouring Sarah rose up behind Kara's eyes. She took a moment to process it. "I'm sorry, David. You must have been in a lot of pain."

He stared out into the crowds of people wandering the streets. "It was a long time ago. But I live with it every day."

Kara couldn't think of anything to say. She watched his pain in the creases of his forehead and remained silent.

Sometime later, David spotted the crane's cable starting to give way. Smaller wires snapped and curled away, leaving the cable thinner and weaker. "Okay, get ready Kiddo. Here it comes." He pointed north on Gosford. "I'll try to stop the crane from moving this way—you look for Mr. Tremblay; he should be walking on Notre Dame Street, coming towards us."

"Right." Kara glanced westwards on Notre Dame Street. "It would help if I knew what Mr. Tremblay looked like!" She stared at the tiny crowds of people wandering the street.

"Look for the one with the name tag...Mr. Tremblay."

Kara sighed. "Very funny, smart ass."

"I know."

"David, w...what about the shadow demons?" croaked Kara. She remembered her last encounter with them. "What am I supposed to do if I see one?"

David plopped his backpack on the ground and zipped it open. He rummaged through it and handed Kara a small fish net and a salt shaker.

"What the...?" said Kara, bewildered. She took them. "Is this a joke?"

"Nope."

"You can't be serious? Have you *seen* what shadow demons look like? How am I supposed to protect myself with this?" she cried, as she waved the fish net in the air. "I'm going to get killed!"

"No, you won't; you're with me. Stop freaking out."

"I am freaking out! I'm not out here to catch *butterflies!*"

"Just relax..."

Kara couldn't believe how cool David was. This had to be some sort of mistake. "Why can't I get a proper sword like you? Didn't you pack the golden one I used for training?"

David zipped up his backpack and threw it over his shoulder. "Nope. You don't have the proper training yet. I don't want you to hurt yourself."

"Hurt myself! Are you *serious*! I'm going to get *killed*!"

"You're over-reacting. Stop screaming…you're making a scene. Look…the mortals are looking." David curled the corners of his lips. "Ah…women."

"You saw what I can do…you know I can use a blade! Come on!"

"This discussion is over. Nothing's going to happen, just keep Mr. Tremblay out of harm's way. See, we have plenty of time to stop the crane and…"

David's jaw dropped. His eyes were focused on something.

"David? What's the matter?" Kara followed his gaze. He was staring at a mortal man across Gosford Street. The man was in his mid-thirties, tall with powerful shoulders. He wore an expensive-looking gray suit, tailored perfectly to his muscular body. His white hair was cut short and styled neatly. His skin had a grayish-blue tint to it, like a few-hours-old corpse. To Kara, he looked like a regular business man, except…

He has black eyes.

Like endless black pits, it was like staring into two black holes. And the man stared back at them. In the pit of her non-existent stomach, Kara felt something was wrong. He stood there without moving, watching them.

"David. The man with the black eyes…he's a demon, right? Like the ones my mother…David?"

David's terrified expression sent panic waves through Kara's body.

"David!" shrieked Kara, "Say something!" She frowned. Another man wearing the same gray suit with the same short white hair emerged slowly from the crowd and stood a few feet away from the other man. His eyes were as black as midnight, and he was identical in every way to the other black-eyed man.

"I don't understand?" David said. "How did they find us so fast...?" he whipped his head towards Kara. "How is that possible?"

"Why are you *looking* at me like *that*? I didn't do anything!"

"It doesn't make sense ..."

"What doesn't make sense, David? You're scaring me!"

He pressed his hands on Kara's shoulders. "Listen. I don't have time to explain. We won't have time to save Mr. Tremblay anymore...but we *have* to save the soul, you hear me?"

Kara turned her head. She could see that the crane's jib was pointed in their direction now, the cable holding on barely by a thread. "But how?" She looked down and waved her sad fish net. "With this?"

"Do exactly what I say and you will. Do you understand?"

She nodded. She glanced back at the black-eyed men. A third one emerged. He crossed Gosford Street, coming towards them. Kara looked around at the faces in the crowds. "The mortals can't see them. David, what are they?"

"They're called higher demons," said David, "and I can't fight them alone with you here. Okay, here we go..."

SNAP!

The cable broke. A large concrete boulder fell from the sky. It reached the man called Jean Tremblay and crushed his entire body in half a second. It was like dropping a heavy book on top of an egg. People screamed and ran for cover, away from the rubble of concrete and body parts, for all of Mr. Tremblay's limbs lay severed from the rest of his body, which was flattened under the concrete block like a juicy raspberry pancake. Mortals threw up their lunches. They stared at four perfectly cut limbs resting by the block of concrete, as though they had been cut with giant scissors. Within seconds, light covered the skin from Mr. Tremblay's arms and legs. A shower of little glowing particles flowed from his dead body and hovered a few feet in the air above the concrete boulder. They came together slowly and formed a ball.

Kara studied the mortals gathered around the body. The soul was invisible to them, she realized.

David twisted through the crowd and ran towards the boulder.

A higher demon walked away from the soul. "David!" Kara yelled. "It's coming after you!"

The higher demon made its way towards David, who had jumped over the dead body and ran in the middle of the street to meet it head on.

"Open the shaker!" cried David. He lunged at the higher demon, a long sword in his right hand. A small group of mortals jumped out of David's way, their eyes glued to his sword.

Across the street from them, the other two higher demons approached, their black eyes fixed upon Kara.

"Okay…here goes nothing!" She twisted the metal shaker top and looked up for a second. David fought off the demon. He pushed him away from the body and from Kara as she walked forward towards the soul.

"Great…I'm going to die—again." She held the fish net in her left hand, and the salt shaker in the other.

One of the two remaining higher demons stood but a few feet away from her. An evil grin flashed across its face. It only had to leap, and it would be on top of her. Its hard body was posed in anticipation.

"THROW THE SALT AT IT!" She heard David yell over the panicked crowd.

Without thinking, Kara dropped the fish net, fumbled with the salt shaker, and threw the metal cap—right in the middle of the higher demon's forehead.

SMACK!

The demon froze, as though expecting something to happen. After a moment, it glanced down at the tiny metal cap between its shiny black shoes and kicked it. Its thick shoulders moved up and down as it laughed. Then the demon looked up at Kara, its ebony eyes glittering. It cracked its face, bared its teeth in an evil grin and took a step forward.

"Oops. That can't be good."

"THE SALT! THROW THE SALT!" she heard David howl.

Kara threw the shaker at its face. The salt exploded all over it. The demon screamed as it covered its face with its hands. Black smoke emitted through its fingers; its skin melted away, exposing

106

rotten flesh beneath. The horrid smell of burnt flesh surrounded her.

"The soul! ...Use the net!" David gasped. She saw him lash out at the demon and cut it, right across its chest. The creature screamed in pain and anger as it backed away, shaken for a moment.

Kara bent down and grabbed the fish net. She pushed her way through the crowd that was growing by the minute. She kept her eyes on the hovering soul. From the corner of her eye, she caught sight of the other higher demon running towards her. She waved the fish net before her with her right hand.

"Do it now!" cried David.

Kara leaped into the air, unaware of the strange looks the mortal crowd gave her seeing a strange girl with a fish net jump into the air as she tried to catch invisible butterflies. Like an overhand softball throw, she swung her arm and caught the brilliant ball of light in her net. She landed with a hard *thump* on top of the concrete block. The soul bounced lightly in her net. The size of a large grapefruit, it weighed less than a roll of toilet paper.

She sat on the boulder and brought the net closer to her face for inspection. Like a miniature sun, the soul's light warmed her face. "Hey, I caught it! I really caught it!" She looked up as mortals appeared. They screamed and yelled at her, their faces screwed up in scowls of horror as they pointed to the pancake man below. "Oh no."

David appeared to her side. "Run!" He dashed off.

"Huh?" She stared at David running away.

Kara swung her legs over the boulder, jumped down, and sprinted after him. They ran all the way down Gosford Street to the Old Port. They turned right onto De La Commune Street. Her mortal legs didn't tire. She ran fast, leaping over benches and dumpsters along the way like a gazelle running away from a predator and clutching the fish net against her chest.

"What just happened?" yelled Kara as she galloped behind David. "Why didn't they try to get the soul?"

"They're not after the soul." David yelled back. "They're after *us*!" He stared up ahead as he ran.

Kara looked back. She wondered why these demons were chasing them. Two higher demons ran after them at an incredible speed. She turned her head and ran close to David, a bit awkwardly as her right arm held the soul protectively against her chest.

"David...we're not fast enough. They're going to catch up!"

"Keep running!"

"We're dead in about fifteen seconds! I don't even want to think about what they're going to do to us!"

"Keep running...and stop talking!"

Thirteen . . . twelve . . . Kara counted backwards in her head as she ran behind David. He ran in a straight line onto the Promenade Du Vieux-Port. They zigzagged through the roller blading kids and tourists. Kara followed David as he pushed his way through the crowds and headed straight for the...

Water, said Kara to herself.

"DAVID!" cried Kara, as she realized what he was about to do.

But he wasn't stopping. Soon they'd reach the end of the Old Port, where the concrete ended, and where the Saint-Laurence River began. A thick metal railing ran the length of the port along the walkway, protecting the people from accidentally falling to their deaths into the chilly gray waters. They were running right for it.

Three . . . two . . .

And just when they were about to hit the metal railing, Kara felt David's hand wrap around hers. He squeezed hard and jumped, pulling her along with him...and flew over the edge.

One . . .

Kara heard screams from above as she hit the water and plummeted twenty feet into the deep dark Saint-Laurence River. Instinctively she looked up, half expecting to see the higher demons cascading above them. But all she saw was the sun's beams reflecting on the water's surface above her. Then everything around her went dark.

CHAPTER 8

DAVID, THE CELEBRITY

KARA OPENED HER EYES. She stared at a brass ceiling that was divided into perfect rusty squares. She lay on the bottom of an elevator and clutched the fish net with the soul inside it against her chest. She lifted up the fish net, suspended it in front of her face, and gazed intently at the soul. It was unharmed, lighting up her face with its brilliance. Rolling over, Kara pushed herself up and looked at a grinning David.

"That was awesome!" He jumped lightly up and down, looking thrilled. "I haven't had this much fun in years!"

"Don't get too excited, cowboy. We barely made it." Kara suppressed a laugh.

There was sudden *snort* and Kara stepped to the side.

A medium-sized gray monkey sat in a chair near the control panel behind David. It had large, square shoulders and a powerful chest. It scratched its bare purple behind while it stared at David and Kara. Its long face was hairless, and sported a furrowed brow. "What floor?" said the monkey, sounding annoyed.

Kara flashed her eyes at David. "I don't think I'll ever get used to monkeys talking…"

"It's *baboon*, not monkey! Baboon L006, if you please," hissed the primate.

David jumped to the opportunity. "Level Four, then…*good looking*," he said. The baboon screwed up its face.

"Careful," said Kara, "it looks about to spit in your face."

"You GAs are all the same," said the baboon. "No *respect*!"

David dusted off his jacket, not paying any attention to the baboon. "Sure thing, hot stuff. Level Four…we're waiting …"

For a moment nothing happened. Then the baboon spit on the floor, an inch beside David's boots. It stared at him, its face crinkled in hatred. Grimacing, it bared a row of large sharp yellow teeth. This baboon looked dangerous. It puffed out its chest, showing off its hard body, and turned around on its chair. Lifting a long arm, it pressed the brass button.

After a few seconds of uncomfortable silence, Kara followed David off the elevator to Level Four, still clutching the soul against her chest as a mother would her newborn child. They walked through the Hall of Souls. The vast space sparkled and shimmered as though it rained diamonds. Millions of hovering souls illuminated the way as they walked up to the dais where a great glass desk glistened. The Archangel Ramiel was busy writing in a large book. He did not look up.

"Ahem, Oh Blessedness!" said David as he smirked and curtsied. Kara hid her smile in her hair.

Ramiel lifted his eyes in David's direction. A frown materialized on his brow. Suddenly, moving with incredible speed, he pushed back his chair, stood up, and threw a newspaper at David, barely missing his face. "YOU FOOL!" he roared. "You were SEEN!"

Kara picked up the paper from the floor. It was today's Montreal Gazette. She and David were on the front cover holding hands, falling into the Saint-Laurence River. The heading read:

Couple's suicide!
A young couple in love plunge to their deaths off the Old Port in Montreal.

"Uh oh," said Kara, "this can't be good."

David grabbed the newspaper from Kara. "Hey…I look *good!*"

Ramiel slammed his fist on the desk and a loud *boom* echoed throughout the chamber. "What were you *thinking?!* You know our laws! You were not to be seen going into water!" If Ramiel was warm-blooded, Kara was sure his face would be red hot with large veins pulsing on his forehead. Instead, there was a terrifying white coldness. It wasn't natural.

"You've been warned before, *David McGowan!* Your days as a guardian angel are numbered!" He growled and pointed a long finger at David. Kara was almost certain laser beams were about to shoot out of Ramiel's eyes and strike David, melting him on the spot. The Archangel's face twisted in fury.

"David, we're so screwed," whispered Kara.

112

"Don't worry...I got this," he whispered back.

David smiled and puffed out his chest. "Relax, Your Holiness . . . see here? My rookie saved the soul." He gestured towards Kara's chest, where she kept the soul protected inside the fish net.

With Ramiel's attention suddenly on her, Kara cringed and backed up. "David! What are you doing?" she said through the corner of her mouth.

She felt her nerves starting to act up. The Archangel's flaring blue eyes made her nervous, but she found she couldn't look away—some sort of eerie hypnosis. She was suddenly made aware of his power, as though he made it known to her somehow with his mind. She tried to speak, but the words would not come.

The Archangel cut the silence. "It doesn't *excuse* what you did. You broke the law!"

This time David's smile disappeared. He looked at Kara, then back to Ramiel. "Listen...there were three higher demons. They attacked us. There was no other way...we *had* to jump."

Ramiel backed up, as though getting a blow from an invisible force. He narrowed his eyes. "W...what? Higher demons? That's impossible!"

"Yup. Three of them. It was like they knew we were coming. You know anything about that?"

"What? Of course not!" Ramiel shouted, his face twitching.

Kara watched in silence as the big Archangel seemed to battle something from the inside. He paced up and down. He rubbed his head, and his eyes and brow narrowed. He seemed angrier than before, if that were even possible. Kara took another step back.

Finally, after some time, Ramiel spoke. "I need to speak to Michael about this. Here, give the soul to the cherub," he said, as he gestured to one of the golden-haired persons, who came at once with a glass jar. The cherub placed the jar in front of Kara and it waited.

"Huh?" Kara said. She thinned her lips and glared at the cherub. "Why should I give it to him? I saved the soul...and I nearly died saving it. No ... I'm not giving it to him. What if he drops it? What then?" She reached into the fish net and grasped the soul in her hand, letting the light shine though her fingers. She looked at David for help.

He tapped her shoulder. "It's ok, kiddo. You did *good*. Now, give the shiny white ball to the cherub." The cherub tapped its foot on the ground. It cocked an eyebrow, clearly annoyed by Kara's reluctance to give up the soul.

She dropped her shoulders and looked down at the soul. The glowing ball emanated light onto her frowning face. Kara pulled her hands away from her chest slowly, and gently dropped the soul into the glass jar. Immediately the cherub turned on its heel, strolled away, jumped into a tiny vehicle, and drove off, leaving Kara staring after it. A sudden feeling of sadness washed over her, as though she had just lost a part of herself.

"What's going to happen to it?" Kara asked, as the cherub disappeared into the walls of light.

"It'll be reborn, like every other living soul," answered David.

A thought nagged at the back of Kara's mind. "David. You think you can ask Ramiel about my mom? Maybe he knows something?"

"Sure." David cleared his throat. "Excuse me, Your Highness, but Ms. Nightingale here has a question. . . about her mother."

"Yes?" said the Archangel heavily and leaned forward.

"Well, she told me that her mother can see demons—so she's probably a Sensitive—but then the interesting part is that her mother likes to...*disappear* at times. Reappearing at different places. So, you see . . . I believe she might be a guardian."

The Archangel's face was impassive, apart from a light twitch in his lip. "I will consult her profile."

He moved his hands over his keyboard and started typing. He looked up at Kara. "Is your mother's name Danielle Dubois?"

Kara's jaw dropped. "Yes."

"She is indeed a guardian angel. She's back on Earth in her mortal body, waiting for her next assignment."

"I knew it!" David's face lit up. He nudged Kara on the shoulder. "How cool is that! My parents are just regular mortals. My Dad's a mechanic and my mom's a teacher...nothing special."

But Kara didn't feel the news to be special. Things just started to make a lot more sense to her, now that she knew why her mother behaved so strangely. Somehow she felt a lot worse.

"My mother—a guardian angel. It explains a lot. I wish she could have told me somehow." Kara dropped her eyes and stared at the floor.

"She couldn't," said David with kind eyes. "We're forbidden to reveal ourselves to mortals. It's one of the laws or something. Plus, it was for your own good. I doubt you would have believed her anyway. It's like you said...you thought she was mad."

But Kara thought otherwise. She would have believed her. She knew it somehow. She looked up at Ramiel. With his eyes closed and his head arched up, he looked as if he was meditating. She studied his perfect face as he opened his eyes again and spoke.

"The Archangel Gabriel is waiting for you. Your *rookie* needs more training. Don't make him wait."

"No worries, Your Divineness...your wish is my command!" David bowed and flashed his teeth.

Ramiel stepped forward, looking down upon David with flares in his eyes. "*You're* still here only because your rookie shows a lot of promise. Don't disappoint her by being a fool!"

"Ah...but I'm the best damn fool in all of Horizon," said David. "Later, Your Worship."

And with that, David whirled around, grabbed Kara by the elbow, and steered her back towards to the elevator.

"You're a real ass, you know that?" laughed Kara. She knew David was way too cocky with the Archangels, but at least he made her smile.

"I'll take that as a compliment, thank you very much." He lifted his chin and smiled into the black skies. "I'd like to think of myself as an entrepreneur...a visionary."

"Keep it up and you'll be visioning Ramiel's fist when it makes contact with your face."

The elevator ride back to Operations was a silent one, apart from the loud scratching noises coming from a chimpanzee in a blue fisherman's hat that kept rubbing its behind. Kara pressed her head against the wood panel at the back on the elevator, closed her eyes, and thought of her mother.

"What are you thinking about?" asked David. He leaned against the panel beside her.

"Oh, nothing much…the usual."

"And … what's the usual?"

Kara opened her eyes. "Just that I was flattened by a bus, got a new job as a guardian angel, souls are everlasting and reincarnated into body suits, my mother is an angel, demons are freak'n real…and some, apparently, are out to get you."

David scratched the back of his neck. "You'll get used to it."

"So you keep telling me."

They jumped off the elevator and walked along the red sand.

"Um, David?" Kara brushed a long strand of brown hair behind her right ear. "Uh…those higher demons…you said that they were after *us*? Why?" She felt a slight shiver pass through her body. Their black eyes still haunted her.

David looked intently at Kara. "Not *only* after us, but after guardian angels in general—especially the rookies, since you're easy targets."

Kara frowned with curiosity as she walked. Puffs of red sand escaped her feet as she kept up the pace with David. "So they were after my mother, too. But why? I thought demons were only after *souls*…like, to eat or something?"

"Well, they do eat them, sort of." He combed the top of his hair with his fingers. "Lesser demons, like shadow demons, devour souls. Souls are a life force. The more they feed on them the more powerful they become, and it gives them longevity on Earth. Without the souls, they would die."

Kara stared at the salt pyramids as she and David walked past them. She reflected on this new information. White puffy clouds ran across a perfect blue sky, shaped like wild animals. An ocean fragrance surrounded them.

Kara raised her brow. "This place is even creepier than I could have imagined." Her mind flashed to thoughts of the black eyed demons. "So, what about the black-eyed monsters? Higher demons?" As she said that, a guardian angel with two stars tattooed on his forehead approached them. He smiled, lifted up his hand, and he and David high-fived one another. They exchanged a few words. The angel patted David on the shoulder and then walked away.

"So, I see you're a celebrity in Horizon," laughed Kara.

"Huh?" A smile reached David's lips. "Right…the higher demons. Yeah, they're nasty," said David as he lifted up the collar from his leather jacket. "Can't be too careful when they're around." He gave Kara his wink *du jour*.

She sighed and rolled her eyes. "Wow, you're so full of yourself. I could slap you!" She kicked up some red sand with her shoe. "But why were they after us? After me?"

"'Cause, you have something they want. Your GA life source is like a thousand regular souls. One guardian angel soul can make a higher demon almost as powerful as an Archangel—and trust me, you don't want that." David looked away and seemed lost for words.

"You said that the higher demons knew where we were? That seemed to disturb Ramiel a little...why's that?"

"Well, for starters, that's never happened to me before. It usually takes hours before the higher demons—or any demon—can sense us back on Earth. They don't just show up like that, a few minutes after we show up. I don't get it." He searched Kara's face, with that same puzzled expression on his face.

"Don't look at me like that! It's not like I *announced* our arrival or anything. Besides, I'm new here! How would I know anything?"

David shook his head. "I don't know, but it smells bad."

Kara felt that was probably true, but there was nothing she could do about it. This new job came with a lot of unanswered questions and a lot of new dangers.

David raised his eyebrows. His blue eyes glittered. "It almost feels like...someone from the Legion told them."

"What? But that makes no sense?"

"It makes perfect sense. And it's happened before." His face hardened. "Traitors, working for the demons from inside the Legion. They're fallen angels who go over to the dark side, their heads filled with a lust for power."

Kara stayed where she was, frozen, as her mind strained to process all this new information. "But why us? Who would do this to us...to me? And why?"

"I can think of someone." David stepped beside Kara. She saw a flash of anger in his eyes. She knew exactly who he was referring to...someone tall and powerful who happened to hate David's guts.

"Benson? *No* . . . are you sure?"

David's tone was sharp. "Positive. This is his chance to get rid of me for good. It's his *payback* for what I did to Sarah."

If what David was saying was true, that meant Benson was going to get her killed as well—caught in the crossfire—just to get to David. She had just barely escaped with her angel life on their last job. *It's just going to get worse.* A part of her felt betrayed. She hadn't done anything to anyone; she had just *died* recently. And now her life was in danger. Another part of her was angry that someone wanted to hurt David. She looked up into his clear blue eyes. "So ...what do we do?"

He looked fierce. "We get him...before anything else happens. We'll need proof, obviously, or to catch him in the act. I'd love to see how Gabriel fries his ass!"

"So, should we follow him?" asked Kara.

David narrowed his eyes. "Yeah...he'll probably have to rendezvous with the demons back on Earth. We should find out what his next assignment is and follow him there. He's bound to make contact with them sooner or later."

Images of the higher demons flashed behind Kara's eyes and she started to feel anxious. "But shouldn't we tell Gabriel, or one of the Archangels? This is pretty serious, David; shouldn't we tell them?"

He looked down at the ground. "No, they'll just think I'm up to something because of our *history*. They won't believe me. Don't think I'm Mr. Popular with the Archangels—or haven't you noticed? And if Benson finds out somehow, we'll never catch him. No one can know about this."

Kara knew David was right. They'd never believe him, or her. They would have to do this on their own.

They wandered through the twisted rows of blue tents, watching the ongoing combats. Operations was full of noises: bursts of combat cries, the clatter of metal on metal and the raised voices of the oracles teaching classes, and then forgetting what they were supposed to teach. The fragrance of salt drifted in the air.

She followed David into the weapons tent. Two guardian angels were making their selection of weapons and looked up as they saw David and Kara enter.

"Yo, Dave! What's up?" said the taller one. "We heard about your *jump*. Awesome! It's spreading all over the Legion already."

"Don't think Gabriel's too happy about that," laughed the smaller one, as he eyed Kara. "He's in a *really* bad mood. You sure you want to be here right now?" he slapped David on the arm.

David lifted his chin and puffed out his chest. "Gabe *loves* me. He just doesn't know it."

The three young men laughed stupidly while hitting one another. To Kara, it was like watching the end of a winning basketball game, where all the boys danced around excitedly after the match. David, so it seemed, had won the popularity game—David versus the Archangels.

More and more guardian angels stopped their training and came to congratulate David on his wild escape. Some even congratulated Kara. She turned around quickly and became very interested in a short silver dagger. She flicked the blade with her fingernail. The sound was drowned by sudden loud cheers. She looked back towards the crowd. She saw David jump down from one of the large tables. He was surrounded by an animated group of predominantly male guardian angels. He re-enacted their suicidal plunge off the Old Port. His cronies giggled excitedly, like a pack of wild hyenas. He bowed after each performance…which were many.

Kara wondered if she was really stuck with this idiot for all eternity.

CHAPTER 9

A TRAITOR AMONG US

TIME PASSED IN HORIZON. From time to time Kara thought about her painting, and about the life she left behind. But now her old life seemed insignificant and dull compared with the busy new life she led now. Every now and then, when she thought of her mother, the feelings of guilt and homesickness would start. But with all she had to learn at combat training and her new lessons with the oracles, Kara didn't have time to feel sorry for herself.

She learned from Gabriel that the Legion was nervous about the fact that higher demons kept showing up whenever she was on the job. They feared a connection between Kara and the demons. If they suspected a traitor they didn't mention it to her, or to David. Instead, they had her spend hours on end trying to *connect* with her other souls…which wasn't happening. It was not until she cussed out the oracle for getting her name wrong for the hundredth time that he finally dismissed her until their next lesson.

Before long, Kara started to adjust better to the new life and job in Horizon—she even saved three other souls. But she soon found out, according to the Archangel Gabriel, that this wasn't good enough—she had to try to save the mortals first, before the soul.

Otherwise, her training sessions with David proved to be fruitful and enriching in every respect. Her senses became more powerful, and so did her instincts. Kara was getting better with each lesson, and in a short time David began training her on different weapons. She even surprised herself a little when she began to enjoy herself and even began, if only slightly, to accept her new fate as a guardian angel.

Then David broke the news about Benson to Kara.

"He's on his way now—566 Saint Catherine Street East," he informed her. "Apparently the Legion's got him on a Scout mission."

"What's a scout mission?"

"Scouts gather info for the Legion…like detective work, but GA style."

"That sounds cool!" Kara imagined herself in a dark trench coat and black fedora hat, spying on would-be traitors in a dark alley way, snapping pictures with her sparkling new iPhone.

David made a face. "Na…it gets boring sometimes. Too much paperwork…it's pretty *geeky* if you ask me. But we know what he's doing, eh? It's so clear now! I can't believe no one suspects him. But we'll get him." David's face cracked into a grin. His eyes glittered in anticipation.

Kara liked how his lips curled when David was enjoying himself. He reminded her of a little boy in a toy store, going crazy as he played with all the new gadgets his little hands could hold. She couldn't help but smile back. "Good job, inspector. Is he near the pools already?" Kara nodded her head towards the hundreds of pools beyond the red hills.

"Yup…let's go get him."

Kara jogged behind David. As they approached the pools, she could make out Benson's silhouette on the ledge of one in the first row. She saw him squat, pinch his nose, then leap into the air and disappear with a splash.

Kara narrowed her eyes. "You really believe this creep is the traitor?"

"Without a doubt."

"I wonder what is going on in his head. How can he risk the lives of other angels?"

"'Cause he's a douche bag."

"He must really hate you." Kara bit her lip. "Maybe he has an entirely different agenda? Maybe he wants me dead and not you?"

David shook his head. "Don't be ridiculous…he's after *me*. You're only involved because of me."

A moment later, Kara and David took their turns and jumped into the salty waters.

As if an army of ants had poured out of their hills in search of food, Saint Catherine Street was a mass of crawling mortals. Kara blinked. Red, green, and yellow flashing street lights illuminated the busy street. Kara passed pawn shops, strip clubs, and bars, as the humid air stuck to her M suit. A stink of exhaust fumes lingered and a smell of moist soil filled the air.

The street was alive with the energy of young people. Kara felt it prickle her M suit. The night was young, and like any Friday, the street vibrated with the sounds of motors running, squeaking brakes, and kids on full party mode.

Teenage girls walked in groups attached at the waist, their faces painted in layers of makeup. With barely-there tops and the shortest of skirts, which Kara liked to call *under-skirts*, they approached the nightclubs. They batted their eyelashes at the bouncers who then let them in without question. Kara felt a slight ache of envy in her chest as she watched them.

She brushed off the feeling and followed David. "So what's 566 Saint Catherine?"

David turned back and looked at her before turning back and looking straight ahead. "It's a nightclub. I have a feeling he's meeting someone there—probably a demon." David glanced at his watch. "He should already be there," he looked up. "Ah...there it is."

Kara followed his gaze and saw a crooked gray building. The windows were painted black, and a large metal sign hung from the top. It read, *The Club*.

"Wow, how original—must have taken weeks to come up with that name." Kara turned her head. A long line of teenage hopefuls waited to get in. "Ah, David ...where are you going? Aren't we going to wait in line over there?"

David grabbed Kara by the hand and pulled her with him to the front entrance. A man the size of a small SUV waited with his arms crossed over his chest.

"Hey man, what's up?" said David as he walked right in. The bouncer didn't pay any attention to them.

"Wow! How did you do that?" asked Kara as David dragged her. "Do GAs have some kind of hypnotizing abilities?"

"Sort of...but my good looks got us in."

They passed through the front door. Music exploded all around them. Kara felt the ground shake beneath her as hundreds of dancers hit the floor. Not wanting to miss anything, she turned her head every which way as David pulled her along.

"I've never been inside a club before," she yelled over the music.

David turned his head and frowned. "Never?"

"No. You have to be eighteen to be allowed in."

"Yeah, but you never made a fake ID?" bellowed David.

Kara shook her head. "No...guess that makes me a loser, right?"

David's white teeth flashed in the darkness. "No, not everyone likes to go clubbing. Besides, you were probably too busy with your art to want to join a bunch of talentless fools jumping up and down in a tight space."

Kara smiled and looked down. "Yeah, I'm sure that's the reason."

Strobe lights illuminated faces, as David pulled her through the tight crowds. The salty smell of sweaty armpits and the thick stink of booze were like an invisible wall of stench.

The further they ventured away from the dance floor, the more Kara could hear over the music— faint sounds of bottles that clashed together and mumbles of conversations.

David pulled her along. She felt her body stiffen as crowds of people brushed up against her. But then David squeezed her hand gently and her skin tingled. She liked the feel of his M skin against her own. It wasn't the same feeling as back when she was alive, of skin brushing up against skin. This was different, and to Kara, much better—like her sensations were ten times as strong. She wished silently that she could hold on to his hand forever.

Kara made faces at the gorgeous girls that eyed David as they passed. They all gave Kara the what-are-you-doing-with-such-a-hottie look. And when David wasn't looking, Kara whirled around and gave them the finger…followed by the biggest smile she could muster.

David pulled Kara towards a round metal table in a back corner of the club, beyond the crowded dance floor and lost in the shadows. Benson sat two tables down from them. He was huddled over the table, presently engaged in a conversation with a dark-haired man in his late twenties. They did not look up.

"Be right back."

Kara watched as David disappeared into the crowd. He came back two minutes later with two drinks. "Here…gin and tonic. Have you had this before?"

Kara shook her head. "Uh...no, but can we actually *drink* liquids?"

David laughed. "Not really, but it is fun to pretend. The best part is that you can actually start feeling the alcoholic effects after a few drinks. Here...have a taste."

Kara leaned in and took a sip. The liquid evaporated in her throat. The alcohol vapor lingered for a moment and then made its way up slowly to her head. It wasn't at all like drinking real liquid, but it still felt nice. She grinned at David. "That was weird." She licked her lips. "But I like it."

"Good. Listen. Let's move in closer to hear their conversation." David drank the entire contents of his glass in one shot. He smacked his lips and slammed the glass down. "Follow me."

David sneaked closer towards the table that Benson and the stranger occupied. Their heads were huddled together, deep in conversation. David walked with exceptional stealth through the crowds to get to the next table without Benson noticing. He sat with his back towards them and leaned against the seat just a little for better hearing. Kara grabbed the empty seat next to David and sat down. She sipped her drink. Her eyes were on the young crowds dancing in front of her, but she strained to hear behind her. She heard Benson speak first.

"...it's not good enough. I need more information." Benson said.

"That's all I know, man," answered a deep voice.

"But you can't be sure it was the same *child?*"

"Hey man, it's like I said. I'm *not* sure."

"In what warehouse was this? What part of the city? I need to know!" Benson asked.

"I've given you all I've got," said the stranger. "If the demons knew I was speaking to you, I'd be a dead man."

There was a pause, and then Benson spoke again. "Yes, I know, but this is really important."

"No you *don't!* I'm not *paid* enough for this shit." Kara heard something slam down on the table.

Kara couldn't make out the rest of the conversion as the music thundered around her. She bristled with anxiety and was pleasantly excited—she was detective Kara Nightingale, bad-ass profiler vigilante. But something troubled her. The stranger had mentioned a child. What was Benson involved in?

Out of the corner of her eye, Kara saw Benson get up. In a flash David had squeezed himself against her. With his right arm around her shoulder, he pressed his hard M suit against hers, his face close enough for a kiss. Her mortal skin prickled with his nearness. She knew not to look into his eyes, for fear she might give her true feelings away. And just when she thought she would burst, David released her and backed away.

"Okay, he's gone. I think he's going towards the washrooms...be right back!" And with that, David disappeared into the crowd.

Kara clasped her forehead with her hands. She wasn't prepared for the intense feeling she felt. If romance was forbidden between angels, then why did she have feelings for this guy?

She moved her hands away from her face and looked down at her glass. "Why not?" She drank the last of her gin and tonic. She felt calmer. Then David squeezed out from a wall of mortals, with four more gin and tonics in his hands.

His face cracked into a wide smile. "Benson went down the toilet. So, the night's still young…no reason to let it go to waste. Right?"

"Right." Kara grabbed a glass and took a drink. She wanted to stay here with David for as long as she could.

"David…did you hear them talking about some *child?*"

David smacked his lips together. "Yup…don't know anything about some kid, though. I'm not sure what that means." He screwed up his face and gawked at his drink.

Kara swirled the straw around in her glass. "Do you think maybe we were *wrong* about Benson? If he's looking for a kid, then maybe he's not the one involved in trying to get us killed? I didn't hear anything about a plot to get *us* killed. Did you?"

After a pause, David brushed the top of his hair with his fingers. "Nope. I don't know. Maybe he was finished with his plan before we got there, and we only heard part of something else."

"Or maybe it's not *him.* Maybe we have it all wrong."

"It has to be…no one else in the Legion would do this to us! I'm sure Benson is the one."

But Kara was unconvinced. If Benson truly was behind the strange demon attacks, then why would he risk a meeting with some creepy mortal just to talk about some kid? It didn't add up. But Kara didn't press it any further.

Soon Kara was on her fourth drink. She laughed away at David's silly jokes, the kind of laughing which would normally have made her innards ache. But without innards, Kara only felt a slight tingle in her chest. She couldn't remember the last time when she had so much fun.

The music changed, and she felt David's hand on hers as he pulled her to her feet.

"Time to go."

"Huh? Already?" Kara hit her glass on the table.

They pushed their way out of the club and walked back along Saint Catherine Street. "We'll go through Berri Park, towards the water fountain." He told Kara. "The park will be deserted…perfect for a skinny dip on the way back to Horizon—ouch!" cried David. He rubbed the back of his head.

Kara pursed her lips. "Serves you right, Casanova."

They reached the park after a short walk. The only sources of light came from the moon and the one flickering park light at the entrance. The trees cast long, ghostly shadows on the ground. Male crickets chirped in the night as they tried to attract a female. A raccoon the size of a small dog enjoyed an early morning feast in a city garbage can. He hissed at them as they passed.

"Can animals see who we really are?" asked Kara.

"Yes. Animals are sensitive to different energies…they can sense us."

The raccoon kept hissing. "I don't think he likes us very much."

David laughed. "Poor little guy. He probably just doesn't want to share his meal."

"Gross."

Kara returned her attention to David. She watched him strut beside her, grinning. She liked how his shoulders moved back and forth as he walked, with his head in the air, like a proud peacock...

"AH!" Yelled Kara, as her foot got caught in a tree root. She went straight down to the ground. After a moment, she hauled herself up and sat on the grass. She giggled. "Oops."

"I love ladies who can hold their liquor," laughed David. He grabbed Kara by the arm and pulled her up—just a little too hard, for she flew into his arms. David wrapped his arms around her and pulled her against him. She looked up. His blue eyes sparkled in the moon light. Kara blinked. She thought his face was even more beautiful close up. His full lips parted slightly, as he stared at her mouth. His face was closer now. Warmth spread through her mortal body. She felt on fire. And then she felt his lips pressing against hers; softly at first, and then harder.

The kiss was sudden and fast.

The next thing Kara knew, David had released her and backed away, his face intense. He had a fiery look in his eyes. Her body exploded in tingles and he broke into a wide grin. He knew she was his.

But Kara was in shock.

David was still holding on to her, as though he were reluctant to let her go. She had never been kissed before. It felt amazing. She grinned.

What the...? Kara felt a sudden sharp pain in the back of her neck.

She reached back with her hand, and was suddenly propelled back with incredible force. She crashed onto the hard floor. If her body had been human, it'd have been broken. She rolled over. She felt something hard tightening around her neck, like a thick rubber hose. Her neck burned, as though the mortal flesh was on fire. Her body lifted off the ground as she twisted her M suit, trying to break free. But the hold was too strong. Kara looked down and got a glimpse of her attacker.

A shadow demon, three times larger than the ones she saw in Mrs. Wilkins' apartment, glistened in the moonlight. It had her wrapped around her neck with one of its tentacles. Kara could smell the foul stench of blood and rotten flesh. The demon let out a loud shriek that sounded almost like a laugh.

"Let her go, demon!" David ran towards her, his sword shimmering in the moonlight. He leaped into the air behind her. Kara heard a *swish,* and then felt a release. She hit the ground hard. She rolled over and tugged at her throat, and pulled off the foul tentacle. She scrambled to her feet and watched as the demon flickered, and its solid form disappeared into a black mist.

"Stay behind me!" yelled David, as he ran towards the demon. Kara stared in horror as he threw himself into the black fog, arms flailing as he struck at the creature. "I...HATE...DEMONS!" he panted. And then he disappeared into the mist. For a moment nothing happened, and then David came into view as he jumped out of the black fog. The demon shimmered and flickered into its solid form again. Wailing, it lashed out at David with its many limbs and knocked him off his feet. His sword flew out of his hand.

"DAVID!" screamed Kara. With incredible speed, the creature wrapped its tentacles around David's body. It lifted him up...and started pulling.

Panicked, Kara understood that the creature meant to rip him apart. She searched frantically for the sword. *Where is it!?* "Crap! Crap! CRAP!"

Kara caught a glimpse of something silver flash in the moonlight. Like a bullet, she bolted after the sword. She grabbed it, the blade heavy in her hand, and turned back. She ran towards the demon, the sword held high in her hand. She wasn't sure what she was going to do with it once she got there, but she knew she had to save David, no matter what.

The demon slammed David's body hard on the ground. It lifted him up and started to pull his limbs.

Kara saw her chance. She took it.

She pushed off the ground and jumped into the air, landing on the creature's back. She thrust the blade down into its head.

Black ooze poured out of the wound like thick tar, drenching Kara in black blood. She pushed off and landed back on the ground. Immediately, the demon wailed and let go of David. David fell to the ground and rolled on the grass. The demon reached behind and pulled out the blade. It shrieked and threw the sword aside. Then the shadow demon flashed, changed into a black cloud, and with a last flicker it disappeared.

Kara ran to David. "David! Are you all right?" She knelt beside him, searching his body for any missing limbs. "Your mortal body seems to have all its parts."

A silly grin materialized on his face. "I am now," he laughed. "Man, I've never seen a rookie take on a shadow demon like that! Kara, you were fierce! Wait till I tell the guys what you did! That was awesome!"

Kara shook her head. "What, are you *insane?!* You were almost killed!"

"But I live to tell the tale—this is better than the soup I created with demon blood!" David jumped into the air, with no signs of injuries, and started to dance. "We make a great team. We'll be the talk of the town!"

Kara shook her head and sighed. "What am I going to do with you?"

"Skinny dipping, here we come!"

As they walked towards the water fountain in silence, David's face was twisted in a wide grin. And Kara's mind was loud with thoughts only of the kiss.

CHAPTER 10

OODLES FOR NOODLES

IN THE FOLLOWING DAYS, neither of them mentioned the kiss. Kara wasn't sure if she should bring it up. She couldn't shut her mind up on the subject either. Maybe David regretted doing it? Maybe it was the aftereffects of the gin and tonic, and he thought he was kissing some gorgeous voluptuous model instead of her? And now, realizing the truth, perhaps he was embarrassed and hated himself for kissing a girl whose feminine curves had been flattened by a giant spatula. She decided to wait for the perfect moment to bring it up, if he didn't bring it up.

And so, she and David submerged themselves in their work.

After a good combat training workout, they strutted away from the great white tent at Operations with their next job. David handed Kara the file, and they made their way towards the pools.

Kara's jaw dropped as she stared at the paper. "A drunk city bus driver is going to crash his bus into a busy Chinese restaurant— Oodles for Noodles. Ten dead mortals, including children!" She looked up at David. "*This* is my next assignment? Are they mad? I don't want to be responsible for this!"

David took the file back from Kara, folded it, and hid it inside his leather jacket. "We all get tough assignments like this once in a while. It's part of the job." He clasped his hands on the metal railing and pulled himself up the four sets of stairs onto the pool's platform. "We stop the accident, we stop all those people from dying," David said, as Kara climbed up behind him.

"I'll never get used to this new life," said Kara. "The life I had before was *so* simple ... I didn't have to save anyone from dying...I just...ate ice cream and painted...." She stared down at the caustics rippling along the surface of the light blue waters as her mind flashed back to the remnants of her mortal life, the simple life. "... and demons didn't want to suck my brains out and have them for lunch."

David ignored her and stretched, preparing for the jump. "You have your gear?"

"Yup." Kara slid a blue and white backpack from her shoulders and rummaged through it. "I got my map, sword, salt shakers, and my *bad-ass* butterfly net," giggled Kara, as the idea of salt shakers and fish nets as gear was still a little outrageous to her.

David stepped up to the ledge of the pool. "Let's go. On three—one...two...three...!"

Kara and David strutted up Decarie Boulevard. They zigzagged through crowds of students who were cutting class, and some elderly shoppers who dragged their feet as they went. The busy street overwhelmed Kara's ears with loud honks and running motors. They made their way north, taking in the stink of exhaust.

"What's the address again?" asked Kara.

"674 Decarie Boulevard, near the corner of De L'Église Street."

Kara looked up the street. "And we have to be there for 3:45pm…what time is it now?"

"It's 3:38pm," said David, as he glanced at his watch. "And I can see the address from here."

He pointed with his right arm to a one-floor stone building, where Oodles for Noodles was squished in the middle by shops on either side, like the custard from a giant *mille-feuille*. It was just a block away, and they reached it within two minutes.

Kara stared at the oncoming traffic. "Do we know what city bus we are looking for? The number or something?"

"204," said David. "It should be an out-of-service bus."

She turned her attention southwards and searched the boulevard for the bus. She felt an excitement growing in her breast. The idea of being responsible for so many mortal lives made her truly nervous.

"Uh, David?" asked Kara after a moment. "How are we going to pull this off? How can anyone pull this off?" She let her hands fall to her sides. "What's the plan?"

David turned to face her. "Well, we know the bus loses control and crashes into the 674 building on Decarie, precisely at 3:45pm. So …we have to stop it before the crash."

"Duh, I *know*. But how? What's the *super* plan?" She watched David's eyes flicker as he thought.

"I don't think out-of-service buses stop for anyone. And the guy is drunk, right? We'll have to force it." David scratched the back of his neck as he surveyed the boulevard, his brain working at a million miles an hour. "We have to stop the accident from happening—so we have about five minutes to figure it out."

At that moment, Kara felt a sharp pain starting to throb on her right ankle. She wiggled her leg, trying to shake off the pain. After a while it seemed to do the trick, and she focused on the job again. Kara searched the oncoming traffic. Her mind flashed back to the day she died and she saw the huge bus coming straight at her. She forced the thought out of her head and focused at the task at hand.

"Are you okay?" asked David, his face concerned. "You look a little upset."

Kara met his eyes. "Yeah, I'm okay. I was just thinking about the day I died. I didn't think seeing a city bus again would make me so nervous."

"It's normal. It was a pretty traumatic experience," said David.

"I keep seeing huge headlights coming straight at me." Kara looked at her feet. "Then I remember feeling hard metal—and then the darkness. I just...I just can't stop thinking...why didn't I look before crossing the street? I might be alive again, with my whole life ahead of me."

"I can see how this assignment has you a little anxious. But you're a guardian angel now...that is your new life."

Kara let out a sigh. "I know. I'll be fine in a minute...I'll try not to think about my body splattered under a bus."

"Oh yeah, I remember that."

Kara frowned. "What? How did you know that?"

"Because I was there." David turned his attention back to the street.

Kara's eyes widened. "What? What do you mean *you* were there?"

She stood frozen in place, her mind working overtime, playing back the events of her death in her head. She remembered a hand reaching out and grabbing her. "That was you?"

"Your soul was my assignment—I see it!" yelled David, "Look!" He pointed southwards on the street.

Kara followed David's gaze and spotted the bus. It swiveled left and right as it made its way north, just a few blocks away from them. "David! We *have* to think of something fast!" She brushed the hair out of her eyes. "What if we can't stop the accident...what...what would happen after? Would all those dead mortals attract a whole lot of demons? David?" yelled Kara.

In a flash, David ran across Decarie Boulevard. His backpack bounced behind him. He got to the sidewalk and turned around. He watched the oncoming bus and then glanced at Kara for two seconds before looking back at the bus. "We only have one option," he yelled from across the street.

"What's that?" Kara struggled with her nerves.

"I'm going to jump in front of it...hopefully he'll turn the opposite direction and hit the parked cars. That should stop it."

"That's your *master* plan?" Kara shook her head. "What if it doesn't work?" she yelled back, as a group of people eyed her strangely. "What if it crashes into the oncoming traffic? That's not better!"

David paced on the spot, his hands on top of his head. "Well, if you come up with something better, you better tell me in about ten seconds, kiddo, 'cause here it comes!"

Kara turned her head. David was right. She could read the *Out of Service* sign at the top. The bus was almost upon them. She looked behind her at the restaurant and saw shadows of people inside, not knowing that this might be their last meal. It was packed.

Kara hit her head with her fists searching for a solution. She bit her lip and looked up the street. A red fire hydrant stood but twenty feet from her.

Without breathing a single word to David, Kara turned and bolted towards the restaurant. With her super-hero-chick M suit, Kara plowed through the glass front door, which shattered with a loud *bang*. Chopsticks fell onto plates as the customers stopped eating and stared wide-eyed and open mouthed at the crazy girl who had just interrupted their meal. Kara knew she only had seconds before the bus came crashing in, killing everyone—including the children.

There was only one thing she could do. She roared, "FIRE!!!!!!!!"

No one moved. They all just stared.

"FIRE!" screamed Kara again. "FIRE! QUICK...GET OUT! GET OUT!" She jumped up and beat the air with her arms.

But no one moved.

Kara searched the small restaurant for any kind of alarm system and spotted one on the wall near the entrance. She sprinted towards the red little box fixed to the wall and pulled the lever. Immediately, an ear piercing ring engulfed the tiny restaurant. The customers looked at each other, and then they all jumped up and started to run. Mothers cradled their babies as they hurried out the door; even the cooks at the far end of the restaurant jumped over tables and pushed their way through.

"Fifteen...fourteen...thirteen..."counted Kara. She waited until everyone was safely out of the restaurant.

"Five...four..." Kara ran out of the front door.

"Two..." The front of the bus rolled up onto the sidewalk and came straight for her.

"One!" She jumped out of the way, and the eight-ton metal monster plowed into Oodles for Noodles. Glass and bricks flew everywhere as a thundering *crash* exploded all around. The bus shuddered to a stop, but not before demolishing a path to the far end of the restaurant. The ground shook as walls and ceiling came crumbling down. The bus was flattened like a soda can by the weight of the structure.

Kara pushed herself up. Rubble was all that was left of the restaurant. She wiped the dust from her face and turned to look at the many stunned faces. Remarkably, no one was hurt. She even spotted the driver of the bus, staggering his way out of the restaurant. "It'll be the twelve-step program for you, buddy," she called out.

Kara smiled. She had accomplished her task. It felt great. She heard David's voice over the chaos.

"Hey! You're a *genius*. The fire alarm! Why didn't I think of that?" David beamed as he ran towards her. He put his hands on his waist and cocked an eyebrow. "Gabe's going to be *very* happy." He watched the crowds of people who were now taking pictures of the wreckage with their cell phones. "Told you it was going to get better!" He patted Kara on the back, like you would a dog that had performed a task. "You did *really* good, kiddo."

Kara smiled. "A good day on the job, wouldn't you say?" she laughed. "I'm just really, really happy no one was hurt." She looked around. "And no demons showed up...now that's a first."

"Yup." David dropped his bag on the ground. "It's times like these that make it all worth it, you know... almost as good as...thirty gin and tonics."

Kara gave David a light shove. "You're an idiot." A smile reached her lips. "But an idiot—on a rare occasion—can be right sometimes."

Kara's attention went to a mother comforting her crying child. "This does feel awesome."

"Told ya."

"Ouch!" A stinging pain erupted on her right ankle. Kara bent over and pressed her hand over it.

"What is it?"

"I don't know...I have this thing here..." she pulled up her pant leg and heard David gasp. The mark had grown. It was the size of a fist now, sprawling up and around her calve like a spidery hand. It was mad and ugly.

"You're *Marked!*"

"I'm what?"

"You're a *spy!*" hissed David. He pushed her roughly away from him. His wide eyes flashed with anger. "How could you? A demon spy! *You're* the traitor! You've been the traitor this whole time, haven't you?!"

"What? David, don't be ridiculous...I'm not a *spy.*"

He was yelling now. "YOU'RE MARKED! Only demon *spies* are Marked!"

Kara frowned. "Stop it! You don't know what you're saying. I can't be a spy... I just got here! This must be some mistake...it's probably not even a Mark, as you say...maybe it's something else?"

David's expression darkened. "Don't try to *fool* me again, traitor!"

His words cut through Kara's being like a knife. What is going on? Her new angel world was crumbling down just as she had finally felt part of it.

Kara felt her soul breaking. "This can't be happening to me." She closed her eyes and then opened them again. "David. I...I'm not a traitor," she croaked, her throat tightening up. "David...listen to me, please ..."

"When did it happen, eh? When did you *sell* your *soul* over to the demons?" He shook his head. Disgust wrinkled into his face, as though Kara was the foulest thing he had ever laid eyes on.

"Please stop! Listen to me. I don't how I got this. I felt some pain on my leg, and then there was this tiny mark...but it didn't hurt, so I forgot about it. It didn't hurt again until today." She stepped towards David.

"Get away from me!"

Kara recoiled, she felt like she just got punched in the gut. "David, please. This is a mistake...I would never do anything to hurt you."

David studied her face. "All this time I wondered how it was possible that the demons sensed us. Why the higher demons were up our asses all this time? You've been playing me this whole time, haven't you? You were Marked, and you led them to us."

Panic consumed her as she realized David wasn't going to believe her. "No. Why can't you believe me? I'm innocent! I don't know why I have this thing. It's not my fault!"

"Don't play innocent with me, *Kara*. The Legion will take care of you. Mark my words."

A few days ago David had kissed her, and now he looked at her with such loathing...she wanted to stop existing entirely. She closed her eyes.

"Ah...your friends have arrived!" said David.

Kara opened her eyes and looked around. "What? Who's here?"

"Have you sent them to kill me!? To finish the job!?" He shouted behind a huge group of people as he backed away from her.

"David! Wait!" Kara took a step towards David and stopped. Two higher demons walked in her direction. They pushed and shoved through the tight crowd, their black eyes fixed on her. She felt a wave of panic wash through her as she backed away. She reached over her shoulder for her bag—but it was gone.

Kara jumped up. She looked over the many heads for David. She spotted him. He was staring at her, a frown on his face. He glanced at the demons before looking back at Kara. A shadow of confusion flashed across his face. He read her true panic. And then he was fighting his way back through the crowd, towards her. Three other higher demons broke through the mob of people and made their way towards David.

"David!" she yelled. He vanished under a wave of mortals.

Kara trembled as she backed away, her eyes on the two higher demons marching towards her. The world around her grew still. She felt helpless and stuck, like a mouse caught in a trap, as she stared at the black-eyed monsters.

One of the demons pulled out a long black blade from his jacket. It was opaque, and a black mist emitted from it, like rippling black smoke. She felt a strange prickling from the inside, as though tiny electric shocks were going off all at once inside her mortal body. The demons broke into a run.

"DAVID!" she cried desperately. She waited ten seconds. Then she ran.

Kara bolted down Decarie Boulevard. She ran without looking back, and pushed her mortal legs as much as she could. Her M suit, it turned out, was better than she could have hoped. Her powerful legs moved with incredible speed. She glanced back and nearly fell as the shock of the higher demons being so close took her by surprise. They were faster than she was.

Kara pressed on. She knew she wasn't trained to fight these demons…not yet. She imagined demon torture. That gave her the fuel to keep running.

She had been running non-stop for so long that she felt her spirit starting to dampen. Her M suit didn't tire, but she didn't know how long she could keep this up. How long could she stay in her suit? She knew they didn't last long. What was going to happen when she outlived it? She knew she had to do something, fast. Dread overwhelmed her whenever she looked back and met those evil black eyes. And David hated her now. The unfairness of it all filled her with rage.

A bright red neon sign, Stan's Diner, appeared in front of her. Kara saw her chance and took it. She ran into a large group of teenage girls, stole a blue jacket from one of them, pulled it on and squeezed herself in with them. She hid with the giggling girls until she was right in front of the diner. Ducking her head, she sprinted straight for the front door and nearly collapsed as she rushed in. She crashed into a few people. "Oops, so sorry! Excuse me!" Kara whirled around and looked out the front glass door.

The higher demons passed Stan's Diner. They ran along the sidewalk, then they stopped. Their heads moved around, as if to follow a scent.

She ran towards the back. A waitress walked down a hallway. "Toilet!" yelled Kara. "I need a toilet—hurry!"

The waitress stopped and pushed up her glasses. Her white hair was pulled back in a tight bun. "Okay. Keep your pants on," she laughed. "The washrooms are over there," she pointed behind her, "but they're out of order."

Kara stared. "Are you kidding me?"

"You'll have to try Stone Grill down the street," the waitress told her.

"I'm not going to make it!"

The waitress blinked. "Are you sick?"

"Something like that." Kara ran past the waitress and stopped in front of a wooden door. Two small paintings of a man and a woman with each sitting on a toilet reading the paper were nailed to the door. A paper sign taped on the front read: *Out of Order*. She tried to force the door open, but it wouldn't budge. "Oh no, this can't be happening!" cried Kara. She pulled on it again as hard as she could—and lost three fingers.

"AHHHHHH!" screamed Kara. She watched her fingers fall to the ground and bounce to a stop. Her index, middle, and ring fingers lay by her shoes, looking like a couple of merguez sausages. A flash of blinding white light radiated from her severed hand, illuminating the entire hallway as if someone had just turned on a huge spotlight.

Kara bent down and scooped up her mortal fingers with shaking hands. She squeezed them with her left hand. They felt like rubber. They were hollow, like empty shells. She dropped them in her pants front pocket. Then she shoved her glowing hand underneath her shirt and turned to check if she had been seen.

A man in his fifties with salt and pepper hair appeared in the hallway. He smiled at Kara as he passed by her. Kara put on her best fake smile and pretended to be talking on the phone. He disappeared into the kitchen where the smell of grease was as thick as tar. A metal coat rack stood against a wall, near the entrance to the kitchen. Kara dashed over to the rack and grabbed a pink silk scarf. She quickly wrapped the scarf around her glowing fingers.

Kara jogged down the hallway to the front of the restaurant. A faint clatter came from the dining area, where customers enjoyed their greasy meals. She saw a young waitress setting up a new table. Kara looked out through the tall glass windows which ran the length of the diner. A higher demon searched the grounds outside. It prowled down the block searching, like a wild animal sniffing out its prey.

She hid her pink hand under her shirt and leaned back against the wall. The waitress filled the empty salt shakers with a large bag of salt.

Kara ran to an empty table. She grabbed a salt shaker and shoved it in her pocket. She knew what a bit of salt could do to a higher demon. But this time she was alone. And there were two of them. She ran to the next empty table and grabbed another salt shaker. There were only two empty tables in the diner. But she needed salt.

The men and women in the restaurant eyed her suspiciously. Kara flashed them a smile. "I have low salt levels."And with that, Kara rushed over to a booth with a family sitting comfortably inside.

"Hi there," she said as she grabbed the salt shaker, "do you mind? I'm all out. Thanks a lot." She shoved the shaker inside her other jean's pocket. And just when she was about to turn around— her right ear fell onto the table.

"Crap!" yelled Kara as she scooped up her ear. She looked at the terrified family.

"Ah…it's just a rubber ear," she smiled, "nothing to worry about. Stupid little prank."

But a beam of light had exploded from the right side of her head. A look of complete shock masked the faces of the family. Their eyes were glued to her head, at the glowing hole where her ear used to be.

Wide-eyed, Kara smacked the right side of her head. She pressed her hand against the hole. "I'm having a seriously *bad* day!"

She swung herself out of the booth and threw her mortal ear on the floor. She ran to another booth and scooped up three more salt shakers. Satisfied, she headed towards the back of the restaurant, but not before grabbing a knife from one of the tables.

A bell rang, and she turned to see a demon pushing the front door open. He stepped into the diner. His black eyes locked onto hers and grinned. Kara pushed open the back door and ran into an alleyway.

The other higher demon stood in the back alley. Hands in his pockets, he waited calmly outside for her. His pale face cracked in an evil grin. His black eyes watched her every move.

"I'm *so* not ready for this!" Kara put as much distance as she could between her and the demon. She knew running was not an option anymore. Her mortal body was shutting down. With her butter knife in one hand and a salt shaker in the other, she waited for the demon to attack.

A door slammed shut behind her. The second demon stepped into the alley with a black blade smoking in his hand. Kara blinked and backed away.

"How about playing by the rules?" said Kara. "Two against one, that's hardly fair!"

Rotating his dagger skillfully between his fingers, the demon took a step closer. Kara watched silently as he positioned his body in anticipation.

And then he struck.

But Kara was ready. The demon lunged forward, his weapon going for her stomach. Kara side stepped and thrust her knife into his side, cutting away at his flesh. She rolled and stepped back, watching in horror as black blood oozed from the cut. The demon clasped his wound with his hand, with a stunned expression on his face. Black blood dripped between his fingers. Then he came at her swinging.

Kara went into defense mode; positioning her right foot in front of her while adjusting her weight with her left, she blocked his hit. The impact nearly forced her to her knees—but she held on. She felt the mortal body strain…she knew it wouldn't last long. With all her strength, she pushed off and backed away, watching the demon's corrupted face screwing up in anger, its upper lip trembling.

The demon attacked again. He swung his blade with brutal force, aiming for her head. She blocked it, but the force of the strike forced her to the ground. Her butter knife flew out of her hand. Blinking, she looked up at the demon, its black eyes filled with a mix of hatred and hunger. She felt a cold fever rushing through her. She trembled. She felt the M suit weakening beneath her, melting away. Her vision blurred. She blinked desperately, trying to see clearly. The second demon walked slowly towards her, a smile materializing on its face. It opened its mouth to speak.

"The end is near, *angel*," hissed the higher demon.

Kara opened a salt shaker.

"You can already *feel* it. We will *drink* your essence, little one...and you will be no more!" Its jaw dislocated and opened abnormally long, all the way down to its chest, like a ventriloquist's dummy's wooden mouth. Kara could only stare. It lunged at her...

Kara threw the salt shaker in its mouth. The demon fell over and screamed. Convulsing on the ground, his mouth sizzled and popped. Black smoke rose from his body like burnt toast. He howled in pain.

Kara grabbed another salt shaker and readied herself as the other demon attacked. She threw the salt at it, but the demon brushed it aside with its blade. With lighting speed, the demon struck and sliced off her right arm.

"Ahhh!" Agonizing pain surged through her M suit. Her body burned, the poison of the blade eating away at her soul. She stared at the hole where her right arm used to be; black mist emitted from the wound like smoke from a candle. A kind of acid surrounded the cut, eating its way around the stump, leaving it blackened. The pain was so intense that Kara shut her eyes and rolled on the ground. She was burning alive from the inside. She felt the poison of the blade spread through her M suit...and into her soul. She was dying, for a second time.

Kara . . . Kara . . .

Kara turned and looked at the demons. Their lips didn't move.

Kara . . .be strong . . .

"Who—where are you...?" She whirled her head around.

We are here with you . . .

Kara trembled. "I can't s...see you. H...help me. Please."

Feel your strength, Kara. Don't be afraid . . .

"What d...do you m...mean?" She shook uncontrollably.

"Who are you talking to, little *angel?*" The higher demon tossed her severed arm in the air. "No one can help you now."

The demon stretched open its mouth and swallowed her arm. Its eyes suddenly glowed white, before going back to black. The demon grinned. It turned its attention to the remaining parts of Kara. "Your essence tastes great," said the demon. "You will make me very powerful, little *angel*. You should be happy your *meaningless* angel *soul* will have served a purpose."

Kara blinked as she forced herself to sit up. She cradled the stump of her arm. Part of her wanted to die, to stop the excruciating pain. She waited.

Kara . . . don't let go . . . you can do this . . . hang on a little longer . . .

"M...my head," breathed Kara, "I'm hearing voices in my head."

154

A door opened with a loud creak on the opposite side of the alleyway. A man dressed in white threw some large black garbage bags on the ground, plopped a large bucket of soapy water with a wet mop beside it, and slammed the door shut.

"Hmmm," continued the demon as it approached her, "how splendid you will taste."

The bucket, Kara, said the voices. *The water . . . run to it. Feel the strength in you, Kara, run!*

Kara couldn't explain it, but she suddenly felt stronger, as though the strength of a hundred people burst into her. The higher demon's jaw loosened up grotesquely as he prepared to eat her, and Kara mustered the last of her energy and ran towards the bucket.

She plunged her head in the water. A sharp pain erupted in her legs—and the darkness took her.

CHAPTER 11

MIRACLES DIVISION

IT SEEMED LIKE DAYS had passed when Kara finally opened her eyes. Her body was enveloped in something soft. It followed her every move like the waterbed she had once tried at her Aunt Tracy's house. Kara turned her head in every which way and saw only orange. As she moved, a semi-liquid substance pressed against her like jell-o. She reached out. Her hands stopped at a harder subsurface. She felt up and down and around. She was inside a globule. She opened her mouth to scream, and liquid poured in. She closed her mouth again.

Kara strained to see past the semi-translucent shell. Shadows of bubbles floated all around her. She looked down at herself; her clothes were gone. She was completely naked. She whirled around inside her bubble, kicking with her legs and flailing her arms.

There was a sudden loud *pop*…Kara felt the bubble break below her, and she slipped and fell into a pool of water. She struggled to the surface, where buckets of the jell-o substance came drooling down on her.

"Gross!" she yelled, as she wiped her eyes. She was inside a massive warehouse-like building made of shimmering brass metal. A great metal contraption of interwoven pipes and wires stood at her left, reaching all the way to the top…like her uncle's car garage, but without the oily cigarette smell. The pool ran the length of the building and sparkled in the sun light, which spilled from the skylights above.

Thousands of soft orange spheres the size of a person hovered in the air, like giant soap bubbles. They bounced off of each other in the crowded space.

Kara heard a shuffle of feet and turned to see a cherub with a glass jar full of souls stop at an operational panel on the left. With some effort, the cherub stood on the top of its toes and dumped the souls into an opening. They flowed up through a pipe, where she couldn't see them, to a giant translucent tube extruded from the top of the machine. The souls rolled inside the machine for a moment and then popped out, one by one, enveloped by orange bubbles. She could make out the silhouettes of GAs wiggling inside these bubbles, as they grew slowly into their human forms.

Something moved in Kara's peripheral vision. A group of guardian angels stood below one of the globules, looking up. Suddenly the bag broke, and with a *splash*, a naked GA plopped into the pool. She heard buzzing as she read a huge flashing neon sign, Healing-Xpress.

Kara made a face. "Whoa…I think I swallowed too much of that orange stuff."

Kara brought her hands to her face. Her body gave off a strong citrus smell, as though the orange substance was some sort of fruit punch. She heard the faint patter of some walking behind her. She turned and looked up into sparkling blue eyes.

"Here…" David threw her a towel and turned his back. "You can cover yourself with that until we get you some clothes."

Kara's mouth seemed sewn shut. She struggled to open it.

"Thanks," she croaked. She pulled herself up and over the ledge into a sitting position. She wiped her body down. "And you've been here for how long…staring at my naked body, if that's what this is?" She wiped her face with the towel and then carefully wrapped herself in it.

"I just got here."

Kara studied David's back. He had come to see her. Maybe he believed her now?

She brushed a sticky strand of hair behind her ear. She felt prickling all the way down her back as she tried to come up with something to say. She was never good in these kinds of awkward situations. But then again, *she* was dead, and she had been naked and covered in sticky orange slime; what could be more awkward than that?

"You can turn around now." Kara watched as his body shifted and turned.

"Hm." David thinned his lips, a scowl materializing on his brow.

She studied his face for a moment. She had never seen David look so troubled. It was as though he was fighting something from the inside. When she couldn't bear it anymore, she asked the one question she'd been dying to ask since he arrived.

"So…do you believe me now? About the demon's mark on my leg?"

David stared at the floor, his face expressionless. "It doesn't matter what *I* think. The Legion is divided about what happened. They haven't come to a decision. Not everyone believes you're innocent."

Kara looked into his face. She wanted David to believe her. It was the truth, after all.

"You still don't believe me…and you think I'm some *spy*?" she said angrily.

"It doesn't matter what I think." His quiet tone was worse than if he'd been yelling.

"Right…you said that. So then, why are you here?"

David met her eyes, an unreadable expression on his face. "I'm still your Petty Officer…it's my job to make sure you're okay."

"Right." Kara narrowed her eyes and shook her head. "You said the Legion was *divided—the Legion*—does everybody know about this? And angels have taken sides?"

A loud *splash* cut the uncomfortable silence between them. More GAs plopped into the pool, their naked bodies struggling to a sitting position as they wiped the orange liquid from their supernatural skin.

After a long pause, Kara turned her attention back to David. "So, how did I get here—in these *bag* things?" She pointed to the floating orange bubbles. "The last thing I remember was being attacked by higher demons and reaching the bucket of water. Then everything went black."

David looked up as more GAs plopped into the pool.

"Your soul was in a bad shape...you needed to be healed. This is where all angels come to get fixed."

"Oh." Kara felt like a car that needed an oil change. She cleared her throat.

"Um, David? Something...something *strange* happened to me when...when I thought I was going to die ... when my soul was dying."

"What do mean, *strange?*"

Kara blinked. She wasn't sure whether hearing voices in your head up in Horizon could mean the same thing as hearing them back on Earth.

"What is it?" said David. "You look like you've seen a ghost."

"Kinda." Kara sighed and closed her eyes. "You're going to think I'm crazy, but I...I heard voices."

She opened her left eye and peeked at David.

"What?" David cocked an eyebrow. "Maybe you just bumped your head or something."

"I don't think that's it. I really *heard* voices inside my head...they...they helped me escape. You think I'm crazy, don't you?"

David's expression was distant.

"I've never heard of guardians hearing voices. I'm pretty sure it was your own voice, Kara. Remember...you were weak, and you thought you were dying. Our minds do strange things when we're about to die."

He threw out his hand. "Come," he said as he gestured for her to take it. "The Archangel Raphael wants to meet you."

Kara took David's hand and pulled herself to her feet. She realized she should be more cautious about what she said from now on. Hearing voices was not common among the angels. She feared it might make her look more like a traitor. So she dropped the subject.

"Who's Raphael?" she asked instead. She pulled her towel tighter around her.

"An Archangel," David squeezed her hand.

"I know…but who is he? What does he do?"

"You'll see."

They left the Healing-Xpress building through giant metal doors, and Kara stared up into a scarlet and orange sky. Like a rainbow, the colors chased one another, twisting and swirling as they spread above and beyond. In the forest before them, tall green trees rippled in a light breeze.

Surprisingly, Kara felt great. She kept the towel wrapped tightly around her body and followed David through the forest. The dirt path led up to a clearing where they looked out across a valley to a mountain that rose high above and was lost into a sea of red clouds. As they neared the base of the mountain, Kara realized that a city was carved from the mountain's core. Groups of oracles and guardian angels poured out from the many stone edifices, going about their business.

"What is this place?" asked Kara.

David seemed to relax a little. "Miracles Division…where the *magic* happens."

"Huh?"

"Just a handful of GAs get to work here," explained David. "Sometimes—but it's very rare—we get to perform miracles. Usually by healing the sick. What the mortals can't explain with their science…how a person is suddenly cured of cancer…that's us."

Kara thought of all the sick people she had seen in the hospital last year when she had cut herself and needed a few stitches…back when she was alive. She remembered *a lot* of sick people. "But…there are still *so* many sick people in the world? Why aren't they cured?"

"I'm not sure," answered David. He passed a hand through his hair. "All I know is there are only a few special cases . . . and that the orders come from The Chief himself."

"Oh." Kara followed David down a small slope. Her bare feet pressed against a smooth stone path. "I feel kinda awkward in just a towel… everyone else is dressed." She tugged the top of her towel and held it in place with her right hand.

"You're not the only one…look." David pointed to another group of GAs waddling down a path in white towels.

"Thank God. I don't feel like such a moron now."

When they reached the opening of the city, two giant man-like rock sculptures stood on either side of the entrance, like soldiers guarding the entrance to the palace. Their rough faces were carved into downward grins.

Kara stared at the jungle of winding and turning walkways that wound between buildings carved from huge walls of rock, as though chiseled by gigantic hands. Other buildings were wood and stone, molded into perfectly balanced designs.

Kara followed David inside a massive stone structure, down a hallway, then finally into a large chamber. Red rays of sunlight poured through square openings at the top, like stained glass windows. Five guardian angels in blue lab coats worked on wooden tables cluttered with plants and pots, mixing and measuring elements in glass containers. The liquids morphed into green and orange colors.

A beautiful Asian-looking woman, draped in white linen, examined the contents of a square glass container, which looked to Kara like a small trapped rainbow. Red highlights reflected off the jet black hair that spilled all the way down her back. She towered over David and Kara.

"So, this is Raphael?" whispered Kara. "She's a woman."

David had a huge grin plastered across his face, his eyes fixed on the beautiful lady.

Kara rolled her eyes. "You're so predictable."

They walked towards the impressive woman. She looked up, and her perfect face melted into a brilliant smile.

"Ah, David." She put the glass container on a table and walked towards them. "I'm so glad to see you again." She reached out and hugged him.

Kara noticed a golden shield crisscrossed with two silver swords marked on her forehead.

"I'm very happy to see you too, Raphael," David was smothered in Raphael's bosom as he spoke. She let him go, and Kara thought she could see the blush on his cheeks.

Raphael's brown eyes locked onto Kara. "So, this must be Kara...let's have a look."

She took Kara's hands in hers as she examined her closely. Kara felt a strange ripple pass through her body, as though she had just gone through an internal x-ray.

"Well, then...I'm going to put my hands on your face, okay? I need to make sure there aren't any traces of the death blade inside you."

"A what kind of blade?" Kara wrinkled her face.

"A death blade...a demon blade. It's poisonous to any angel," answered Raphael, "it can kill you."

"Right . . . I remember those."

The Archangel studied Kara's face closely. "Are you ready, Kara?"

Kara blinked and looked over at David. He gave her a reassuring nod and then his eyes darted back to Raphael. Kara bit her lip and turned back to face the Archangel.

"I feel a little weird with you staring at me like that," she said.

Raphael smiled. "Don't worry. It won't take long," she laughed, "I promise I'll stop staring at you in just a minute."

Raphael's almond eyes hypnotized Kara, and she could only nod.

Raphael pressed her hands around Kara's face and then closed her eyes. Immediately, Kara felt a soothing warmth spread from her head to the rest of her body, as though someone had just poured a bucket of warm water over her head. The sensation turned to little pricks inside her, like tiny lightning bolts bouncing on the inside walls of her core.

And then it stopped.

Raphael took a step back and her face broke into a smile. "Wonderful. You show no signs of the poison. And the demon's Mark is gone. *That*, is *very* good news, Kara." She turned around gracefully and walked over to the large wooden table.

Kara bent over and stuck out her right leg. She twisted it inwards so that she had a clear view of the bottom part. She smiled. It was olive colored, smooth and clean. The mark was gone. She danced around on the spot, flashing her clean leg. She locked eyes with David and smiled. But he didn't return her smile. Instead, he focused on Raphael.

Raphael rummaged through piles of clothes neatly placed on long wooden shelves. Kara studied her angelic face, wondering if she thought her a spy or not. Raphael didn't act as though she thought Kara was a traitor. Raphael was kind to her and wasn't giving her the cold shoulder like David was.

"Raphael, is there a way you can sense…I'm not a traitor somehow? That I'm telling the truth when I say I'm not a spy?"

The Archangel turned to stare at Kara. Her eyes switched to David's momentarily, then back to Kara. "I'm afraid I cannot help you with that. I'm a healer. I don't get involved with Horizon politics." She smiled. "I cannot read your mind."

Kara sighed. "Oh. Well...thanks anyway." She stared at the floor.

Raphael stacked a pile of clothes and handed them to Kara. "Here, these are your new clothes. You can get changed in the back." Her voice was so soothing and motherly; just having Raphael close to her made her feel as though she was with her own mother.

"Thank you. I can't wait to be out of this towel."

Kara took the clothes and went to change in a small room with a round door and no ceiling. Red light flooded from above, and a smell of moist soil filled the air. She pulled on some undergarments, a cami, blue jeans and a gray hooded sweater and walked back to join the others. She smiled as she watched David with the Archangel Raphael, putting on his best moves: the winks, the famous smile, the cocking of the eyebrow. Kara felt a little jealous.

"I'm back," announced Kara, "but I'll need some shoes." She wiggled her toes.

"Here..." David handed her a pair of running shoes.

Raphael clasped her hands in front of her and cleared her throat. "The Archangel Gabriel is expecting you both back at Operations shortly. There are lots of jobs for the two of you."

Her eyes shifted to David and didn't move again. "And please, *try* to be nice, David."

David pursed his lips. "I will, if he will."

The Archangel sighed loudly and shook her beautiful black hair. She looked at Kara. "Please try and talk some *sense* into this

166

one? It's not helping his case to be insubordinate to the Legion commander."

"He's a putz," said David.

"But he's also three times your size," said Kara. She pushed her feet into her new shoes.

Raphael placed her hands on her hips. "Gabriel is a bit intense at times, but he is your superior. Come now. He is waiting. I will accompany you back to the elevators."

Her long, white linen dress swished behind her. "Oh, I almost forgot," said Raphael as she turned around. "He has also informed me that the two of you will be summoned to the Council of Ministers."

David jogged to catch up to her. "The Council of Ministers? Are you sure?"

"Yes," answered Raphael and kept walking.

Kara ran next to David. "Why do you look so worried?" She studied his face. "And angry? What's going on, David? You're making me nervous! What's this council?"

David turned to look at her. "It's where all the big decisions are made in Horizon."

"And this is bad?"

David's face was grim. "It is when you're *summoned*."

CHAPTER 12

THE COUNCIL OF MINISTERS

AFTER KARA AND DAVID left the Miracles Division, they went back to Operations. They could only wait until the Council of Ministers decided to summon them. Gabriel handed them piles of new job files instead, never mentioning the demon's Mark. It was as though it had never happened.

Their first assignment: Mr. John Yong, 1240 Peel Street, sidewalk, 1:24 pm. Suffocates due to a severe allergic reaction to cherry gum. And while David was on the lookout for demons from the shadows of a building, Kara sneaked behind Mr. Yong as he popped in his gum and gave him the Heimlich maneuver of his life. The gum came rocketing out of his mouth and landed in some woman's hair. Too shocked and confused to speak, Mr. Yong's bulging eyes were a good enough sign that he was alive and that the job was done.

Moving on, they then tackled: Mrs. Rose Roy, at 359 Messier Street Apt. # 34, 6:12pm, who fries her brain by using the convection oven to dry her new perm. Impersonating students selling the local newspaper, Kara and David were able to sneak into the retirement home, go up the third floor, and talk Mrs. Roy out of using the oven to dry her hair.

During all this time on the job, David gave Kara the silent treatment. Kara stuck to small talk and work-related conversations. She hated him one day, and was totally into him the next. She hated herself for being so *sensitive*, so typically *female*.

At times she wanted to give up and leave him to hate her and to ask for a new Petty Officer. But Kara was determined to prove her innocence to David and to the rest of the Legion.

Kara and David hopped out of the elevator back to Level Two when they had completed their rescue missions. Gabriel greeted them with a scowl.

"Files!" he barked. He took the job files from David and waited for the oracle to roll over and take them away. Kara watched the Archangel as his dark eyes darted from David to her and back again. The look in his eyes was fierce, and it frightened her.

"It is time," said Gabriel, his perfect face showing no emotion.

"Time for what, Big G?" David flashed a set of pearly whites.

Gabriel fixed his eyes onto Kara. She shook as she felt a tickle inside her, moving from the top of her head to her toes. Then her forehead got really cold, as when you eat ice cream really fast and get brain freeze. She looked at Gabriel. He wasn't blinking, as if he were in a trance. Somehow, she could feel a part of him inside her, searching her core. And for a long moment, he didn't speak. He turned his attention back to David as he spoke.

"The Archangel Uriel is ready for you. The council will see you now." And with that, Gabriel turned and left Kara and David to contemplate their fate.

"Why was he staring at me like *that?*" she shuddered. "I feel a little violated. It was like he was trying to see through me—a bit freakish."

David flipped the collar from his leather jacket. "I don't know, but we better get going."

Kara searched David's face. "So what is the Council of Ministers going to do?"

David turned around and started to walk back to the elevator.

Kara ran to catch up. "Do you know why we have to go?"

"It's a *council*. And we're going because we have to," said David, back to his usual avoiding-Kara game.

"Right…but why? This has something to do with the demon's Mark, hasn't it?"

David kept staring at his boots as he pattered onward. "I'm sure it's because of the Mark. You don't just get summoned to the high council for tea."

"I knew it! Everyone thinks I'm a traitor!" Kara could feel herself starting to shake. "I'm starting to *flip out* here…what are they going to do to me?"

"I don't know."

"Is this like a trial? Am I going to be able to defend myself?"

"I don't know."

"Great. I feel so much better."

The ride up to Level Six, the Council of Ministers, was a silent one. Kara glanced angrily at David. He looked as though he was frightened, too. He stared at the floor with his arms crossed over his chest.

A large brown monkey operated the elevator. Its orange eyes darted back and forth from Kara to David. It adjusted its purple bowtie around its neck, mumbling to itself. After a moment, the monkey picked at its tail and popped things Kara couldn't see into its mouth. It checked its fingernails, and then scratched its bottom.

"You're disgusting, you know that?" Kara made a face.

The monkey lifted its chin. "You're just saying that because you can't have some."

"I don't want some, that's the point. It's gross."

The monkey smacked its lips. "You don't know what you're missing!"

When Kara turned away from the monkey and looked at David his brows were scrunched, and he was staring at the floor again...*so* not him. She missed the old David...the new one hated her guts.

"What happens to traitors in the Legion?" she asked.

David stared at the floor. "They're thrown out, banished forever ... never to return. They're left to serve their demon masters."

Kara clasped her trembling hands behind her back.

"Level Six! Council of Ministers," called the monkey at the control panel.

The elevator jolted to a stop. Kara stared straight ahead as the doors slid open. Blinding white light came flooding in, and she had to shut her eyes. Gradually she adjusted to the light and could see. She stepped to the door and peeked out. She looked down. Tiny puffs of clouds spread out sporadically above a vast plane of greens and beige, divided into rectangles. Dark blue curves wiggled through the landscape and out of sight. Miniscule cities were surrounded by monopoly-game houses that disappeared over the horizon.

The bottom of the elevator rested on a soft white cloud, the size of a small car. They were floating in the air. Kara started to feel unsteady and grabbed the sides to support herself. She felt *really* dizzy. In the distance, mountains hovered in the air, kept up by some sort of magic.

"You okay? You look like you're about to be sick," David said, as he rested a hand on her shoulder. She winced, totally unprepared for him to touch her so suddenly. She tingled at his touch.

Kara nodded, keeping her eyes straight ahead on the bright blue sky.

"Don't worry, we're not going to *fall*. We're just waiting for the sky-car."

Kara frowned and turned to look at David, not sure she heard him correctly. "The what?"

"The sky-car." David pointed out towards the sky.

Kara followed his gaze. Something white and small floated their way. It maneuvered easily in the open air at great speed. Kara could hear the soft *tat tat ta* sound of a motor getting louder and louder, until finally the sky-car lingered at their door. It was an oval-shaped cloud, the size of a normal car, with four upholstered blue seats in two rows in the middle. A metal T steering gear stood at the front. Puffs of white clouds shot out from the back, like balls from an automatic tennis ball launcher.

"So, how does this thing—what the...?" Kara noticed the driver.

"Sky-car 2555, at *your* service!" the driver said.

A large white and black bird was perched on the steering gear. On the top of its head rested a red cap with the numbers 2555 stitched across it in gold letters.

The bird puffed out its chest and opened its beak. "Step right up, step right up! Sirs and madams!" He spoke perfect English. He pulled out his left wing and bent it at the elbow, flapping it, gesturing for them to come aboard.

David jumped down easily with a loud *thump*. He turned and gave Kara his hand. "You won't fall. Just don't look down if you're scared."

"I'm not scared!" Kara forced herself to look only at the sky-car. "I'm just not used to getting into flying cars, that's all." She grasped the door's frame. "I don't remember seeing it in the job description."

"Let's go, Miss," said the bird, "I have other appointments..."

"Okay, okay!" said Kara. "So what if I fall ... I'll just reappear in an elevator, right?" she whispered to herself. She took David's hand and jumped into the sky-car. She was relieved to land on solid footing.

"The name's Sam," said the bird. He jumped up and twirled around in the air, landing with his back facing them. With his feet clasped tightly around the steering bar, he swung upside down and extended his right wing in greeting.

"Pleasure to meet ya," he blinked several times.

David shook his wing. "I'm David, and this is Kara," he said to the upside down bird.

"Okay then! Now that we're all acquainted..." Sam flapped his wings, swung his body back upright on the steering gear, straightened himself, and said formally, "Please take a seat! Take a seat!"

Kara and David sat down together. "There are actually seat belts on this thing? Why?"

David put his belt on. "Trust me...buckle up." He raised his eyebrows. Kara clipped her seat belt together and pulled it tight.

"Now should I be scared?"

Sam flapped his wings excitedly. He adjusted his hat.

"Ready?"

David nodded. "We're good to go."

Sam used all his weight to push the accelerator.

"Hang on to your *butts*!" The motor kicked into life, and the sky-car rocketed towards the floating mountains.

"HOLY CRRRAAAAPP!!!"

Kara's head was pinned to the headrest, as though she was on a circus ride. The wind whistled in her ears, and she squinted her eyes into slits. The sky-car flew across the sky. Soon, the mountains came more in focus and Kara realized that she had been mistaken. What she had believed to be huge mountains were in fact parts of a massive city, floating on individual clouds.

174

When they reached the floating city, Kara felt a cool spring breeze. Sky-cars flew in and out of buildings and disappeared between the clouds, picking up and dropping off guardian angels and oracles. The huge city sparkled in the sun like massive pieces of jewelry. The sky-car swayed and hovered over a large concrete landing zone, then dropped and settled onto a platform.

"You okay? You look green." David grinned and combed his hair with his fingers.

"Peachy," grunted Kara, as she swayed on the spot.

Sam the bird swung around and around on the steering gear. "Don't forget to tip your driver!"

He beat his black wings, hopped to an upright position, and held out a tin can in front of him.

"We have to leave a tip? Are you serious?"

"Oh, yeah…I almost forgot." David ripped a button from his shirt. He dropped it in the can.

"Buttons are tips?"

David flattened the front of his shirt. "Tips can be anything…just as long as you give them something."

Sam shook the can, delighted. "Smell ya later!"

The sky-car lifted up, hovered for a moment, and raced off.

"And I thought the monkeys were the ones on crack!" Kara stared after the flying car until it was just a gray speck in the vast blue sky.

There was a sudden *click*, and a door at the far end of the platform opened. An oracle appeared and maneuvered his giant crystal towards them.

"Ah! Here you are at last." He crumpled the front of his robe in his excitement.

"Quickly now…the two of you should know that you are going to be questioned about the demon's Mark situation…the council is waiting…this way please." The oracle steered his crystal around and made his way towards the door at the end of the platform.

David sighed and followed the oracle.

Kara jogged over to his side. "So . . . what do you think is going to happen to me?" asked Kara as she studied David's face.

David looked into Kara's eyes as he walked. "I'm…I'm not sure exactly. But I know it has to do with the demon's Mark. A spy in the Legion … is some serious stuff."

Kara felt the anger rising inside her. "But I'm *not* a spy!" she hissed between her teeth. "I haven't done anything wrong."

David turned away from Kara slowly. "That's for *them* to decide. You'll have to convince them, not me. I'm not on the council."

"Right. I forgot. You *hate* me."

David grabbed Kara by the elbow and pulled her around to face him. "You *betrayed* me!" he growled, trying to stay calm.

"*I* betrayed *you?*" Kara narrowed her eyes. "You won't even believe me when I'm telling you the truth! You pretend I don't exist!"

"The truth is that you're *Marked!*" said David.

Kara made fists with her hands. "It's not my fault! I didn't know I was Marked! How many times do I have to tell you?"

"You *played* with my emotions," said David, recovering his composure. "You used me." His voice was almost a whisper.

"What...?" Bewildered, Kara just stared at David, not believing she had just heard what came out of his mouth.

"Ahem...am I *interrupting* something? Are you in *control* of your feelings?" The oracle tapped his foot on the glass sphere.

David straightened up. "Yes, oracle."

The oracle glared at the two of them for half a second. Then his face broke into a smile. "Was that convincing enough? I used to think...if I were born mortal...I'd be a swell actor."

"It was great."

"Yeah, you were really convincing." Kara put on a fake smile. She was still shocked by David's words.

"Well, I've watched myself perform this very act hundreds of times—oh, dear." The oracle screwed up his face. "I can't remember what I'm supposed to say next? My mind is blank. Are we on our way to an exhibition?"

"No, you're taking us to the High Council," said David.

The oracle's eyes widened. "Right, that hasn't happened yet. So mixed up, so mixed up. Well then, let's get going. The council won't wait for you." He tossed his beard over his shoulder, spun around, and rolled away, mumbling to himself.

David was silent as Kara followed him and the oracle through the gray metal door at the end of the platform. Her mind was numb and her body fluttered with the words he just said. They moved through a great hall with colorful carpets and portraits of oracles, Gas, and important looking Archangels hanging high on the walls.

Haunted eyes stared back at them. They passed many doors with golden signs nailed above them, stenciled in black letters. Kara stopped to read: Council Officer # 78-ORC. She peeked through the open door and spotted an oracle sitting on his crystal ball before a long wooden desk, going through some papers. They darted along to the end of the hall, where they met two massive brass doors.

"Well then, here we are," said the oracle as he pushed open the doors. "The Minister will see you now." He disappeared behind them, leaving Kara and David standing alone.

Kara gasped.

Fourteen eyes stared back at her. She blinked. A group of seven determined-looking Archangels sat upon a dais at the opposite end of a large round chamber. The room had a rounded glass dome, and Kara could see the blue sky and hints of other tall buildings floating around them. Rays of light spilled through the glass. The Archangels sat around a black half-moon desk, which sparkled in the light like a huge black diamond.

Kara staggered behind David as they walked through the majestic doorway. Her skin prickled all along her back, as she felt the entire room go still around her. The only sound was the echoing patter of their feet.

Rows of wooden seats were angled along and around the chamber, like seats in a stadium, but this time they were all empty. She started to feel extremely cautious. A long bench was placed ten feet away from the dais, anticipating their arrival. David walked casually to the bench and faced the group, mouthing to Kara to do the same. She flicked her hair behind her ears and waited. And as she looked up, seven pairs of eyes were still watching her every move. Kara bit her lip, feeling small and insignificant. *I'm so dead.* She couldn't remember feeling this nervous before, even when she first presented her paintings. She wished she could throw up.

The largest of the Archangel males, who sat in the middle, stood up and spoke.

"Welcome, guardian angels, to the Council of Ministers. I am Uriel, the Minister of Ministration and Peace."

Uriel's voice was soft and almost musical, not at all like the booming voices of Ramiel and Gabriel. His dark brown wavy hair sparkled in the light. There was something very soothing about his presence. Kara felt herself relax a little. He was also very easy on the eyes. A long golden robe swished and swayed as he lifted his arms.

"Let us begin," he called back. "Please, sit down." He threw out his arms, gesturing for Kara and David to take a seat.

Kara fell into the chair with an echoing *thump.* The sound cut through the thick wall of silence like a knife. The hairs on the back of her neck prickled. She felt the energy of the council focus upon her. Kara flinched.

"Ahem...members," said Uriel, "there are two matters to be discussed regarding guardian angel, Kara Nightingale, of the class order # 4321. First, let us begin with the delicate subject of the demon's Mark."

Kara lifted her eyes and gazed at the speaker. Uriel sat back down and brought his hands together in front of him. For a moment, he considered the council, his face stained in discountenance.

An Archangel with a shaved head and dressed in a long gray robe pushed his chair back and stood up, his hands clasped together in front of him. "Let me be the first to object to bringing her to the council. She is a demon spy! She wears their *Mark!* We should cast her out to join her filth!" He turned his attention to Kara and glared at her with deep-set eyes.

Kara bit her lip. "This is not so good," she whispered.

A woman stood up. Her curly red hair rippled all the way down her back. Her robes were green, and her skin gave off a milky glow. "We understand your concern, Zadkiel. But under these new circumstances, I feel it is our obligation as elders to this council to seek the truth and believe in our guardians. From what Gabriel has told us, she had no previous knowledge of the Mark. There is no evidence that implicates her in any demon activity. The demons could have Marked her without her knowledge. Without any proof, I must believe she is innocent."

There were a few mumbled consensuses amongst the council members.

Zadkiel pressed his lips together. "Camael, do not be fooled. The Marked are best at concealing themselves...they are true chameleons. She is a danger to us all. Having her here will only bring death to our world! Can you not see this? Her soul is evil!"

Those last words rang in Kara's brain. She felt herself sinking on the bench.

Camael lifted her hand in a calming manner. "There's no need to shout. I understand the dangers involved if we are wrong. But I believe she is innocent. There is no evidence that points to her deceiving us."

Kara's anxiety rose to an uncontrollable level; her head was spinning. She rocked back and forth on her chair, fumbling with her fingers.

"This is against all High Council laws. Never before have we permitted a Marked angel to stay in Horizon. This cannot be! I forbid it!" bellowed Zadkiel. His lips trembled as his face was cloaked in a scowl.

Another member of the Council stood up. His night black skin contrasted against his blood red robes. His face was twisted in contempt. "I agree with Zadkiel. Letting this angel stay amongst us will only result in our *ruin*. She should not be permitted to stay!"

"She will be killed if we cast her out. She must be allowed to stay!" protested Camael.

Kara heard some members gasp.

"Members," said Zadkiel. His tone had changed into a soothing melody of words. "How can we trust this angel? We know nothing of her. Who is to say she is not a spy? She might not look evil, but do not let your eyes deceive you ... evil has many faces."

"I'd like to hear what Petty Officer David McGowan has to say about this," Uriel's voice silenced everyone in the room. Kara felt its power. His eyes darted over to David. "He's been with her since she arrived in Horizon, some short time ago. He's watched over her. I'm sure he can give us a better understanding of her temperament. David?"

Wide-eyed, Kara shot a glance at David. His expression was unreadable.

David stood up. "Um...she seems to be a regular sixteen year-old girl—a bit of a loner at times—but I haven't seen her do anything suspicious ... or against our ways. I don't sense any evil in her heart."

Kara frowned. Did he just call her a loner? She searched David's face.

"How can you be sure? You cannot know what's in her heart! No! We cannot allow this!" Zadkiel hit the table with his fist.

"This angel is innocent!" said Camael. "There is no proof supporting your claim!"

"She is a *traitor*! Have you already forgotten that she was Marked?!" shouted Zadkiel.

"ENOUGH!" said Uriel. His voice thundered through the great dome. "Let us vote on the matter now. All those in favor of banishing Kara Nightingale from Horizon, raise your right hand."

Panic moved down her body slowly. Kara counted the hands. Three.

"All those in favor of keeping her in Horizon so that she may continue to excel as a prominent GA?" continued Uriel, and he raised his hand. He pulled back the corners of his lips and showed her his teeth.

Kara waited patiently as she watched the hands go up. Four.

"The council has spoken...Kara Nightingale will stay in Horizon. Without conclusive evidence, we find no fault in her actions, nor do we find any in her Petty Officer."

Uriel looked at Kara, his deep-set eyes searching. She felt as though he was trying to see through her. Uriel lifted his brow. "And so, the council has closed this matter...let's move on to the next."

Kara had only just begun to feel calm again when she realized it wasn't over yet. The Archangels who were standing seated themselves. She looked at David for help. But he wasn't looking at her. He stared at the floor.

Another woman Archangel from the council stood up. Her long blonde hair covered the front of her white robes. She was looking at Kara.

"The council has been informed about a grave matter. An elemental child, born of mortal and angel parents, has gone missing. The elemental are very powerful creatures. They possess power of great magnitude. The mixing of mortals and angels is forbidden, but unfortunately it has happened, and we have to deal with the consequences. And to make this serious matter worse, we have now learned that the child has been taken.

"This child is *very* special, both to us and to the demon ruler, Asmodeus— for the power it can give the demons is unimaginable. Asmodeus and his kingdom of demons could perpetuate their stay in the world of the living. He wants to create havoc and take possession of Earth. It is our belief that the child is being held by some demon troops, hidden in the mortal world. When the time comes, Asmodeus will kill this child and use its power to rule the mortal world."

There were a few acknowledgments among the council.

Kara's head was spinning. An elemental child? Was this the same child Benson had mentioned? Twisted images of demons torturing a child flashed before her eyes, as a faint echo of a baby's cry made her shiver. A feeling of dread crept inside her. She looked across at the council members. Her eyes rested on Uriel; his face was unreadable. Amongst all these wise men and women she felt insignificant, as if her body had melted into the bench.

The Archangel Uriel glanced over at the speaker and motioned her to sit. "Thank you, Jophiel," he said, as he placed his hands flat in front of him. "And now, at this time, you have been summoned to the council, Kara Nightingale, to be given a *life-quest*."

At these words she heard David gasp. She turned to see his eyes bulging out of his head. He mouthed the word, "*What!*"

She heard another gasp behind her, then a *thump*. And when she turned, she could see that the oracle had fallen off his orb. He clambered back up on his crystal and threw his arms around it.

Kara shook her head. "David!" she whispered, "What's a life-quest?"

David spoke with the side of his mouth. "It's a special assignment. If you succeed, you get your life back...your mortal life back as it was before you died!"

Kara could only blink.

"It's very rare," he continued whispering.

Kara's jaw dropped as she let David's words sink into her brain. "*Your mortal life back...are they serious...?*"

"Kara Nightingale," said Uriel quietly. "Your life-quest will be to retrieve the elemental child. We have called upon you to fulfill

184

your duty as a guardian angel and to complete the life-quest which is now appointed to you."

His dark eyes glittered, and he waited to meet Kara's eyes. "Will you accept this quest?"

Kara had lost her voice. She stared at the council, wide-eyed, with her lips glued together. She looked up at Uriel. His face was lost in shadow. Visions of her past life came crashing down upon her, nearly knocking her off balance on the bench.

"I...I can have my life back? Is this for real?" her voice cracked.

"It is very real," answered Uriel. A hint of a smile reaching his lips.

"And I can see my mother again?" She hoped for the chance to make up past wrongs.

"Yes. You'll have your whole life ahead of you."

As crazy as it sounded, she had already made up her mind. She just couldn't utter the words. She forced open her mouth and stammered, "Y...yes? Yes. I'll do it."

Uriel nodded, apparently pleased with her decision.

"Good. And for your information, this life-quest has also been appointed to five other guardian angels. This will be a *difficult* challenge, and we will need as many chosen angels as possible. Each guardian was chosen for their specific skills."

"Elementals are very rare—and very dangerous," he continued. "They are not born evil, but their power tends towards the darkness, unless we can prevent it. But I must warn you: Elementals can only be touched by mortals. If an angel or a demon touches an elemental, they will die. You will be given a pair of silver gloves to wear. With these gloves, the elemental's touch cannot harm you."

All eyes were on Kara. She hated being the center of attention. She felt like a mutant. She cast a quick glance in David's direction, but he did not meet her gaze. She did not know what would happen next. She felt her body jolt as an electric shock burned from the tips of her toes to the top of her head.

Uriel cleared his throat.

"As the appointed minister of this council, I call this meeting adjourned. We will look forward to your progress on this quest, Kara Nightingale. You will report to the Archangel Gabriel for your briefing with the others. That is all."

Kara watched David stand up. She heard the echo of an oracle's orb rolling towards them.

"Well now, that wasn't so bad. This way please," said the oracle with his tiny arms outstretched, "no point in hanging around…the meeting is over."

He pointed towards the door. "Let's get going, angels. There is work to be done!" The oracle rolled away.

Kara pushed herself off the chair and followed David. Before she left the room, Kara turned around and stared back at the council one last time. Uriel fumbled with some papers, but did not look up.

As silent as a grave, the threesome walked and rolled back down the hallway leading to the landing zone. Kara stole a sideways glance at David. She could see that he was preoccupied with thought. And she was doing some thinking of her own. Dizzy with the events that just happened, Kara's mind was on but one thought only...to be with her mother again.

CHAPTER 13

LIFE QUEST

ON THE RIDE BACK to Operations, travelling by sky-car and then the elevator, Kara relived the events from the council in her head. If she succeeded in her new mission, she would be with her mother very soon. It was her only chance to make things right. Failure was not an option.

But some of the events with the High Council had left her feeling less than perfectly happy. Clearly, some of the members didn't believe her and wanted her *dead*, which meant a big part of the Legion was also in doubt. But Kara was even more determined to prove her innocence. She wasn't a liar, or a traitor. Her new mission, this life-quest, was the perfect opportunity to show them all...including David.

Kara thought of all the possibilities that having her life back again would offer her: She'd be with her mom again. She'd have a chance at her career as an artist, and she could maybe even slip into a little love? She stole a look at David and felt herself go limp. He had accused her of playing with his emotions—of using him—did that mean he cared for her? Now he was giving her the cold shoulder again. And something was different about the way he looked at her. She thought she saw fear flash behind his eyes a few times. But why? What was he so afraid of?

They strolled along in the ruby sand on their way to the large white tent. Gabriel hovered over a table and examined some documents. Five other guardian angels lingered around and talked amongst themselves. None of them turned to greet Kara and David. They all ignored her. Some smiled at David, but most of them avoided eye contact with Kara.

She felt a sting in her chest. "Does the entire Legion know about the Mark?" she asked David.

"Words travel fast here. I'm sure everybody knew about it before we were called to the council meeting."

"Great," she sighed. "They're all treating me like I'm guilty. But I'm not!"

"Don't waste your time with them...you need to stay focused on your new mission."

She stared at the small gathering of angels. "Hey? I'm the only rookie...everyone here is a Petty Officer? Is that normal?"

"I don't know."

"And look...Benson is here."

David scowled. "Well, well ... my favorite douche bag. What were the odds of him showing up?" Benson looked at David with contempt. He puffed out his chest and squared his shoulders.

Kara bit her lip and followed David towards the group. Gabriel lifted his head as they approached and met her eyes. She looked quickly away and stood next to David.

"Kara Nightingale," said the Archangel, "glad you could join us."

He waved a large hand over to the group. His attention then turned to David. "You don't have to stay with Kara, David. She will be well taken care of."

David kicked some red sand and looked up. "I'm here for *moral* support, Gaby," he grinned. He met Benson's glare and blew him a kiss.

A moment later, Benson sneaked away from the group and moved closer to David so that only he and Kara could hear what he had to say. "Didn't know you liked your women *dirty*, David?" Benson cracked a smile.

Kara saw David's jaw tighten. "You've got five seconds to get lost."

"I would have never pictured you *frolicking* with the enemy," said Benson, as he cocked an eyebrow and stared at Kara, before looking back at David. "I didn't think it was your *style*."

A cool smile curled David's lips. "My *style* is my foot up your butt if you don't leave."

Kara sensed a rush of anger spilling inside her. "Stop it! Why are you doing this? I haven't done anything..."

"I don't speak to traitors...I kill them." Benson smacked his fist into his hand and his face twisted in an almost animal expression. He looked at David. "I'd watch my back if I were you."

Rage flashed in David's eyes. "Thanks for the advice, *dumbass*, why don't you run along now…I hear your mother calling."

"She'll have you killed, you know." And with that, Benson walked back to the group.

It was worse than Kara had hoped. If Benson openly loathed her, who else did? David looked in a worse mood than when they left the council. His expression was livid as he stared at the ground.

"You're…you're never going to believe me, are you?" Kara's voice started to crack. "You still think I'm a traitor … don't you?"

"I don't know what to think anymore," said David softly.

What was more frightening than the dangerous life-quest was losing David's friendship. Kara felt him drifting away from her. She forced herself to look away from David. Gabriel was about to begin his briefing.

Gabriel straightened himself, a scowl on his brow as he pursed his lips. He placed his two hands on the table facing the angels and addressed them. "Listen up, guardian angels! You are gathered here now because you have all been chosen to carry out a life-quest. Do not be mistaken. This is no *ordinary* assignment—and some of you will not return…"

At that moment there was a sudden collective silence. Kara looked around at the five guardian angels' looks of bewilderment spread across their faces as they gawked at Gabriel.

"We have acquired information regarding the whereabouts of the elemental child," continued Gabriel, his dark eyes darting from face to face. "Our Scouts inform us that the child is in the hands of some higher demons and is being held in one of their many demon safe houses. They move the child around from house to house…and they use decoys, so we're not sure in which safe house the child could be." Gabriel paused as he concentrated.

"You will be put into pairs and assigned to three different locations," continued Gabriel after a short moment. "All of you will be geared up with the weapons and tools you will need to survive. We know this is probably the hardest assignment of your GA careers, but remember, you have been chosen out of thousands because we *know* you can succeed. You all have what it takes."

The last time she checked, Kara didn't have any special talent. Could she paint a demon to death? Drown it in some gouache?

"Keep in mind that you are responsible for your partner. Let's not make this harder than it already is. Good luck." Gabriel stepped back and folded his hands in front of him.

An oracle steered his great crystal ball to the front of the table carrying a folded piece of paper. He opened the paper and cleared his throat. "The groups are as follows," he called, holding the file in front of him.

"Benson Henderson and Ravi Aruna!" Kara watched as Benson walked over to stand next to a thirty-something East Indian man.

"Lindsey Steel and Carlos Lopez!" Lindsey was a thick, forty-something brunette who stood at about five foot ten. To Kara, she looked more like an Amazon than a guardian angel. She turned her head as Carlos walked over to Lindsey, his five-foot-five frame appearing fragile beside hers.

Kara blinked as she looked around, realizing that this meant there was only one guardian angel left to be paired with her: a twenty-something woman, who was probably regretting her acceptance of the life-quest right about now.

The oracle's eyebrows shot up on his forehead as he continued. "And for our last group, Brooke Miller and Kara Nightingale!"

Kara bit her lip and shot a glance at David, who gave her a reassuring nod. Fidgeting on the spot, she moved towards her new partner who was walking towards her. Kara saw a reflection of disappointment in Brooke's eyes, for just a second, but it was long enough for Kara to see. Then Booke's face cracked into a wide smile and she extended her hand. "Hiya! I'm Brooke," she said. Her long blond ponytail bounced behind her.

"Kara." The two girls shook hands and turned to face the oracle.

Kara blinked as she watched Gabriel stepping forward.

"And one more thing," declared Gabriel. "As you know, if you succeed in this life-quest, you will indeed get your mortal life back as it was. But if you decide to stay in Horizon, the Legion will promote you to First Officer. So, you will have a choice." He stepped back, clasped his hands behind his back, and lifted his chin.

The oracle fidgeted on the spot and cleared his throat again.

"Guardian angels...each group will have *precisely* two hours to complete their mission. If you stay longer than that — pay attention now— your M suits will *expire*...did you all hear me? Good." His blue eyes glistened with unease.

For a moment he studied the three groups, and then he grabbed three separate files which were piled on top of one another on the table. He opened the first file and glanced quickly inside before shutting it.

"Group 1—Benson Henderson and Ravi Aruna. Here is your assignment," said the oracle, as he stretched out his tiny arm and waved the closed file in their direction. Ravi walked up to the oracle and took the file from him, opened it, and read it while returning to his spot. Once Ravi had finished reading the file, he handed it to Benson. Kara watched Benson's eyes widen as he kept on reading.

"Group 2—Lindsey Steel and Carlos Lopez!" he called. Lindsey broke away from Carlos and took the file from the oracle. She opened the file only when she was back beside Carlos. Their heads nearly touched as they absorbed the information on the file.

One group left, thought Kara. Her eyes flashed to David. He stood with his arms crossed, scowling at the oracle.

"And lastly, Group 3!" the oracle called as he opened the remaining file. He took a quick look inside before closing it again.

"Brooke Miller and Kara Nightingale...here is your assignment."

Kara couldn't move. Brooke gave Kara a nod and then hopped over to the oracle. She grabbed the file and came bouncing back, her large blue eyes glistening, as she settled beside Kara. She and Kara opened it and read:

Group 3: Life-Quest

Guardian Angels: Brooke Miller, Kara Nightingale

Rank: Petty Officer W-2, Rookie 1ˢᵗ year, W-1 Guard squad

Assignment: Rescue Elemental child, from Demon safe house #3;

1228 Pine Avenue West. 9:00 pm.

Kara pulled out a blueprint of a house.

"Please report back here within two hours," the oracle told the groups. "You will be debriefed and sent out again if the child is still missing. Quickly now…report to the weapons tent for gearing right away!"

The old man clapped his hands. "Off you go! Off you go!"

Kara watched the other groups breaking away and marching towards the weapons tent. David jogged over to her.

"So … do you know what to do?" he said, as he jammed his hands into his front jean pockets, avoiding her eyes. "You think you can handle this?"

"I think I can manage." Kara watched David as he eyed the file in her hands. "Uh…you want to take a look?"

"That won't be necessary." Gabriel came striding behind them. "This isn't your assignment, David. And the location isn't of your concern."

David turned to face Gabriel. "It is when *I'm* her Petty Officer, Gabe!"

"You're not on this assignment." Gabriel towered over David, his dark eyes threatening as he tightened his jaw.

"Um…it's okay." Kara lifted her hands in protest. "I don't mind David taking a look…seriously, it's fine."

David took his hands out of his pockets and made them into fists. "You know as well as I do that this is an *impossible* mission!" he yelled at Gabriel, his face cracked in contempt.

"*You* shouldn't even be here, David."

"YOU'RE SENDING THEM TO THEIR DEATHS!" said David angrily.

Kara thought it strange that he was pointing only to her at the mention of *them*. She could see that David was really concerned.

"What?" asked Kara, puzzled. "What are you saying, David? The Legion wouldn't send us on a suicide mission, would they?"

Gabriel pulled out a massive hand and grabbed David by the arm with such force that he lifted him off his feet, as though he were a toy soldier.

"I've had enough of you today! It'll be a pleasure to escort you out personally."

Kara took a step back as Gabriel started to emanate a golden glow. The air around them tightened and the light dimmed.

David kicked his legs and shot Gabriel a dangerous look. "Go ahead, *Your Holiness* … I'd like to see you try."

"Enough!" shouted Kara, her eyes wide, shocked that the words had actually escaped her lips. "Uh, sorry…Mr. Archangel, sir, uh, Your Majesty," she stammered. "Um…I'd like David to help me choose my weapons … please?" Kara pursed her lips, scrunched her forehead and tried her best to make sad puppy eyes.

Gabriel studied Kara for a moment, still holding David off the ground with one arm.

"If you think *he* can help you…then I will let him stay." He dropped David to the floor and bent over him. "Open your mouth again, and I will rip out your tongue."

David stuck out his tongue in Gabriel's face when he looked away for a second.

Kara walked over and pulled David back on his feet. "Very mature, you know that? You'd think you were twelve." She looked across to the weapons tent and could see that Brooke was already gearing up. "Let's go, I need some weapons…and I'm running out of time."

"Sure," David said. He and Kara marched up to the weapons tent, with Gabriel following closely behind.

Kara could see that the GAs from the first group had finished gearing up and were headed down towards the pools. She watched Group 2 stuffing blue arrows and daggers into their duffel bags. And over at the far end of the tent, Brooke was trying out a long silver dagger. She sliced the air with it. She looked up and saw Kara and David approaching. Her face broke out into a grin.

"Hiya, what do you think of this one?" Brooke jumped into the air and stabbed the invisible foe in front of her. She landed with a slight *thump* and looked up at them, eyes blazing. "I think I can cut me up some shadow demons with this little baby!"

Kara had a strong feeling that she and Brooke were going to get along just fine.

"Awesome," said Kara, as the corners of her mouth lifted. Brooke looked bad-ass with that dagger in her hand, and she moved with great skill. As a Petty Officer, she was a few years ahead of Kara in terms of combat training. She was also strong and athletic.

Having had hours and hours of combat training herself, Kara felt pretty confident that she and Brooke could rescue this elemental child. How hard could it be, really? She hoped that they would get the real safe house where the child was being held captive. Her instincts and her strong desire to get her old life back were strong motivation to rescue the child.

Kara smiled as she grabbed a long curved silver sword from the weapons stand. She brought it up close to her face and saw that the stars embedded along the blade formed seven tiny circles. She rotated her wrist and watched the blade flicker in the light. It was as light as a feather and cool against her skin.

"It's a soul blade. Usually rookies aren't allowed to use them—too powerful—but I think in *your* case, they'll make an exception," David looked over to Gabriel and raised his voice to make sure that Gabriel had heard him.

Gabriel, who seemed very interested in a white globe on one of the many littered tables, didn't look up.

"You're going to need these, too." David pulled off Kara's backpack and started to fill it with red and white orbs. He held up one of the red orbs. "The red ones are called firestones—smash it near a shadow demon and it will implode, swallowing the demon with it." He arched his eyebrows as he waited for Kara to respond.

"Okay," Kara said.

He placed the red orb in her backpack and then held up a white orb. "The white ones are moonstones—they give off rays of light that are harmful to any demon, even the higher demons. Like this…" David's arm shot up in the air with the orb within his hand. "You don't have to be too close; I've used it at about fifty feet away, and it worked."

"I've packed a whole bunch, too!" Brooke bounced into view, her ponytail flailing behind her. "And…one of these!" She pulled out a white net, the size of a large trench coat. She looked at Kara and David, her blue eyes sparkling, "Shadow chains. I've used them once before and they were *amazing!* We trapped the shadow demon in it, and it couldn't transform into shadow anymore…and we killed it!"

She flashed a smile at David as she stuck out her hand. "Hiya, I'm Brooke."

David took a step forward and took Brooke's hand. "David," he said, as he gave her his trademark wink. "David McGowan."

Kara was jealous of the attention he showed Brooke. He used to bombard her with his winks, but he hadn't winked at her since he had seen the mark on her leg. She'd been feeling disconnected from him ever since, like she'd lost a best friend. She looked up at his beautiful face and his lips. The memory of the kiss flashed before her. She shook her head, trying to clear it, but other images came flooding in…images of his strong arms wrapped around her body, of him holding her close. It was too much. She looked away.

"You're *that* David?" Brooke raised her eyebrows. "You're kidding!" She let go of the shadow chains and pressed her hands against her shaking head. "I can't believe it's really *you*!" She studied his face, "I'm a *huge* fan!"

David flipped his leather jacket collar up and jammed his hands in his pockets. "Yup…that's me." He cocked an eyebrow.

"Okay, lover boy…we…" said Kara, as she pointed to herself and then to Brooke, "gotta go save the kid! Life-quest, remember? Chosen ones?"

"I know, I know."

David helped Kara finish packing her bag with some extra salt shakers and an extra soul blade, the size of a dagger. She hid it under her jeans, strapped around her calf.

"Kara Nightingale! Brooke Miller!" An oracle rolled towards them. Silver cloth glistened in his hands. "Your Sparks…here." He stretched out his little arms and handed them their gloves. "Hurry up now! You don't have much time left. Off you go! Off you go!" He waved his arms impatiently.

Kara stared at her Sparks. Twinkling like diamonds, they hardly weighed anything.

"Ready?" said Brooke.

Kara shoved her gloves in her backpack, zipped it up, and threw it over her shoulders. "Ready."

She followed Brooke and David and the three of them walked over towards the pools. They passed tents with groups of guardian angels practicing their combat training. She could hear the clangs of metal on metal.

They approached the first rows of pools. The air was thick with salt and loud *splashes* and *plops* surrounded them. Kara looked up and saw Group 2, Lindsey Steel and Carlos Lopez, standing near the edge of a pool. Their lips moved in unison…and then they jumped. With a *wallop*, they hit the water at exactly the same time. A second later a brilliant light shot up through the water, and they vanished.

Kara bit her lip and followed Brooke to the metal staircase, David at her shoulders. Brooke climbed the steps easily and waited for her on the platform.

David grabbed Kara's arm. "Hey." David turned Kara around to face him. "Remember what I taught you in combat training…how to parry, how to riposte, and how to attack?"

She nodded. "I do."

"There's still so much we didn't cover yet…you're just a rookie." David's face twisted in a frown. "You shouldn't be doing this!"

"I *want* to do this, David. And I'm happy I was chosen. This is my chance to go back home…to finish my life…to have my life back. There are so many things I still want to do…to experience. Don't you understand how important this is to me?" She searched his blue eyes. "Besides, why do *you* care? I'm a *traitor*, remember?"

David winced and stepped back, his face wrinkling into a scowl. They stood staring at each other for a moment without moving, without saying anything. Kara saw a shadow of pain glistening behind his blue eyes. "Just be careful," he said softly.

Kara studied David's face for a moment. She could still sense his suspicion, as though he wore it like a heavy coat.

"I will," she answered.

Securing her backpack, Kara grabbed the metal staircase and pulled herself up to the top. She stepped beside the grinning Brooke. The pool's reflections rippled along the water's surface. The smell of salt filled her nostrils.

"You ready?" said Brooke.

Kara took one last look down at David. She watched him as he gave her a slight nod. His face had no expression. "I'm ready," she said as she turned to face Brooke, and cleared her mind of thoughts of David.

Brooke flashed her teeth. "Okay, on three?"

Kara nodded.

"One…"

She blinked.

"Two…—"

If she had any spit, she would have swallowed.

"THREE…—!"

Kara pushed herself off the ledge of the pool and plunged into the water beside Brooke.

CHAPTER 14

ELEMENTAL

KARA OPENED HER EYES and blinked in the blackness. Vega still made her feel a little dizzy, but right now the darkness troubled her. She tried to blink the blackness away, but it didn't work. She wiggled her mortal suit's hand up to her face, but she couldn't see it. There was only blackness. The air was tight, and she could hear the faint drippings of a water pipe.

"Brooke?" whispered Kara. Her eyes strained to adjust themselves to the darkness that they couldn't penetrate.

"I'm over here," Brooke whispered back.

Kara heard the scrape of feet on concrete, and after a moment she felt a hand touch her shoulder.

"I think we're in a basement. See if you can find a light switch on the wall to your left…I'm gonna try over to the right." Brooke let go of Kara's shoulder, and Kara heard her footsteps go in the opposite direction.

"Okay." Kara was in complete darkness. She forced herself to calm down and thought about what she was going to do once she was alive again. When her nerves were calm, she struggled to move her feet. After five steps, her hands touched a cold hard surface.

"I've found a wall." Kara slid her hands up and down and tried to feel for a switch of some kind. She heard a faint *click* behind her, and the lights went on.

"Found it," declared Brooke, at the opposite end of the basement.

The basement was unfinished, with a dirt-filled concrete floor and open walls with exposed insulation. Cobwebs fell from the ceiling like see-through curtains and covered some scraps of old wood furniture that were piled in the corners. The room looked forgotten.

"There's some stairs over here." Brooke pointed to her right and waved Kara to follow. "Let's get out of here."

"Wait!" said Kara. "Is this 1228 Pine Avenue?"

Brooke shook her head. "No. The Legion wouldn't transport us to the safe house directly. But we're probably really close."

They climbed out of the basement, pushed open a heavy wooden door, and found a hallway. The old oak floors creaked as the girls sneaked down the hall, trying to find the way out. A musty carpet smell lingered in the air…just like in Kara's grandma's house. She loved that stink. She was certain this house belonged to an elderly person. They came to a foyer, which opened to the front door. Even in the dark, Kara could make out the flowered wallpaper covering the walls. Brooke mouthed, "This way," and trod towards the door. She turned the lock very slowly and pulled open the front door.

They stepped down three concrete stairs onto a sidewalk. A full moon shone down from a black sky. The cool September wind, carrying the smell of wet pavement, caressed Kara's cheeks, while a light drizzle of rain patted her hair. She wiped the wet from her cheeks and turned to face Brooke.

Brooke turned her head, "Look...we're on 1194 Pine Avenue West." She pointed to the black numbers that were nailed to the front of the Cape Cod style house they had just left. "We're just a few blocks away."

Kara glanced at her wrist watch. "It's 8:40 pm. We have 20 minutes to get there."

At that moment, thunder exploded above their heads and released a deluge of rain. The angry skies had sucked in the moonlight, and only the old street lamps showed them the way.

Squish, squish.

Their shoes pattered onward, squashing the water out as they trod up the street. Crooked gray maple trees swayed back and forth in the wind.

After only a few minutes, Kara was drenched. The rain felt strange against her mortal suit. It felt cool, but it was as though the wetness didn't seep through, like it stopped midway. Glancing down at the sidewalk while she walked, she saw two dead birds: red cardinals, their necks twisted, resting in small puddles of water. A feeling of dread crept inside her. She kept thinking back at what David had said to Gabriel...that this was an impossible mission, and that the Legion was sending them to their deaths.

Brooke stopped abruptly, and Kara nearly walked right into her. They had arrived at a street corner. The heavy rains had turned to a soft drizzle. Kara glanced up and read the street sign: Cedar Avenue. They were close.

A tingling sensation spread inside her as she surveyed the area. She imagined her old life, where she painted and had a family. *I'll have my family again soon.* A group of teenagers appeared on the opposite side of the street, giggling without a care in the world. *That'll be me soon enough.*

They crossed Cedar Avenue and were back on Pine Avenue. After four strides, Brooke stopped again. She stared in front of her. Kara followed her gaze.

1228 Pine Avenue was staring back at them. It was an old Tudor-style home with a worn down paver walkway covered in black puddles. An overgrown cedar hedge covered most of the front of the house. There was no light coming from inside. It stood alone in the dark. And all the curtains were drawn.

"Come..." whispered Brooke, as she steered Kara by the elbow towards the neighboring house's cedar hedge. She crouched down, peeking through the trees. Kara followed her example. There was no movement inside the house, from what Kara could see. Brooke slipped her backpack from her shoulders, settling it on the wet grass. She opened it and pulled out the blueprint of the house. Kara leaned in for a closer look. She could see that there were three floors to the house: a basement, a ground floor, and a second floor. She could see a back door exiting from the kitchen area.

"Two ways out," whispered Kara. "The front and back doors."

After a moment, Brooke looked up and met Kara's eyes.

"What do you think if we separate?" she whispered. "If the elemental is here, they probably put him in the basement," she pointed to the blue rectangular shape on the paper with "Basement" written under it.

"Demons like dark and dingy places, and my feeling is that he's there."

Kara looked down and studied the blue print. "Okay."

Brooke raised her eyebrows. "So, since you're still a rookie, I was thinking you could check out the ground floor…" Her hand moved over a few inches as she pointed to a new drawing, "Check out that area, and then we'll rendezvous back near the front door in about ten minutes. The child might not be here in this house. But if you see the child, come back to the rendezvous spot, wait for me, and we'll go back in together with our Sparks." An intense look flashed in Brooke's blue eyes as she stared at Kara. "You think you could do that?"

A gust of wind brushed Kara's bangs into her eyes. "Yes," she whispered back as she glanced at her wristwatch. She sensed that Brooke had faith in her abilities and wondered if she should tell her about the demon's Mark—that she was innocent—but decided against it. Tiny rain drops started to fall again.

"I'm ready," Kara said after a moment. "I can do this. I know I can."

She studied Brooke's face. "But, are you sure you can handle the basement alone?"

"Don't worry about me. I haven't lost a fight yet!"

With determination spread across her face, Brooke shoved the blueprint back in her bag. She rummaged through it and pulled out a long soul blade and two firestones. She pocketed the firestones in her blue jeans and grasped the soul blade in her right hand. Kara copied her and pulled out her soul blade from her backpack. She jammed two firestones into the large front pocket of her hoodie sweater.

Brooke nodded and the pair threw their packs on their shoulders and stepped out of the cedar hedge. Glancing around, Brooke went up the front stairs first. Kara followed a step behind, the hairs on the back of her neck standing up. With her hand gently placed on the door handle, Brooke turned it slowly counter clockwise, and with a soft *pop*, she pushed the door open.

Their eyes were already adjusted to the darkness around them, and they could see the inside of the house in shadows of gray. They walked into a large foyer, which opened up into a hallway with two rooms on either side of them. The air was stale, with a lingering faint stink of mildew. Although it was dark inside, Kara could tell the house was abandoned. The stairs to the second level stood at the end of the foyer. She knew from studying the blueprints of the house that the entrance to the basement was through the kitchen. She turned and looked at Brooke, who gave her a nod. Kara nodded in return, and with her soul blade in her right hand she pulled out a Firestone from her pocket, grasped it tightly, and stepped into the room to her right. She felt Brooke moving on her left, but she was as silent as a cat.

Kara glanced at her watch: 9:02 p.m. She had ten minutes to scout out the first floor and then rendezvous back in the foyer. She sneaked inside the large room. She could make out a large sofa and chairs. The air was stale as she crept on. Keeping close to the walls, Kara saw an opening at the left end of the room. She walked carefully towards it. She gripped the soul blade tighter in her hand...any tighter and she was sure her mortal fingers would snap off. She stepped into the opening to her left and was in a hallway. She blinked. To her right was the kitchen. A soft ray of street light came in through the kitchen window above the sink...enough to make out the old nineteen-fifties style kitchen with metal kitchenette table and matching vinyl and metal chairs. She brought her left wrist to her face and glanced at her watch: 9:06 p.m.—she still had five minutes.

Straight in front of her was a room, probably a bedroom. The door was closed. She strained for any sound and heard nothing. Nervously, she turned the door knob and pushed open the door. The door swung open and revealed an empty bedroom. Kara dropped her shoulders and closed the door. Moving down the hallway, she came face to face with another closed bedroom. She pushed open the door, and again it was empty. She shut the door behind her and glanced at her wrist watch: 9:12 p.m. She turned to her right; the foyer stood empty. Kara walked back into the foyer and watched the faint light in the kitchen down the hall from where she stood. She would see Brooke coming back from the basement from here.

9:15 p.m.

Kara blinked and looked up at the stairs leading to the other level.

9:22 p.m.

The rain hit the foyer windows with soft continuous taps. Kara started to feel uneasy. Brooke should have been there by now.

9:31 p.m.

Something was definitely wrong. *You're responsible for your partners,* she remembered the oracle telling them.

CRASH!

The loud noise came from the basement, as though a wall had come crashing down.

Kara sprinted down the hall and entered the kitchen. She turned to her right and saw the doorway to the basement. She rushed to it and started to descend to the basement. She could hear muffled voices…male voices. Quickly, she stepped down the rest of the stairs. It was darker down in the basement. The windows had been covered up with newspaper. She followed the voices, her soul blade in front of her as she stepped deeper into the blackness.

BAM!

Kara jumped. She heard a woman scream. They were torturing her. Kara ran blindly into the dark, following the voices. A faint light shone from a room at the end of the hall. She ran towards it; the door stood ajar. The voices were clearer now.

"Commander Urobach…kill the angel female! I want to *taste* her soul…" said a hoarse voice. Kara could hear someone moaning. Brooke.

Heavy boots thumped the ground. "Not yet, Zelar," said another voice, as smooth as silk. "Be patient. She still hasn't told us what we need to know."

"You want me to rip off another arm, Commander?" said a high-pitched third voice.

Trembling, Kara edged forward and then flattened herself on the wall. She inched forward. Hidden in the shadows, she stared in horror. Brooke lay semi-unconscious, spread-eagled on the ground. Her left arm was missing, a luminous hole near her shoulder. Three men stood around her. Even from a distance, Kara could see their black eyes—higher demons. Two were dressed in the same gray suits Kara had seen before, and both carried death blades. Black mist emanated from the shafts. But the third man stood out. His long leather jacket swished at his heels as he paced around Brooke. Standing about six-foot-seven, he towered above the other two. His black, oily hair hung loosely over his shoulders. He carried no weapons. He crouched down near Brooke's head, wiping her wet hair off her face.

"Come on now, little *angel*...tell me, who else is coming?" asked the same silky voice. "How many guardian angels has the Legion sent after the elemental?" Urobach turned his attention away from Brooke for a moment and looked over to the opposite side of the room. A rusted metal cage about the size of a large bird cage rested on the floor.

And inside the cage, Kara saw a young child. He was wearing only a thin pair of white and blue pajamas. She could see him shivering. His eyes were red, and dried tears smeared his dirty face.

Urobach turned his attention back to Brooke. "How did the Legion know where to find us, eh?" He stood crouched over her, his black eyes searching. "If you don't answer me, I will hurt you."

After a moment, Brooke struggled to open her mouth. "I...I don't know," she croaked. Pain flashed in her eyes. "I was given an assignment...they told me where to go ..."

The Commander's lip curled into a smile. "Tut, tut, tut.... I'm afraid, little *angel*...that is not a good enough answer for me..." With frightening speed, he jumped up, and black electricity shot out of his fingertips and attacked Brooke. Her body convulsed up and down. She cried out in pain. Kara watched in horror as Brooke's mortal body sizzled. Brilliant light shone through tiny holes all over her body. Her angel core was spilling out. She was dying.

Without another thought, Kara jumped through the door frame. "STOP! YOU'RE KILLING HER!" She lifted her weapons in front of her and prayed silently that she was going to make it out alive.

Urobach snapped his head around towards the doorway. He stopped his attack on Brooke. His eyebrows shot up on his forehead, and an evil grin materialized on his face. "Well, well, well ...what do we have here, my friends?" The Commander's black eyes widened, as though he was trying to suck her energy out. The other higher demons turned to face her, their bodies bent.

The Commander came closer to Kara. He flashed a crooked smile. "Hello, little one. Aren't you a pretty thing."

Kara glanced over at Brooke; was she still alive? She tried to move, but her legs seemed to be glued to the spot. She turned her head and met Urobach's black eyes again. "W...what do y...you w...w...ant?" was all she could muster.

He moved a massive leather boot a step closer to her. "Want?" answered Urobach. "My friends and I just want to have a little chat."

The demons nodded in agreement. Their bodies started to sway from side to side, their eyes glaring at her, anticipating an attack.

A tiny voice inside her head told her to run. She blinked hard and struggled to find her voice. "S...stay away from her!" She yelled as she thrust her soul blade into the air.

At this, Urobach chuckled. He wrinkled his forehead. "I like this one better."

And before Kara could react, he reached down and lifted Brooke's rag doll body up above his head, smiled at Kara...and ripped the body easily in half, as if it were made of paper.

"NOOOOOO!" screamed Kara. She watched hopelessly as Urobach threw her friend's severed body to the higher demons. They snatched up the body parts from the floor and opened their mouths. Their jaws extended grotesquely down to their waists as they swallowed her friend.

Kara's knees buckled beneath her. "Brooke!" She cried. She trembled uncontrollably. She stole a glance at the child. It cried silently, eyes wide and on Kara; a silent pleading. They were both going to die.

One of the higher demons stepped forward, close enough that Kara could smell his foul breath. "So, the question is, will *you* play with us now?"

Licking his lips, he displayed rows of rotten teeth. "My Commander requires some information."

Urobach cocked an eyebrow as he strolled over to Kara. "I will not lie to you, little *angel*. It will hurt…yes. And you will die, eventually. My *master* wouldn't have it any other way. Pain is necessary." He was only a few feet away from her.

Kara looked over to the elemental, and she cringed. Fear flashed in the child's eyes; its tiny little hand grasped the metal bars as it whimpered. Kara's training took over, and in one fluid movement she threw her firestone at the Commander's feet. It shattered as it hit the ground. A red mist engulfed the demon.

But then it evaporated. Urobach was still there. He grinned at her.

Kara shook her head in disbelief. "What…?"

The Commander wiped down his jacket, as though specs of dirt clung to it. "Your little toys don't work on us," he laughed. He glanced at his cronies and snapped his fingers. They charged.

Kara ran out the room and raced up the basement stairs, the demons at her heels. Summoning all the strength she could muster from her mortal legs, she pressed on as fast as she could. Jolting down the hallway, she ripped open the front door and bolted down the street.

Kara ran down Pine Avenue West and headed towards the Mont Royal Park. She knew the park well. She'd come here by herself during the summer holidays. She knew perfectly well what lay beyond the forest...Beaver Lake.

She reached the park, hopped the fence, and ran into the thick forest. It was an uphill run from here on, and she prayed her mortal legs could keep up. She ran for her angel life. She knew if they caught her, they would kill her. She shot a glance behind her and spotted the higher demons, just a few yards behind. She knew it was only a matter of time before they caught up. Images of Brooke's pale face pulsed in her mind, and a feeling of hopelessness washed over her.

"You cannot hide from us, little angel!" yelled one of the higher demons from behind. "And since you won't come quietly, it gives us great pleasure to use force!" The demon wailed a high-pitched screeching laugh.

His laugh echoed in her ears. But Kara pressed on. She could see a clearing up ahead. *Almost there.* Straining her mortal suit with everything it had, she ran for her soul, and for Brooke's. She reached the clearing at the top of the mountain. She spotted Beaver Lake, its oval shape reflected in the moonlight. Kara rocketed downhill, concentrating hard not to trip over tree roots or rocks. She could hear the demons behind her, so close.

The lake was getting bigger and bigger, bouncing into view. It was only a few yards away. Soon she would be safe.

A sharp pain shot into her back, and she stumbled to the ground and rolled to a stop. Dizzy, she pushed herself up; the pain was so intense that her vision blurred. She blinked. She could make out dark shapes running towards; they were almost upon her. She felt sick and weak. Excruciating pain shot from up her back. The poison was paralyzing her.

Run, Kara, said the voices inside her head. *You're almost there.*

I can't. I won't make it, answered Kara.

Yes you can. Remove the death blade . . . it's making you weak. You can make it. Run.

She felt a sudden rush of new energy and hope. She reached around and felt the blade in her back. She wrapped her hand around it and pulled. She stared at the black blade gleaming in the moonlight. She pushed herself up, threw the dagger on the ground, and started to run again. Kara felt the blade's poison inside her, eating away at her soul. She knew she only had a few seconds.

Little waves rippled in the moonlight as Kara reached the lake's shore. She heard the demons' breathing behind her. She heard a hiss in the air, and something stung the back of her neck. Then, with one last effort, Kara fell head first into Beaver Lake.

CHAPTER 15

LAST HOPE

KARA RECUPERATED IN A rejuvenating orange bubble, at Level Three of the Miracles Division, in the Healing-Xpress. When she was herself again, the Archangel Raphael sent her to Operations on Level Two to debrief.

Kara ran out of patience with the elevator's operator: a huge gorilla, who tried to steal some of the dried flesh from her scalp. When the gorilla had turned around, she grabbed a handful of fur from his butt.

"Take that, King Kong!" said Kara as she flicked the black fur from her fingers and watched it fall on the ground. After that, King Kong did his best to ignore her and kept to himself, rubbing the bald spot on his bottom.

She jumped off the elevator and headed towards the white tent. The air was thick with salt. Kara quickened her pace. She could see David at the head table, speaking to another angel. She felt a stinging in her chest. She was a bit mad that she had awoken at Miracles Division without a David to accompany her. But why would he be there, anyway? He had labeled her a traitor. Maybe he'd hoped she wouldn't make it back? She watched Gabriel converse with another Archangel whom she had never seen before. He was even larger than Gabriel. His golden brown skin shone brightly in the sunlight and contrasted with his silver and golden robes. Silky, dark brown hair brushed his muscular shoulders, and his face was the fairest Kara had ever seen…a male model fresh out of a fashion magazine.

Kara walked up to the table. Her eyes turned to David immediately. He turned towards her.

"Hey…how you feeling?" He lifted his hand, but as he was about to place it on her shoulder he withdrew it, as though her body was contagious, still hot with the Mark. He let his hand drop at his side. His face was screwed up, as if he had bitten into something sour.

Kara looked away, hiding the pain in her eyes. "I'm okay, I guess."

She turned her head around and looked for the members of the other two groups. Images of Brooke haunted her. Maybe she could have done more to try and save Brooke. She searched the tent. There were angels in combat practice, but no recognizable faces from the life-quest mission.

"Where is everyone?" Her eyes locked with David's. "Am I the first one back?"

David threw a quick glance over to the Archangels, before turning back to Kara. He dropped his shoulders.

"They didn't make it." He spoke in a whisper.

The floor started to spin. Kara blinked several times, trying to compose herself. "What do you mean...*they didn't make it?* What are you saying?"

Although she had no lungs, at that moment she felt as though she was suffocating.

"They were all killed." The husky voice came from the handsome Archangel, as he broke away from Gabriel and took a step towards Kara.

"You're the *only* survivor, Kara."

He wiped a long fringe of hair away from his face as his piercing green eyes studied her closely, as if she were an abstract painting.

"I'm the only survivor?" Kara croaked, "No...that can't be ... I don't believe it."

"It's true," said David.

Kara shook her head stubbornly. "No! The elemental child was at the safe house where Brooke and I went, not the others. They're probably late...yeah, maybe they're on their way back now."

"They didn't make it, Kara. They're all gone," said David.

"What...?" Her mind wandered to Benson, and she felt a sting in her chest. She didn't really like him, but he didn't deserve to die.

Kara cleared her throat. "I...I don't understand." Brooke's death flashed before her. A chill rippled through her being.

"I'm just a rookie . . . I'm the one who should be dead...not them." She felt numb all over.

"The Archangel Raphael informed us about what had happened to your partner, Brooke Miller, when you arrived at the

Miracles Division," said Gabriel. His black eyes glowered beneath his scowling brow. "Raphael told us what you told her, before you entered the Healing-Xpress shop. We knew then that you were the *sole* survivor."

As the words reached her ears, Kara flinched. How was this possible? She shook her head, frowning, and looked at David. His face was twisted in sadness as he met her eyes. But when Kara turned and looked at the Archangels, they weren't looking at her with sadness as David did; their eyes were filled with bewilderment...and was there also fear? She forced herself to look away.

"Kara Nightingale," declared the larger archangel. "I am the Archangel Michael, the Legion's commander."

He bent his head, looking down on the rookie, like a redwood tree towering over a misty shrub below. "I would like you to tell us what happened. And don't leave *anything* out."

Kara watched Michael's full lips compress, his eyes locked onto hers. She couldn't look away. She recalled the events of the assignment, starting with the killing of her friend, Brooke, to the caged elemental child, and finally to her escape from the higher demons into Beaver Lake. When she had finished, the Archangels were silent. They looked at each other with disbelief.

"We will send the Scouts out again," Gabriel broke the silence. "She came very close...there is still a chance. We should meet with the others."

Kara thought about the life-quest. "So . . . I can still get my life back, right?"

A bit of hope came flooding back into her.

"So...when do we get more chosen GAs to pair into groups?" She wondered who she'd be paired with this time.

She looked at the Archangels' puzzled faces and cocked an eyebrow. "Why are you staring at me like that? What is it?"

It was Michael's turn to speak. "There won't be any other groups."

Kara shook her head. "I don't understand? What do you *mean* by there won't be any other groups?" She looked to David, who avoided her gaze and stared at his boots.

"What are you talking about? Are you saying we're not going to be paired up again?"

Archangel Michael's green eyes fixed on Kara. "There are no other guardian angels on this mission. You are the only one, Kara."

The words hit like a ton of bricks. Her jaw dropped. "What!" She stared at him in disbelief.

"You are the only one left who can save the elemental child. No one else," said Michael.

"But...but can't you *choose* more angels? Aren't there like...*thousands* to choose from?"

Kara felt a wave of panic coming on. Soon she would be drowned in it.

Michael clasped his hands in front of him and closed his eyes for a moment, as if he was listening to another voice from inside his head.

When he opened his eyes he spoke to Kara. "Six were chosen from the entire Legion. Only those special six were destined to save the child...no others. That order comes from The Chief himself."

Kara shook her head. She exchanged a nervous look with David. "But, that doesn't make sense...I can't do this alone. That's crazy!"

"She's right," shot David, "you can't ask her to do this!" Kara was relieved David agreed with her.

David let out a soft yell of frustration as he paced the ground, his hands on his head. "She's just a rookie...it's not right!"

"She was *chosen*, David...this is out of our hands," answered Michael.

"I'm not going to let you send her off like that...I won't!" spat David.

Kara was surprised to see how flustered David was; it almost felt as if he cared, like before.

Gabriel stepped up to David. "It's not up to you. You can't stop this, David."

"There has to be another way!" David shouted. "It was a miracle she came back at all! Now you want to send her back? She...she needs more time to train!"

"You know how important this is, David. You know what'll happen if the demons use the child." Michael's green eyes flashed dangerously. "You know...this *is* the only way."

David opened his mouth to speak, but no words came out. He kicked the ground.

Michael stepped over to Kara and placed his large hand gently on her shoulder. She felt lost in his brilliant green eyes, as though she would do anything he asked her.

She shook off the feeling and looked away. "I'm not going to let you hypnotize me with your good looks."

"Kara," said Michael, his expression softened by a degree. "You are part of this Legion, chosen by The Chief to be a soldier. He has chosen you to do this task—you alone—because no one else can do it."

"The demon leader, Asmodeus, is waiting for the elemental child's power to grow to its full potential, which could be anytime now, and he will use it to destroy us. Elementals are creatures of great power—of wild, uncontrollable power—and if Asmodeus uses it, he will become more powerful than any of us. We will not be able to fight him. If you don't succeed in your mission, Asmodeus will overthrow the Legion and destroy the world of the living. He will bring havoc to the Earth. Horizon's fate rests with you."

Kara's mind was working overtime. "But...you're *stronger* than me," she looked at Gabriel and then back to Michael, "why can't *you* look for the elemental? I'm sure you'll have a much easier time than me."

She stared down at her puny body, wishing it were strong and skilled like Brooke's—maybe then she'd have a chance. She wished she could throw up.

"Because only the chosen can do this task," said Gabriel, his dark eyes piercing through her.

Michael squeezed her shoulder lightly. "That is why, you, Kara Nightingale, are the Legion's *only* hope."

CHAPTER 16

ASMODEUS

KARA BLINKED AS SHE stared at the reflections rippling along the water. She wondered if this was her last time staring down at the shining waters of the pools. Or her last mission jump? The jumps were by far her favorite things so far. She would miss the tingling sensation she felt all over her body, right before she'd disappear. It reminded her of the crazy rides at La Ronde—the saucer-like ride that spun extremely fast, which pinned your back against the wall so that you were unable to move…and when the machine went into overdrive you felt as if your body was coming apart, piece by piece. It was really cool.

The salt water smell filled her nostrils. The *plops* and *splashes* from the neighboring pools echoed in her ears. She tried to think positively about her assignment, even though the outcome was ninety-nine point nine percent sure to fail. She wondered what the Archangels felt about leaving Horizon in the hands of a rookie guardian angel. She was probably going to die today, which meant she'd be responsible for destroying the entire Legion…just a wee bit of stress on her life-quest.

David had taken Kara to train for a few hours before her mission, so that she could practice a few moves before taking the big plunge. She wasn't focused and she kept falling, missing her strikes and landing with her face three inches deep in the sand. Frustrated, she couldn't concentrate on anything except David and how he still didn't trust her. She just couldn't get it out of her head.

He put on a brave face for everyone else, but she sensed the suspicion; saw it flash in his eyes and in his body language. He tried to hide it, even now, with the fake training…the fake caring. She felt betrayed…the kiss had meant nothing to him.

It was a strange thing to fall in love in Horizon, without a heart to break…but a broken soul felt just as painful as a broken heart to Kara. She noticed that David never made eye contact with her either and he kept yelling out words to the invisible person above her head. She felt anger…she wanted to hit him hard in the face.

Soon, David gave up. He sensed she wasn't there in spirit. Kara stopped lifting her blade entirely. They walked back in silence to the big white tent. Kara received her new assignment. The oracle told her that the Scouts had only just arrived back. They had given one positive location of the elemental. She had only one hour to find the child this time. Time was of the essence, and she knew her own time was running out.

To make matters worse, the entire Legion seemed to have come to Operations to see Kara off. She looked around at the hundreds of gathered guardian angels staring at her. She heard them whispering.

"Look! That's her, she's the one…"

"Is she really a *traitor*?"

"Tom says he saw the demon's Mark himself…she must be…"

"Look! I can see the Mark on her…"

"Strange how she was still chosen."

"Yeah, but she's a rookie, she'll never make it back."

Kara stood in silence for a moment, absorbing the stings from the words she had just heard. She wiggled her backpack and tightened the straps. She thought of her mother. If she succeeded, not only would Horizon be safe but she would have her life back. She would take care of her mother. For now, it was the only glint of hope she had left. Her mortal life would have to do.

"You ready?" called David from below. He gave her half a smile, the one where the corners of the mouth stretch out and snap right back. He was joined by hundreds of onlookers. She felt like a celebrity, and hated it.

"As ready as I'll ever be," Kara answered, keeping her eyes on the shimmering waters.

"If the elemental isn't there, you come straight back! Don't wait for things to happen."

Kara turned her head and met David's eyes. She wasn't sure if this was a charade or real concern. How distant they seemed from each other now, not how they had once been…that night at the club when they had kissed. She bit her lip and wiped that thought from her mind. She might never see him again. She gazed into his brilliant blue eyes, stepped off the ledge of the pool, and plummeted to the bottom of the water.

Kara stood in the shadows of Sources Boulevard. She looked up at the brass letters hanging from a black metal gate door: Birch View Cemetery. She glanced at her watch. It was almost midnight, and the eerie garden of dead bodies glowed in the moonlight. Tall dark shadows edged the length of the rock walls around the cemetery. The front gate was padlocked and topped with barbed wire. Through the spaces between the metal gate, Kara could see hundreds of gray headstones with withered flowers lying at their feet. The night air was cool against Kara's mortal suit. The place looked sad and creepy.

Perfect for demons, though Kara.

She couldn't squeeze through the front gate, so she walked around the stone border of the cemetery until she found a spot where she could climb over. She pressed her hands against the cold rock and pulled herself up. She crawled over the edge and jumped down on the opposite side of the wall. She pushed herself up and dusted off her jeans.

She strained her ears for any sudden sound and watched for movement. The park, it seemed, was holding its breath. She walked in the silent darkness, trying to fit parts of a plan together, like a jigsaw puzzle with a missing piece.

Then she heard muffled voices in the dark.

Kara slid behind a large headstone and dropped her bag. She pulled out her soul blade and threw her bag back onto her shoulders. She followed the voices. Sneaking from headstone to large bush to more headstones, Kara edged her way deep into the cemetery until the demons came into view. She counted three higher demons sitting in a circle. The odds weren't good. She recognized the demon, Urobach—Brooke's murderer. She felt her body shake with hatred as she remembered how he killed her. Revenge would be bittersweet.

Kara sighed. How the Legion believed she alone could do this was beyond insane.

She scanned the area and saw the small cage with the elemental child inside. The cage rested at one of the higher demon's feet.

"We should be moving soon, Asmodeus…the angel Legion will have sent Scouts by now," said a voice in the dark.

"Let them come…I'm in the mood for a little *excitement*," answered another voice. "Soon, my friends, when the elemental's power has reached its full potential, we will be invincible! And we will *crush* the Legion and take back what is ours!"

Kara heard grunts of agreements.

One of the demons kicked the elemental's cage. Kara's soul ached as she heard the little child whimper. She crouched in the dark, thinking.

She needed a diversion.

She felt the ground and wrapped her hands around a stone the size of a softball. With the rock in her hand, she crawled out of her hiding place and sneaked behind the demons. With all the strength her mortal suit could muster, she threw the rock past the demons and into the darkness behind them. The rock landed with a loud crash.

The three higher demons jumped up. "Zanu, stay with the elemental...Urobach, take the left side. I'll take the right." With their weapons drawn, the demons ran into the darkness.

Kara grabbed another rock and threw it close to the ground near the one they called Zanu. He whirled around and began searching the ground. Kara threw her soul blade. It hit the demon's chest. The demon cried out in pain, as he fell to the ground convulsing.

She only had seconds to react before the others came back.

Jumping over the body, Kara ran to the cage. The elemental child's eyes were wide and wet. She wondered how a thing so cute could be so deadly.

"I'm here to help you," she said, hoping he understood.

There was a lock on the cage's door. Kara searched the ground and grabbed a large stone. She hit the lock over and over until it broke. She yanked open the cage's door. The little child trembled uncontrollably. She knew she couldn't touch him. She dropped her bag and searched inside it for her Sparks. Seconds later, she pulled out the shinning gloves.

"Ahhh!" Kara cried out as something hit her hard in the back.

She fell over the cage and landed on the ground. The gloves flew out of her hands.

Crying out in excruciating pain, she rolled over and pushed herself up on her elbows. The cage was empty.

Something moved in the darkness twenty feet in front of her. The elemental's bare limbs shone in the moonlight as he ran. He disappeared from sight behind a head stone. He was safe for now.

Kara turned around and faced the demons. They walked casually towards her. Urobach picked up the metal cage as they approached.

"You think you can run away with my *prize*? You *stupid* little angel!"

Kara blinked. She could feel the poison of the death blade in her back. The demon leader's face shone in the moonlight. He looked exactly like an Archangel…unbelievably handsome, with short black hair framing a strong jaw. His gray eyes glimmered in the moonlight. He wore a dark tailored suit. He pulled out a long sword from under his black leather trench coat. He then snapped his fingers and glanced at the other higher demon. "Urobach, take care of this monkey!"

Urobach dropped the metal cage. He brought his death sword up to his mouth and licked the blade. Grinning widely, he walked towards Kara, his long leather coat trailing behind him. "I'm glad we meet again, my little angel. You won't escape me a second time."

Kara wrenched the death blade out of her back, and sick with the pain, wincing, she threw it ineffectually at Urobach. She scrambled for her backpack, digging frantically inside for her soul blade. She pushed herself up and planted her feet. With her body bent, she was ready.

The demon lunged. He stroked downward toward her head, but she wasn't there. She jumped over him, slashing as she came down. But Urobach was quick. He twisted away from her and blocked her blade with the end of his hilt.

His face twisted into an evil grin. "Not bad, little angel. I'm almost having fun."

He came at her again, slashing with force…and cut her in the chest. Kara cried out in pain as she sidestepped, backing away from his killing strikes. She felt her energy drain from her body, as the death blade's poison spread through her core. He slashed again, outmaneuvering her as she desperately concentrated on not getting cut into tiny little pieces…like an angel shish kabob. The poison burned her from the inside, and Kara began to see double. Urobach grinned as he licked his lips when he sensed that Kara's strength was fading.

You've got to put your blade into his head, said the voices inside her head. *Get in closer and strike. Do it now, Kara.*

Kara felt energy surge inside her body, as the voices spoke to her again. Under normal earthly circumstances they'd lock her away in a loony bin, but Kara didn't care. The voices inside her head were like invisible sidekicks, enabling her to see opportunities that she might have missed.

Kara backed away from Urobach, trying to find an opening. And then she saw it. Urobach came forward, grinning confidently as he swung his blade up towards her head. Kara sidestepped, whirled around, and jammed her soul blade into his chin…pushing it right into his head. Black blood spilled around the hilt and down his throat. The higher demon dropped and lay motionless on the cold ground.

Asmodeus screamed with rage. "YOU'VE KILLED MY LIEUTENANT!"

In one rapid movement Asmodeus lifted his arms, and a large jet of black electricity shot out of his fingers. The brute force picked her up and threw her hard against a large headstone.

CRUNCH!

Kara crashed against the hard rock and slumped to the ground like a rag doll. She winced in pain and pushed herself up on her elbows in search of the child. She spotted him crouched in a corner, shaking. His big watery eyes glistened in the soft light. Blinking, she felt dizzy, as her vision blurred. She wasn't sure she was going to make it.

Have faith, Kara, said the voices inside her. *Take the child into your arms.* Kara turned around. "Those gloves! Where are they?" she breathed.

Asmodeus roared with laughter. "Where's who? No one is here. Now, little angel...you *are* going to die. And I'm going to enjoy it immensely. But I think I'll start with the kid. Why wait? I can feel his power strengthening." He took a step forward.

Kara turned towards the child. Her body prickled as she felt a wave of energy wash through her.

Take the child, Kara. Don't be afraid . . . he will not harm you.

Without a second thought, Kara jumped to her feet and ran towards the elemental. She reached out her hand and touched his face.

"What the...? Nothing's happening? I'm...I'm still here!" She held his face with both of her hands. "I can touch you?" She opened her arms. "Come," she said smiling, "we have to go."

A tear escaped the little child's eyes as he stretched out his tiny arms towards Kara. She lifted the little boy in the air and clasped him tightly against her chest.

"Well, well, well...what do we have here?" Asmodeus strolled towards them, a confused look on his face. "How is that possible? You are touching an elemental...and your angel soul is still intact! This is very, very interesting."

The warmth of the child felt good against Kara's cold mortal suit. She felt him shivering and held him tighter.

"I would never have believed it possible, but yet here you are ... with this child against your breast. Only mortals can survive the touch of an elemental. So how can this be? You are an angel, no doubt, and yet you can survive his touch. Tell me, little angel...what is your name? You seem ... familiar." Asmodeus edged closer.

"Stay back!" she yelled. "Don't you touch him!"

The demon lord laughed. "Touch him? I certainly don't want to *touch* him . . . I want to kill him and use his power! With the elemental's energy, I will become invincible! I will destroy the Legion!" His forehead came together in a frown and his evil eyes mocked her.

Kara narrowed her eyes and made fists with her hands. "You will never hurt him!"

"My, my, aren't we motherly...tell me, what is your name, little angel?" Asmodeus walked slowly towards Kara. Pain spilled inside her core, but she wouldn't give up the child.

Asmodeus flashed his white teeth. "No name? Perhaps I can guess. Let me see..." He closed his eyes and lifted his eyebrows. Kara sensed a sudden chill forming inside her forehead behind her eyes, the same kind of brain freeze she'd feel when drinking an iced coffee too fast. And then the brain freeze faded. She felt lightheaded, with a tickling sensation as though hundreds of tiny fingers were going through the files inside her brain, reading all her thoughts.

"Ah, of course. Kara ... Kara ... Kara ... tut, tut, tut. We meet at last."

"What?" Kara backed away, she didn't like anyone prying inside her most intimate thoughts. "How...how do you know my name?" She shook her head, trying to rid it of the awful tickling.

"Kara Nightingale...rookie in the famous guardian angel Legion...on a life-quest," said Asmodeus. "Hmm. This is very interesting."

Kara saw his lips curl. "You're *in love* with someone called David...how very *mortal* of you," laughed Asmodeus. "And he is not returning your *amour* anymore, is he?" He rolled his eyes at the sky. "Romance is *so* overrated. So many insignificant feelings get in the way. It's too distracting. Who has time for love nowadays, anyway?"

He closed his eyes and raised his eyebrows. "Ah, yes...you want your life back. I can feel it...yes, very strongly. You want to be with your mother again, don't you?" Asmodeus's gaze searched Kara's face. "You were going to become a famous painter before the bus hit you, were you not?"

Kara pressed her mouth shut.

Asmodeus closed his eyes again. "Ah...what is this? I feel something else inside you ... something different from anything I've ever felt before. I feel a sense of *power*...of a wild power." He opened his eyes and smiled. "It feels almost ... elemental."

"That's impossible. You're lying!"

"But it's the truth, my dear." The demon lord cocked his head to the side. A strange eagerness flashed in his eyes and his hands trembled. "Such a pity you're playing for the *wrong* team." His face twisted in disdain as he shook his head. "But you're still so *weak*...look at you! Getting *emotionally* attached to the job! Regardless, with your power and my power combined ... we could achieve greatness!"

"No thanks, I think I'll pass," she hissed.

There was a short pause, and then Asmodeus continued, a sly smile forming across his face. "You see...you were supposed to be on *my* team, Kara. I had *chosen* you to be part of my army."

Kara's jaw dropped to the ground. This couldn't be true. "W...what?"

"It's true," continued Asmodeus, his voice pleasantly soft. "Who do you think gave you that Mark?"

"What?" It was as if a ton of bricks had fallen on her. "You ... you gave me that Mark? You did this to me! Why?" She felt paralyzed by his words.

"You have the potential to become a great warrior...the greatest perhaps." Asmodeus placed his right hand on his chest. "I can feel it...just like I felt it before. You are destined for greatness!"

Kara saw him lift his shoulders and then let them drop.

"Some guardians beat me to you. When we got to the crash site, your dying body was already protected. But not before I grazed your leg with my hand. Half a second earlier . . . your soul would have been *mine*."

"I would *never* have been *yours*!" said Kara, her voice shaking.

Asmodeus twisted his face in a smile and chuckled. "Either way, you have something of mine. I'll give *you* what you want, if you give me what *I* want."

Kara shook her head like a stubborn child.

Asmodeus took a step forward.

"I can give you your life back, little angel. Just like that..." He snapped his fingers.

Kara frowned. "No...you can't. You're lying!"

"Oh yes, I *can*. And all I ask in return," he kicked the metal cage between him and Kara, "is that you put this silly little boy back in his cage." Asmodeus's beautiful face creased into a smile.

Fragments of her past life flashed before her eyes. She felt her grip on the child loosen.

Asmodeus spoke softly. "I was an Archangel once...the most powerful angel in all of Horizon! They resented me for it, and that's why I left."

He paused for a brief moment and then held out his arms. "I can give you back your life, Kara, I promise. All I need from you," he said, his voice as smooth as silk, "is to put the child in the cage, and..." he snapped his fingers, "...you'll be back on Earth, in your old body, without any knowledge of your angel experiences. Your life will be as it was. As it should be."

Kara felt sick and confused. She looked down into the child's wet blue eyes and cringed at his tears. She knew the demon would kill the little boy. She couldn't live with that. She might never remember any of this once she was inside her old mortal body again, but she believed in karma. And karma would eventually bite her in the ass. She wouldn't give him up...not even for her own life.

"No ... I will never give him to you. I would rather die." said Kara.

Asmodeus's eyebrows lowered dangerously.

"NO?" he repeated as he came rushing towards her. "PUT HIM IN THE CAGE—OR I'LL KILL YOU!"

She stepped back shaking her head.

"I—SAID—PUT—HIM—IN!" Asmodeus scooped up the cage and threw it at Kara. It hit her hard and then bounced on the ground. He edged closer. He was nearly on top of her.

Kara tightened her grip on the child, cradling him. "Don't be frightened. I'm here with you."

An image of David flashed suddenly before her eyes. She trembled. She was ready.

In a frightening rage, Asmodeus lurched forward and charged. He moved with lightening speed, striking out at her with lines of black electric current.

Kara threw out an open hand protectively in front of her. Her palm hit his chest and golden light exploded from her hand. Asmodeus was propelled back in the air and landed hard on the ground. He rolled over, howling in pain. A golden glow emanated from his chest and spread slowly all the way around his body until he was covered in golden light.

Kara stared at her hand. Traces of gold light hovered over her palm and fingertips.

She backed away and watched as the demon lord convulsed uncontrollably. He spit up a thick liquid that showered the floor in black puddles. He wailed as he clawed at his own flesh, scratching bloody holes into his body and face. He let out an ear-piercing scream. And then his body twisted, bent inwards and with a pop...he vanished.

Kara blinked several times. She walked over to where Asmodeus had stood seconds before. There was nothing left of the demon lord, not even a burn mark. Kara searched the ground with her shoe, brushing away clumps of dirt and dry leaves. The ground underneath was bare.

She stared at her hand again and made a fist.

Pursing her lips, she turned her attention to the little boy. Kara lifted the child by its armpits and searched his grinning face.

"You know, we were really lucky...you're like my good luck charm. But how come I can touch you and no one else can, eh?" She lowered him into her breast. "I guess you don't know either. Boy, do I have a lot of debriefing to do!" She laughed. "I'll be in there for weeks! But the important thing is...you're okay!"

The child grinned and clapped his tiny hands together.

Kara laughed. "We make a good team! Good job, little one. High five…" she held out her hand, palm facing the little boy. He smacked it and giggled.

She studied the boy for a moment, her eyebrows low. "You need a name." She bit her lip and squinted. "From now on, I'm calling you … Lucky. You like that?"

The child smiled and wrapped his small arms around Kara's neck. His cool skin brushed against the nape of her neck. She felt a shiver. She knew that Lucky was part human and was probably cold.

"Here…let me put this over you." She took off her jacket and wrapped him in it. "There you go. I don't want you to catch a cold, now."

Lucky looked up at her and smiled. His big fat cheeks wrinkled his face.

"Okay. Let's get out of here."

She held him tight in her arms as they walked out of the cemetery.

CHAPTER 17

LEVEL SEVEN

KARA DEBRIEFED FOR HOURS back at Operations. Gabriel was speechless when she told him she could touch the elemental without the silver gloves. But when she got to the part where a golden beam shot out from her hand, Gabriel stopped blinking. The three oracles writing up the reports fainted and fell off their crystals.

"Golden light shot out of your hand?"

"Yup."

"It…it came out of your hand?"

"Yes, like I told you … it just sort of came out … and bam! Asmodeus went flying. Then he started to shake and twitch. He was all covered in a golden light, and then he vanished. I'm sure that's happened before, right? Um…are you okay? You look like a little worried?"

"I have to speak to the Council of Ministers. Stay here." Gabriel stormed out of the tent.

"Okay ...?" Kara watched him disappear beyond the red dunes.

A few hours later, an oracle found her and told her to present herself to Level Six, where the Council of Ministers awaited her.

She had succeeded in her mission, her life-quest. Soon she would be reunited with her mother, back in her old mortal body. She needed to make up for all the years she had wronged her mother...her mother who has been a guardian angel all along. She was restless. She ran all the way back to the elevator.

Kara followed the oracle down the platform towards the entrance to the Council of Minister's chamber. Her mind flashed back to Asmodeus and she wondered if she should tell the council that he had given her the Mark, but she decided against it. It didn't matter anymore, she was going home.

The oracle pulled open the metal door to the building and rolled himself back out of the way.

Kara stepped inside.

Cheers exploded all around her, like a sudden burst of thunder. In the thousands, the entire Legion of guardian angels was gathered along the length of the hall to welcome her back. The thousands of clapping hands sounded like firecrackers. She walked through the crowds. She saw angels pushing and shoving each other just to get a look at her. She saw a young angel fall flat on her face in a faint.

"Look, it's her! That's Kara Nightingale!"

"The one who beat Asmodeus!"

"She saved the elemental!"

"She saved us all!"

Kara couldn't help but laugh. It was strange to have her own paparazzi.

The oracle plowed his way through the mob and down the hall to the large council doors. He pushed them open and rolled to the side. Kara left the crowd behind and entered the council chamber. The doors shut behind her.

One by one, the council members stood up and started clapping. Embarrassed, she looked at the floor. A long red carpet spread all the way down to the dais. She'd never thought that one day she'd be walking down a red carpet.

Kara followed the red carpet until she was near the dais. Gabriel, Raphael, Uriel, and Michael stood at the head of the council table, their faces cracked in wide grins. Kara turned her head to her right and saw David. She couldn't believe she had forgotten about him. She felt a tingling of hope. He made his way over to her, smiling broadly. His perfect face was just as she had last seen it. But his eyes seemed darker than usual. She saw a trace of sadness in them.

He stopped at her side and passed his hands through his hair. Lifting his head high, he squared his shoulders. "You did good...and I think you scared the crap out of everyone..."

Kara gestured with her hand. "But I'm okay. See? Still in one piece. So...what happens with Lucky? Is he going to be okay?" She remembered his tiny smiling face and realized that she missed him.

"He's fine. A family of Sensitives took him in. They'll take good care of him, don't worry. They're the best mortal guardians the little elemental could ask for."

"I guess so." Kara studied David's face, searching for a whisper of some sort of affection...anything which might give her the hope she desired. The smallest spark would suffice.

Their eyes locked for a moment, and David looked quickly away. "I'm...I'm sorry, Kara. I should have believed you...I'm such a jackass. Will you ever forgive me?"

Kara felt her bottom lip start to shake. "Of course I forgive you. Besides, what would I do without my favorite jackass?" She strained to keep her true feelings hidden.

David laughed. He fumbled with the zipper on his jacket. "So ... have you decided what you're going to do? Are you staying ... or going ...?"

Kara felt a strange prickling on her cheeks reminiscent of a flush. She brushed a strand of hair behind her ear and sighed. "You know what I've always wanted. I want to go back home...to my mother. I need to take care of her. It's like—I feel I was robbed by having only sixteen years on earth. I want to experience life, my *mortal* life. I want to do all the stupid things that young people do. I need that...before I die...again. I have the chance to get my life back just as it was before I died. I'm going to take that chance."

She felt a sharp pain in her chest. She was glad that angels couldn't cry, otherwise her face would be soaked.

David dropped his shoulders. He was silent for a long moment. "I know. If I had the chance to go back one last time...I'd want to go back too. I miss my dad's purple face when he'd yell at me for using the car." He shoved his hands in his front pockets. "I just wanted to check."

"Maybe we'll meet again?" Kara asked, trying not to sound too desperate.

"I know we will. You can count on that." He looked over to the dais. "They're waiting for you." He stepped back.

Kara stared at David. There was so much she wanted to say, but the words wouldn't come. Someone cleared their throat, and Kara turned her head towards the council.

Dressed in red robes, Uriel lifted his arms before the crowd. His long sleeves brushed the black marble desk. "Welcome, guardian angels, to the Council of Ministers," his voiced echoed throughout the chamber, bouncing off the walls. "We are gathered here at this hour for a special celebration...a celebration of life and of the success of a life-quest. I'm honored to present to you all, Kara Nightingale...a rookie guardian angel who has saved us from great peril. Without her, we would be lost."

Kara pursed her lips, her eyes wide as she continued to stare at Uriel.

"She has shown us the true meaning of courage and devotion—a true guardian angel." Uriel stretched a long arm in Kara's direction and beckoned her to come forward. "Come, Kara Nightingale."

Kara stepped up onto the dais before Uriel. She bent her head back and looked up into his face. She watched him turn around momentarily to pick up a shiny golden medal on a fine golden chain.

"Kara Nightingale," declared Uriel. "It is with great honor, that we, the Council of Ministers, award you with a life-quest. This medal celebrates our world's highest honor." He slipped the chain over Kara's head and smiled. "We are forever grateful to you." He stepped back and clapped. The rest of the council members joined in and clapped enthusiastically.

Kara clasped the medal in her hands, feeling its smooth surface against her palm. She moved it around so that it caught the light. She traced her fingers around the silhouette of a person with widespread wings. "It's beautiful. Thank you."

After a moment the clapping slowly died, and Uriel cleared his throat.

"And now we must discuss something that is most important." He looked at her with kind eyes.

"Gabriel and I have had a long chat with the council members about the events leading to your rescue of the elemental. We have learned of your extraordinary abilities...abilities which are unknown to us. Since the very beginning of Horizon, no angel has ever touched an elemental and survived."

Kara fidgeted on the spot. She felt something was wrong. "So ... what are you saying? That it was a mistake to touch that little boy? I *had* to do something to save him...I'm not sure I understand what you mean."

"Let me explain. That golden beam you conjured against Asmodeus...that is an elemental's power. Only elementals have that kind of immense energy. We believe that your soul is part elemental, Kara. It explains why you were able to touch the child without your Sparks. It explains how you were able to vanquish Asmodeus. It would have taken a team of our most skilled guardians to challenge the demon lord...yet you faced him alone...and vanquished him.

"You are special, Kara. You have powers—strong and wild powers that have the potential to do great things. And that is very unfortunate. You see, Asmodeus desires power above all else, and now he has had a taste of yours. He will stop at nothing to try and possess it."

"Wait a minute...I killed Asmodeus!" said Kara. "I saw him die with my own eyes. He's dead, I swear he is..."

"I'm afraid it's not that simple. Asmodeus is not dead, but simply weakened. We have gathered information from our Scouts which tells us he is back in the Netherworld...weak, but still alive.

"We must send you back to Earth for your own protection," Uriel continued. "You cannot stay here in Horizon, vulnerable and exposed to traitors. We still do not know your full potential, Kara. And while we ponder this, we need to keep you hidden and safe. Asmodeus and his demons will not be able to find you if you are hidden in your mortal body. He will search for you in Horizon."

Kara's eyes flicked at David. He stood tall, his strong shoulders back, his eyes fixed on the council. She didn't know why, but she waited, staring at him. After a second or so she turned to face the council. "So...am I going to remember any of this? When I'm back on Earth, will I remember you, or me—or the fact that Asmodeus wants to kill me? Any of this?"

"No," said Uriel softly. "Once you are back within your own mortal body, you will have no memories of your time spent in Horizon. You won't remember a thing."

She remembered her kiss with David. She was sorry she wouldn't remember it…it was such a good kiss. But something else occurred to her. "What about my mother? I want to remember that I know she's a guardian. I mean…does she know what's happened to me?"

"Your mother knows about the situation. She will look after you. But for your own protection, your memory will be erased. A group of guardian angels have already been assigned to look after you while you are on Earth."

Kara opened her mouth to protest, but shut it again. She knew that things would be different this time around…that she would eventually figure out that her mother was *special*.

"But," said Kara, "will I ever come back here? To Horizon?"

"Of course."

A hint of a smile reached Uriel's lips. "When the time is right, we will call upon your services as a guardian of the Legion again. I'm sure that we will need your special talents again. But for now, it is best that you return to Earth."

"Okay. I understand."

"Although you will be sadly missed by your friends," Uriel's eyes darted to David and back to Kara, "we believe it is the right decision."

He studied her for a moment and then addressed the council. "Let us give our thanks to our fellow angel, Kara Nightingale…who has surpassed all obstacles and proven herself to be a true and devoted soldier. She shall be missed. We salute you!"

Loud voices echoed from the chamber walls as the council members repeated, "We salute you!"

Kara felt very small. She fumbled with her medal. Her eyes fell on David, who beamed at her. She couldn't help but to grin back.

Uriel clapped his hands together. "It is time, Kara. Report to Level Seven."

Kara turned and was immediately lifted in the air in a bear hug.

"See you soon," said David. He let Kara go and stepped back.

She looked into his eyes. Her body tingled, "I hate goodbyes...I never know what to say." Her eyes darted to the council for a moment. She fumbled with her fingers. "Plus, we have an audience."

"It'll be okay, we'll see each other soon enough."

"Just try to behave, David. And don't piss off any of the Archangels."

"I won't, if they don't."

"God, you're such a baby," she laughed. Part of her wished she could stay. But she knew it was impossible. She sighed and looked into his eyes. "Goodbye, David."

"Bye, Kara."

As Kara rode in the sky-car back to the elevator her mind was a storm of thoughts. She was part elemental. She had these extraordinary powers. David was her friend again. And best of all, she would be with her mother very soon. The only down side was that Asmodeus was still alive. She tried not to think about their next encounter.

After a short ride, she jumped off the sky-car and hopped into the elevator. To her surprise, it was chimp 5M51 at the controls. He lifted his eyebrows at the sight of her.

"Oh, it's *you*," said the chimp.

Kara made a face. "Oh, it's *you*, too!" she spat. She stepped to the back of the elevator.

Chimp 5M51 scratched his butt. "I'm told to bring you to Level Seven?" He eyed her suspiciously. "Not many guardian angels get to go to that level. Why are *you* so special?" He frowned as he studied her.

Kara lifted her chin. "Well, I am." Her body tingled in excitement.

"Um...did you ever meet The Chief? What's he like?"

"I have no idea, Miss. I have never met him."

"Oh."

The chimp sighed and turned his attention to the control panel. "Level Seven...The Chief!" Kara watched as his long finger pressed on the brass number seven button.

The elevator rocked slightly as it ascended higher. Kara felt a mixture of excitement and regret. She was excited to go home again, but she already missed David and her life in Horizon. It was impossible to know if she'd ever see him again, and that left a mark on her soul.

The elevator shook and stopped.

"Level Seven!" cried chimp 5M51.

Kara pushed herself off the panel with her hands and walked up to the elevator doors. Her eyes flashed at the chimp. He raised his eyebrows and stuck out his tongue.

She shook her head and laughed. "Moron."

With a swish, the doors swung open. Immediately, blinding white light spilled into the tiny elevator. Kara covered her eyes. A few seconds later, her eyes adjusted and a feeling of warmth spread through her body.

This is it, she said to herself. *I'm going home.*

She stepped into the light.

CHAPTER 18
DÉJÀ VU

KARA RAN ALONG SAINT Paul Street. Her long brown hair flowed behind her. She balanced her portfolio in one hand and pressed her cell phone against her ear with the other. She jumped onto the sidewalk and rushed through the oncoming crowd, her mind on her big presentation.

"Wait for me! I'll be there like in … two minutes!"

"I can't believe you're not here yet," said the voice on the other line. "You had to pick today of all days to be late."

"Okay, okay! I'm already freaking out about the presentation. You're not exactly helping, Mat."

A laugh came through the speaker. "I'm just saying … that this is supposed to be the most important day of your life…and you're late."

"Yes, I heard you the first time…*Mother.* My stupid alarm didn't go off!" Kara dashed along the busy street. "Excuse me! Coming through…coming through…"

She squeezed herself through the crowd and kept running.

"You know, the presentation won't wait for you…"

"I swear I'm gonna kick your butt when I get there!" Kara looked behind her as she jumped back onto the street.

Her heart skipped a beat.

Less than half a block behind, a man with white hair and dressed in a gray tailored suit stood staring at her.

His eyes are black, she realized. A chill rolled up her spine. The man vanished back into the crowd.

"I think I'm being followed," said Kara, after a moment.

"You always think you're being followed."

"No…I'm *serious!* I swear this guy is following me—some psycho with white hair. I've seen him before. Or at least my mother has…"

"We all know your mother is a little nutty sometimes…no offense… I love your mom, but she's been seeing and talking to invisible people since we were five. I think it's rubbing off on you."

"Listen. I was with my mom yesterday, on Saint Catherine Street, and she said we were being followed by someone. What if this is the same guy? Maybe she's not as crazy as everyone thinks." Kara wondered if there was a little truth in her mother's visions.

Mathieu laughed on the other end of the phone. "Are you serious? It's bad enough that your mom sees spirits and demons. If you start believing in all that…they'll lock you up."

"Thanks for the vote of confidence. Remind me why you're my best friend again?" Kara focused on her presentation as she ran. "Okay…I can see you now."

Mat was leaning against the gallery's front brick exterior. "I think it's starting…hurry up!"

Kara took a deep breath and sprinted onto Saint Laurence Boulevard. Her cell phone slipped out of her hand as she ran. It hit the ground with a crash.

"Crap!" Kara crouched down to grab her phone.

A flicker of movement appeared in the corner of her eye.

"WATCH OUT!" Someone shouted. She stood up and turned around.

A city bus hurtled towards her.

EEEEEEEEEEEEEEEEEEHHH!!!

Kara watched in horror as a city bus came charging straight for her. In a second it would hit.

Kara closed her eyes and braced herself for impact…

But the impact never came.

Kara felt something hard wrap around her left arm. She was lifted off the ground. She floated in the air as something pulled her body away from the bus, and not a second too soon. In a blink of an eye, Kara watched the bus as it skidded to a stop and plowed through the spot where she had stood moments before.

She landed a few feet away. Her portfolio flew out of her hand.

Crowds of people ran to her, all yelling at the same time.

"Oh, my God! Are you okay?"

"Is she hurt?"

"Did you see that? That guy saved her life!"

Feeling the touch of a hand still wrapped tightly around her arm, she turned around to get a glimpse of her savior. She met a grinning face. He was young and extremely handsome, with blonde hair and piercing blue eyes. His full lips were curled up into a sly smile. He wore a brown leather jacket, weather worn, with the collar rolled up. He cocked an eyebrow.

"Careful there, kiddo," said the stranger. "It's not time yet...not for a little while, anyway."

He stood there searching her eyes for a moment. His closeness made her skin prickle with goose bumps. She inhaled a strong musky smell.

"Huh? Time for what?" It took Kara a moment to compose herself. "What just happened?" She swayed on the spot.

"Looks like you were almost hit by a bus."

Kara looked at the stranger. Their eyes locked. Her heart hammered at her chest. "Hey...you look familiar ... do I know you?"

"No, I don't think so."

She couldn't take her eyes off his face. "This is going to sound really crazy, but...I feel like...like I know you? Are you sure we've never met?"

"I'm sure."

Her cheeks burned. "Whoa...this is the biggest feeling of déjà vu I've ever had!" She pressed her hands on her head, feeling dizzy.

"Take care of yourself," said the stranger.

He let go of her arm. And with a smile, he turned on his heel and walked away. Kara stared after him until he was lost in the crowd.

"Wait!" she cried. But he was gone.

Kara stood staring at the spot where the stranger had stood.

Then she picked up her portfolio. The pedestrian walk sign flashed green. She took a deep breath, walked to the other side of street, and pulled open the gallery door.

And now a sneak peek of the second book in the

Soul Guardians series

FROM AWARD-WINNING AUTHOR
KIM RICHARDSON

CHAPTER 1

LIGHTNING STRIKE

KARA AND A LITTLE boy stand together, alone in a small river. He clutches her hand. The cool water tickles their toes. A fine mist rises and twines around them, and Kara smells the faint stink of rotten flesh. Something touches her toes. She looks down.

White hands reach up out of the water and claw at her ankles. She jumps back, pulling the child with her. More hands reach out all around her. A thick, black mist rises and blankets the stream. Long tendrils coil around their legs, like white snakes. Kara screams and kicks at the mist.

A stench of iron overpowers her. The mist parts. Kara struggles for her balance. She stands in a river of blood. The little boy has blood to his thighs. Kara is nauseated.

She hears a splash.

A figure, in the river ... a man, no ... the twisted human head and diseased torso that rise up from the river grow out of a confusion of human and insect guts on the back of a hideous monster. Long, insect-like legs thrash towards her, black and razor-sharp. Boils and sores cover the monster's skin, like leprosy. Its red eyes glow in the black mist. It snaps its jaws.

The child lets go of Kara's hand. He is dragged under the bloody river. Kara bends down and waves her hands around in the blood, searching for the boy.

A sob. Kara looks up.

The creature has the child. It grabs the wailing boy by the neck and squeezes. It opens its mouth. Blood trickles down its yellow pointy teeth. Slowly, it brings the screaming child towards its wet mouth ...

Kara woke up with a start.

Her heart pounded hard against her chest as she blinked through eyes crusty with dried tears and sweat. Still half asleep, she sat up on her bed with her arms stretched out before her, ready to save the little boy from the monster. She brushed her sticky bangs from her sweaty forehead and waited, calming herself, till the effects of the dream wore off. She'd been crying.

She wiped her face and her eyes slowly adjusted to the early morning light in her room. Dark shadows became focused. Her demon and angel paintings that covered the walls like wallpaper looked even more sinister in the dim light. She shook off a chill.

The paintings were part of a story Kara needed to tell. Fresh from her nightmares, she had taken her paintbrush and painted the recurring stories again and again. She told herself that it was sort of therapeutic, and that perhaps, one day, the nightmares would stop.

After a while her mother refused to go into her room. Kara remembered that her mother had thrown her hands in the air and screamed that the monsters were out to get them.

But to Kara, they were only paintings. She figured they couldn't hurt anyone.

5:00 am...still too early to get up for school. She forced her eyes shut and fell back onto her bed. The faint snore coming from the second bedroom down the hall confirmed that her mother wasn't awakened by Kara's screams. That comforted her. Her mother worked long hours, so she deserved a good night's sleep.

Every night Kara dreamt of horrifying monsters, and of a scared little boy with tangled blond hair and blue and white pajamas... about to be eaten. She'd wake up screaming the moment the child disappeared into the monster's mouth.

Kara let out a long breath. She couldn't fall back asleep.

She swung her legs off her bed and tiptoed to her dresser. The pine floorboards creaked. White paint peeled from the dresser's top and legs, giving a false antique look. A few knobs were missing from the top drawers, and Kara had used dried up pens as knobs. She picked up a metal picture frame.

The glass cover was cracked and chipped. Kara held it close. A man with disheveled brown hair and a friendly smile held up a little girl with long brown pigtails and yellow overalls. Kara's chest tightened. She could barely remember that day anymore. Her father's image had drifted away. He had died when she was only five, and Kara couldn't remember him at all. She traced his face with her finger. What she wouldn't give to have a real dad! Maybe her mother would be a little saner if there was a man around. Kara felt an ache in her heart, and with a sigh, she placed the frame back on the dresser.

Kara's face stared back at her through the cracked mirror and forced a smile. Today was her seventeenth birthday. Seventeen was supposed to be the age when girls fell in love and went off to college to follow their dreams. Her smile fell. Kara's summer job barely gave her enough to help pay for groceries. She could never save enough for college.

A cockroach skittered up her mirror and stopped right in the middle. It was eye level with Kara; its two beady black eyes stared up at her with eerie intelligence. Its antennae twitched nervously.

BAM!

Kara removed the book from the mirror and tossed the dead roach into her garbage can. She felt guilty about killing the insect. She pursed her lips and glanced at the mirror again. She should be happy, she knew. But she felt empty inside. A part of her was missing, like a car missing a wheel so that it couldn't drive. For months now she had been moping around school, not wanting to do anything besides painting and reading books. Even her best friend Mat avoided her. Two weeks ago at lunch time, he told her that hanging around with her was making his brain melt; she was making him depressed. Without Mat to support her she felt even more lost and confused. She tried to shake off the feeling, but nothing worked. She felt alone.

The soft chirping of birds reached her ears. Kara smiled. Even though they annoyed her sometimes, they sang beautifully. The chirpings became louder, more intense. Then she heard the loud cawing of crows, lots of them ...

Strange, Kara thought to herself.

She sneaked over to her window sill. The wood floors were cool under the balls of her feet. She pressed her head against the glass and looked out. Nearly twenty crows were perched in the tall maple trees. With their heads bent, they cawed at something below that Kara couldn't see. She strained to look through the branches. A chill rolled up her spine.

Her heart was caught in her throat. There in the middle of the road was a little boy...the same little boy from her dreams.

Kara flattened her nose against the glass as she stared at the small figure in pajamas waddling down the street. He was barefoot. In August the Montreal weather was still warm, even in the early hours of the morning. She watched him plant his feet and steady himself. The little boy shuffled past parked cars. Newspapers rolled around him, caught in the invisible wind.

I have to go get him, Kara said to the window. She made up her mind and pulled on a pair of gray sweat pants and a sweater. With a click, she opened her bedroom door and stepped into the shadows. Careful not to wake her mother, she crept stealthily across the dark hall and ran out her apartment's front door.

She jumped down the stairs two at a time and bounced into the lobby. She caught her breath and pushed open the glass doors. The air outside smelled of wet leaves and grass, cool against her skin, hinting of the approaching autumn. Gray puddles littered the sidewalks, and Kara jumped to avoid them. She ran to the spot in the street where she'd last seen the little boy.

He was gone.

The street was very quiet, and Kara noticed that the birds had suddenly stopped chirping. The wind died. Kara shivered. A chill crawled up her back, and her heart hammered in her ears.

"Hey, little boy!" she said in a hushed voice, not wanting to wake up the neighborhood. "Little boy...where are you?"

She jogged past the spot and stopped. She dropped to her knees and searched beneath the parked cars. Nothing.

He couldn't have gotten far. He's just a little boy, she thought. Kara took a few steps forward and stopped. The hairs on the back of her neck stood up. She felt that something wasn't quite right, an inkling that told her to run...

And there he was.

Kara held her breath. She could see him clearly now—not the child, but a handsome stranger she had seen before. He leaned against a parked car, his arms crossed over his chest. The stranger's gaze locked onto her. Kara's heart stopped. He was tall and lean. A brown leather jacket embraced his powerful shoulders, and he wore ragged jeans with a tight T-shirt that emphasized his muscular chest. He stared at her with a silly almost-there grin painted across his face. With barely-there dimples, his face was unmistakably gorgeous. Too perfect. The kind of face that sent millions of butterflies jolting in the pit of her stomach. Kara had given him the nickname "hot stalker" ...her gorgeous shadow.

What is he doing here at this hour?

She scowled. Something didn't make sense to her. Part of her felt the excitement of having such a good looking guy gawk at her like that, but the other part gave her goose bumps…and not the good kind. There was something very creepy about the way he looked at her.

Hot stalker combed his messy blonde hair with his fingers and turned around. He caught Kara's eye and then looked away, pretending to be interested in some parked cars. He didn't look anything like the Jeffrey Dahmer serial killer type to Kara…the kind that dismembered and ate their victims, like some kind of exotic stew. No, he had such a gorgeous mouth that she couldn't bring herself to imagine him eating anyone. Kara couldn't figure out why he was stalking her. With her lack-of-bosom and her invisible curves, she didn't have much to offer the opposite sex in the way of looks. What was so engaging and "stalk-o-licious" about her? Nothing. And that made her very suspicious of him. Things that are too good to be true usually are, she realized, especially when they involved her.

She tore her eyes away from him for a moment to look for the child again. Dark shadows lurked along the quiet street, and Kara felt herself tense. But nothing else moved. The boy was nowhere in sight. And when she looked back at her hot stalker, he had vanished as well, as though he were a figment of her imagination.

I'm seriously losing my mind. Kara thought as she brushed her bangs from her face. A light drizzle cooled her hot cheeks, and Kara welcomed it…

Something moved in the corner of her eye.

At first, she thought it was her hot stalker returning. But she quickly realized it wasn't him. This man had white hair and pale grayish skin. He wore a dark tailored suit, and Kara believed it looked expensive and out of place at this hour of the morning. He leaned against a lamp post across the street. Even from a distance she could tell there was something very wrong with his eyes.

They were black. And they were watching her.

Kara's stomach lurched; she caught her breath and a nasty feeling crawled along the back of her neck, making her hair stand up. Her heart pounded in her ears and she trembled. She recognized that face...it belonged to the foul monster from her nightmares. It sneered and licked its lips, showing off a mouthful of pointed yellow teeth.

Her insides twisted. A sick feeling rose to her throat and Kara bolted down the street.

With her flats scraping the pavement, she picked up speed. Kara became aware of the stillness around her even more. It was as though the world stood still, and only she moved within it. A sudden gust of wind pushed against her back. Darkness grew, sucking out the light. Kara heard thunder rumble in the distance. A large shadow suddenly appeared on the ground before her, as though a bucket of black paint was spilled by her feet. She looked up. A single, dark gray cloud raced alongside her in the pink and blue sky. It travelled fast against the wind and headed towards her.

Kara gasped and focused on putting as much distance between herself and the black-eyed monster as she could. She stole a look behind. Her heart caught in her throat.

The demon was right behind her.

A loud roar made her jump as thunder cracked all around. Kara glanced up. The gray cloud was now above her. She choked a scream. Goose bumps prickled on her skin. *How could a cloud move like that?* She knew it wasn't natural. Panic surged through her body.

Kara made a run towards a bus stop across the street and collapsed into the glass shelter. A shadow covered the ground and darkness crept around her. She looked up and stared through the top of the shelter. The gray cloud was directly on top of it. It had followed her.

Kara followed it with her eyes. A spark emanated from the cloud, and then another, until the cloud was consumed entirely by tiny electric flashes. She shook her head in disbelief.

Something moved in the corner of her eye. She caught sight of the demon...he stood in the doorway. He snarled, bared teeth shining in the darkness. She shut her eyes and willed the nightmare to end. There was a sudden loud crack; Kara opened her eyes.

A bolt of lightning charged out of the cloud.

It hit the demon.

Kara screamed as she watched him sizzle and crackle before her eyes. His limbs crumbled to pieces like overcooked toast. Ashes floated in the air like dried leaves from a tree in a breeze. A pile of dirt was all that remained of the demon. Kara felt a moment of nausea wash over her.

ZAP!

A bolt of lightning struck the shelter. In a flash of white light the entire shelter disappeared, leaving only a few traces of smoke and the smell of burnt plastic. Horrified, Kara glanced around her. How was this even possible? She shivered as her stomach tightened into a ball. Her hands were shaking, and she clenched them into fists.

Kara hopped out of the blackened shelter, back onto the street, and ran towards the nearest house. A sizzling sound, too close ... she felt a sensation of something behind her. Something touched her hair, brushed the back of her neck. She whirled around to look...and nearly fainted.

The demon with the black eyes ran behind her with unnatural speed, like an image being played in fast- forward. He hissed and spit furiously. His pale grimace revealed rows of thin pointed teeth. He didn't have a scratch on him, Kara realized. No signs of any burns from the lightening that had immolated him, not even on his tailored suit.

Kara's knees gave in. She crashed to the ground and cried out. She rolled over and clasped her foot. The skin around her ankle swelled and instantly turned red and purple. She strained to stand, but fell back down. A shadow crept along the ground. Kara looked up. The gray cloud was inches from her head, so close she could reach out and touch it. A loud scraping sound came from behind and Kara whirled around.

The demon was only a few strides away. He would be on top of her in a matter of seconds. A weird smile spread across his face as he ran, like he was about to win the lottery.

"Help!" Kara screamed in desperation. "Someone help me!"

The demon's mouth opened and his chin dropped to the middle of his chest, like a snake unhooking its jaws, ready to swallow his prey. In that horrible moment, Kara realized she was about to be eaten...just like the little boy in her dreams. She could only tremble and watch.

At the same time, the gray cloud settled above her. Blue and white sparks danced in and out of the cloud.

And then another bolt of lightning shot out.

Kara blinked as white light burned her eyes.

She felt a surge of electricity flow through her body. It burned. She didn't have time to scream.

And then everything went dark.

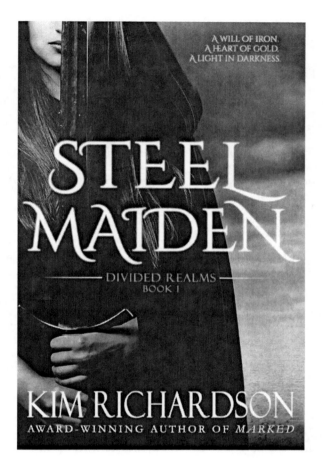

CHAPTER 1

THE TEMPLE VAULT WAS completely dark.

I'd been crouched inside a cabinet with my chin resting awkwardly on my knees for about six hours, and now the muscles in my body screamed and burned. Acid from hunger worked away in my empty stomach, and the air was hot and stale. A cold sweat trickled down my back, but I kept my breathing low and steady, held my position, and waited.

I could hear muffled male voices and the shuffling of feet.

Pricks.

If the temple guards discovered me now, they would slit my throat before I could even begin to explain why I was here, hidden in a cupboard in the vault. The truth is, there was only one reason why someone would sneak into the temple vault at night—to steal the high priests' treasures.

I bit my lip. This was by far the stupidest and most dangerous stunt I'd ever pulled. But hunger and desperation had brought me farther into Soul City than I'd ever ventured before. And now I'd been foolish enough to seek my quarry inside the vault. I knew the risks.

We'd finished the last of the cabbage soup two days ago, and Byron hadn't any bread to spare this week. I'd sworn last night that I wouldn't spend another night with a hungry belly.

A cramp bit into my leg, but I ignored it. Hiding in cubbyholes for long hours wasn't new to me. I was used to small spaces. Thank the creator I wasn't claustrophobic. My heart thumped loudly in my ears as my hunger was replaced by my anger.

The high priests were the reason we were all starving. There were enough precious stones and jewels in the vault to feed the families in the Pit for generations, and yet we were all starving to death. It was clear that the priests wanted to keep us hungry. We were easier to control.

Bastards.

I remember the stories I had heard when I was a child. Three hundred years ago, after the Great War of the Realms, the Temple of the Sun priests had arrived. No one had known for sure where they came from, but the legends told that the kings and queens of the six kingdoms of Arcania had stepped down, one by one, and relinquished their rule to the high priests. Some legends spoke of a dark spell that had been cast on the kings and queens since they had so willingly given their titles and their kingdoms to the priests. But no one knew for sure.

Not everyone was subject to the priests' will, however, and a great rebellion against them had arisen two hundred years ago. Unfortunately attempts to remove the high priests had been in vain. Most of the men and women from the kingdom of Anglia who had joined the rebellion had been slaughtered like cattle by the temple guards.

But the priests did keep some of the rebels alive. As punishment, and to remind those who might dare to oppose them again that their efforts would be futile, the priests created the Pit. They confined the rebels to the district of Anglia where the rebellion had started. Now ten thousand prisoners were cramped into a muddy, filthy shantytown where they were forced to live out their lives as trash. They would never forget that their ancestors had tried to rebel.

There was a saying amongst our kind, *If you're born in the Pit, you die in the Pit.*

But I wouldn't die here. *I* was going to get out.

I couldn't let my anger cloud my mind. I had a job to do, and I needed to focus. It was risky, but this was finally my chance to get out of the Pit, and I had to take it. I wouldn't mess it up. I couldn't.

After a few minutes of careful listening, I heard the screeching of hinges and then the loud thump of a heavy door. I knew there were only two guards patrolling the vault, and I couldn't risk them discovering me. Although I could hold my own in a fight, even with two grown men, I had to go unnoticed if I wanted my plan to work. That meant no fights.

I had been blessed with a talent for hand-to-hand combat although I had never received any real training. My earliest memories were of throwing a set of knives against the trunk of a tree and hitting the makeshift target every time. I was adept with weapons, especially ones with a blade. I never knew where my skill came from, or why I had it, it just *was*. Rose called it a gift—I called it survival instinct.

My heart thundered as I strained for any more sounds. Only the darkness of my cupboard whispered back. It was now or never.

I held my breath and pressed lightly on the door. I peered through the small crack and blinked back the sudden brightness. A series of flaming torches illuminated the vault in soft yellow light.

I was alone. I let out a shaky breath and then slipped into the vault with the stealth of a cat.

My limbs ached and cracked as I stretched and moaned quietly. I took a calming breath, grateful for the gulps of fresh air, and looked around carefully. Bile burned my throat as I took in the shelves that lined the walls. They were loaded with brilliant gems and precious jewelry.

Sick. All of it. The people from the Pit were starving while this useless chamber sat stuffed with enough jewels to feed a nation. It was probably just a fraction of the high priests' wealth, and it was a wealth that had once belonged to our kings.

One, two, three, I counted in my head. I only had about five minutes before the next rotation of the temple guards would check on the vault.

I clenched my fingers as I stared at a large necklace speckled with rubies and sapphires. I could certainly fill my pockets with necklaces like these—they were practically *begging* for me to steal them. But that would be stupid. I couldn't afford to be stupid. Not now when I was so close…

Even if I did take my fill of precious stones and pearl necklaces, I wouldn't be able to sell them. Women in the Pit didn't own jewelry. Where would we wear it if we did? It would raise questions if I tried to sell it. I'd get caught if I were greedy.

There was only one person in the Pit who *would* and *could* buy such trinkets, and he'd already made a deal with me. I wasn't here for a mere necklace. I had *bigger* plans.

I crossed the chamber to the opposite wall and stood before a tall metal cabinet. Two lions, the royal seal of Anglia, were engraved into the metal. I couldn't see any lock or device that secured the doors.

A trap? Why wasn't it locked?

It felt too easy. A treasure of incredible valuable must have some kind of lock. Even if it were a trap, what choice did I have? I had committed to this, and I would see it through—for my sake and for Rose's.

With my heart in my throat I pulled open the doors and stifled a gasp as a veil of green fire enveloped me and licked every inch of my exposed skin.

I panicked and stepped back.

The strange wall of green flames could only be magic. What was magic fire doing in the high priests' vault? Priests saw magic as the devil's work. It was forbidden in Arcania, so why was it here? There was not supposed to be any magic on this side of the world. The legends said that magic came from beyond the mystic mountains in the east, from Wichdom. And yet it was right here, in front of me.

I don't know how long I stood there, watching the green flames dance along the edges of the cabinet, but in my moment of panic I had forgotten to count.

Damn, Elena. I cursed to myself. *You can be such a fool sometimes.*

How many seconds had passed? Twenty? Thirty? My cheeks burned at my own stupidity and how easily I had been distracted.

I took a deep breath and braced myself.

"For a better life," I whispered and stepped into the veil of green fire.

I cringed, not knowing what to expect. The flames tickled my skin and warmth spread on my face as though the sun kissed my cheeks. But it didn't burn, and surprisingly my skin didn't melt.

I couldn't hear anything except the pounding of my heart in my ears, but I could see my quarry through the swaying green flame. It was a golden crown set with gems, and it featured two golden lions facing a large red diamond. It was probably the high priests' most valued treasure, and they had gone to the trouble of conjuring magic fire to protect it. It was the crown of the last king of Anglia, and it had been stolen three hundred years ago by the priests of the Temple of the Sun Empire. They had taken it just as they had taken everything else.

Heat flushed my face as my hatred for the priests mixed with the heat of the flames. Many babies had died of the fever last winter, but no healers had been sent to our aid. With all this wealth they could easily have sent healers. But they hadn't. We didn't matter. And it wasn't just the priests, even the nobles and the lords of Anglia pretended we didn't exist.

Although diamonds and precious stone necklaces, rings, bracelets and encrusted weapons hung on the walls of the vault, I knew they were nothing compared to the value of this crown. *This* crown was my ticket out of the Pit. *This* crown would give me a new life.

The crown sat on a plush red cushion, daring me to take it. The thought of Mad Jack's face when I handed him the crown made me smile. I was almost giddy. I had told him I could do it, but he had laughed in my face. And now freedom stared *me* in the face. It was almost too easy.

And he said it was impossible.

Carefully, I picked up the crown, wrapped it in a cloth, and dropped it into the pouch around my belt. I didn't have time to admire it. I knew my five minutes were nearly up. I had to leave now.

As I turned to leave, my vision blurred for a second, and the green fire began to burn my lungs. Smoke coiled from my black wool cloak like a mist, and the smell of burned hair filled my nose. I fought against the dizzy spell that shook my knees. If I passed out now, I'd either burn to ash, or the temple guards would feast on me. The thought was enough to shake me out of my stupor.

I pulled my hood over my head, spun around, leaped out of the flames, and bolted. I was at the vault's door in a few great bounds.

As I reached for the handle I looked back at all those gleaming diamonds and pearls. It was the richest sight I'd ever beheld. Part of me wanted to reach out and fill my pockets with treasure for the others in the Pit, especially for the little ones, to fill their aching bellies. But I knew it was too risky. I couldn't chance anything going wrong when I was so close.

The only thing left for me to do was to run.

ABOUT THE AUTHOR

Kim Richardson is the award-winning author of the bestselling SOUL GUARDIANS series. She lives in the eastern part of Canada with her husband, two dogs and a very old cat. She is the author of the SOUL GUARDIANS series, the MYSTICS series, and the DIVIDED REALMS series. Kim's books are available in print editions, and translations are available in over 7 languages.

To learn more about the author, please visit:

Website
www.kimrichardsonbooks.com
Facebook
https://www.facebook.com/KRAuthorPage
Twitter
https://twitter.com/Kim_Richardson

CPSIA information can be obtained at www.ICGtesting.com
Printed in the USA
LVOW10s1559220316

480253LV00002B/270/P